If Only He Was Mine

MARIE MCGRATH

Other works by Marie McGrath

The Many Faces of Charlotte Barnes (My Book)
Rosewood County Series
The Fate of a Crush – Standalone Book 1
Honey Cove Series (My Book)
The Fall Changes – Book 1
The Winter Heals – Book 2
The Spring Renews – Book 3
The Summer Unites – Book 4

For the latest news and updates, please check out Marie McGrath's newsletter. Signups can be found on her website.
Twitter: @Marie_McGrath_
TikTok: marie_mcgrath_author
Instagram: marie_mcgrath_
Website:
https://mariemcgrathauthor.wixsite.com/books

Published in the United States by Creative James Media.

www.creativejamesmedia.com

978-1-956183-24-5 (trade paperback)

First U.S. Edition 2023

To all those seeking adventure in love, may you never feel you aren't worthy of it…

Chapter One

At the ripe old age of eighteen I had expected to have a boyfriend, my first kiss, and to have gone on many dates.

But my reality was very different from that.

The flat present wrapped in green taunted me. I hated not knowing what I got for my birthday, but it was from my cousin Andrea and no good ever came from one of her presents. One year she bought me a rubber spider because she knew I would fling it and scream. Another year she wrapped a gift from her birthday that she had broken and didn't want anymore. That was her special touch.

So no, this gift wouldn't be a *gift*. It would be cursed or a gag or meant to humiliate me in some fashion. But my curiosity couldn't be subdued, so I tore at the paper, until a book fell out.

My eyebrows rose. Could it actually be ... and then I read the front cover.

Adventure Book Dates. A leaflet flitted from the inside.

Inside you will find dates to spice up your romance. The dates are adventure themed. Do them in order or do them randomly to bring a little something extra to your relationship. Take a picture then glue inside to hold onto the memories.

This was my gift? Sure, Andrea could be cruel and, in most cases, tended to live up to that reputation, but this?

Andrea smirked from her side of the couch.

I knew what she wanted me to say. She wanted me to admit that I, Marley Wix, couldn't use that gift because I was hopelessly alone. And normally I would have given her that satisfaction.

She was the beauty of the family and I was the brain. Her perfect white teeth with no family freckles and pin straight blond hair set her apart from me. My unruly brown curly hair and face covered in freckles couldn't look more different. I hadn't learned how to grab a guy's attention, but Andrea didn't have that problem. She always had a boyfriend or two at her side, as if they were purses she could interchange like her outfit.

"This is ... great."

She smiled, clicking her tongue against the back of her teeth. "You think so?"

I nodded. "Why of course. I can complete them with my boyfriend."

Andrea's expression soured as the shock of my statement registered. But she couldn't be as shocked as I was.

Why had I said that out loud? I had no boyfriend. I had no hopes of changing that before I graduated either. With barely a month left of school, I had skipped prom and had graduation to look forward to. College could be the time I reinvented myself.

"What boyfriend? I haven't heard anything from Daddy."

I cringed. Who called their dad, *daddy* by the time they

were an adult? "Just because Uncle Steve hasn't told you, doesn't mean it isn't true."

Marley, just take it back.

But it was too late. The humiliation would be worse if I told her I had lied and to be honest I enjoyed that her smug smirk had been replaced with bitter disdain. For once her plan wouldn't work. She couldn't make me feel like more of a dork than I already was. I could beat her at this too.

I just needed a boyfriend.

"So where is he then? Boyfriends should support their girlfriends on such a momentous occasion."

"It's a birthday, not a wedding."

"It's your eighteenth birthday. That is pretty important in my book. And Uncle Hank and Aunt Erin must want to flaunt him."

My cheek twitched at the mention of my parents. What if she went up and asked where he was? Or tried to corroborate my story? They would blow the whole thing.

"Of course, but this is a family get together and he was busy. Last minute trip."

She rapped her manicured fingers over the table. "How convenient he is missing." She stood. "Well, I can't wait to meet him then. Let's say graduation night! You can show me your filled out book by then." Her smirk returned.

She probably knew I was bluffing, but instead of calling me out now, she would wait until I had an empty gift and my tail between my legs.

It was fine. I had four weeks to manage that. No biggie. It was a piece of cake.

"Mar, come in the kitchen. It's time to sing and have cake!" Mom shouted from the kitchen.

Andrea sauntered toward the growing crowd as I lingered, staring at the rest of my gifts. My aunts and uncles had come to spend time with me. The party had been somewhat last minute, and my mom had insisted on throwing a celebration to show how much they all cared about me but having literally only family just made it feel worse.

My best friend Sage couldn't even come.

I pushed up from the couch and walked to the kitchen. Both of my aunts and my one uncle, Andrea's dad, were crowded around my parents and the cake. Andrea and I were the only children so far, which was weird for four siblings, but my aunts hadn't settled down yet. They were also much younger than their brothers and had high ambitions for their careers.

It should have been a dream to have a cousin so close in age to me, but who could ever describe Andrea like that? Even now while it was my birthday, she stood to the side, trying to make it about her. She had always craved the attention and she normally got it too, but it always revolved around her beauty or something crazy she had done to show up someone else. It wasn't for her grades.

I on the other hand had happily focused on my studies. I competed in academic competitions and took APs. My grades were straight As, even with a handful of AP classes over the years. I wasn't valedictorian by any means, but I was still up there.

"On three," Mom said. She counted, then everyone sang me happy birthday. "Make a wish, Mar."

I smiled, closed my eyes and blew as hard as I could to get all eighteen. I didn't usually wish for much, but this year, I needed help.

I wish for a way to prove Andrea wrong. Find me a way to complete that book!

I opened my eyes as they clapped, then Mom shifted the cake to another plate and cut pieces for anyone interested. At least it was my favorite, yellow cake with raspberry sauce and buttercream frosting in the middle and then more buttercream frosting on top. Everyone else left the kitchen, except my parents and me.

"How's your day going?" Dad asked.

I smiled. "Great, thanks."

I didn't want to tell him about Andrea's gift. Not this time. This time I wanted to figure it out for myself. I was an adult now. They didn't need to fight my battles for me. Although I knew what he would have said if he had known. Every year they waited to see if Andrea would grow out of her mean gift giving, and every year it just got worse. He would see it as a passive aggressive attempt to put me down after she didn't get accepted to any of the colleges she had applied to and maybe he was right, but that didn't matter. This would stay my secret, for now at least.

He ruffled my hair as he walked past. "Did you open all your presents?"

"Not yet. Had to stop for cake."

"Well, let's get those presents opened!"

"Okay, Dad."

"Hank, leave the girl alone. You just want to see what your brother bought her."

Dad grinned sheepishly. "Don't use your lawyer interrogation tactics on me, Erin. I just want Marley to enjoy her day."

Mom crossed her arms. "Sure ya do, big guy. Sure ya do." She pushed him toward the doorway. "Go wait out there."

I shook my head. No matter how much older I became, they always acted like that—playful, almost like teenagers. If I didn't know any better, I'd have never guessed they'd been married long enough to have a grown daughter.

Their marriage was solid, envious. If I ever fell in love, that's what I wanted.

Mom wrapped her arm around my shoulder. "Now that he's out. What was the deal with Andrea's gift this year?"

My eyes widened. "You don't miss anything."

"If I did, I'd be bad at my job."

"It's nothing I can't handle."

She gazed into my eyes, searching for any moment of weakness. "If you're sure."

"I am."

Her expression shifted, a lighter smile and not as intense of a stare. "Well, let's go see what else you received. You know your dad. He'll be opening them if we leave him alone too long."

I giggled and followed behind her. I didn't know how, but I meant it. I'd find a way to get out of this mess with that ridiculous book.

My parents waited until everyone had left to give me their gift. They usually wanted it to be just for family knowledge, but I knew it had more to do with not flaunting their salaries, more than it did with prying eyes. My dad's brothers and sisters did well with their lives, despite being poor as children, but he still didn't like to show it.

My dad had worked hard in school and grown up to be a trauma surgeon. My mom was a lawyer and between them, they had earned a fair salary over the years. Our house wasn't a mansion. It was a regular ranch home with three bedrooms and two baths. They had a two-car garage and a basement that wasn't even finished.

We didn't have a pool or live in a gated community. My parents believed in experiences, not things, which was fine by me. We always went on vacation once a year, but to be so successful, their schedules were strange. Half the time, my dad would get in at midnight and my mom would still be leaning over the kitchen table staring at a deposition.

I couldn't have asked for better role models, though.

We sat in the family room on the sectional. They were close together on one side, and I was on the chaise part. I slowly unfolded the wrapping paper, stifling a giggle as my mom wiggled in anticipation.

"Mar, hurry up! I want to see your face."

I laughed. "Okay, okay." I slid out the present, which turned out to be paper. I slowly read it as my jaw dropped. "You bought me a plane ticket to Greece?"

Mom squealed. "I convinced your father to take us to Greece for part of the summer before you go to college. What do you think?"

I jumped up and hugged them both. "This is amazing. Thank you! I have to go call Sage."

"Of course, of course."

"Don't take too long or I'll eat the rest of your cake," Dad called from behind me.

I bolted down the main floor's hallway toward my bedroom. Once I shut my door, I pushed her contact and waited impatiently for the video call to connect.

"Finally," I said when her face appeared.

"What? I haven't talked to you for like five hours and apparently the world is ending?" Her phone's view shifted as she walked. "Sorry, I had to go in the back room so I could hear you. It is crazy out there."

"That many people are busy in your parent's bookstore on a Sunday?"

"You have no idea. Anyway, what's wrong? What'd Andrea do?"

I giggled. I had completely forgotten about that stupid gift in the time it had taken me to open my gift from my parents. Although now that she had reminded me, I needed to tell her about that too.

"We can get to that. I'm calling about my parents' gift."

I waited until her brow rose and she gave me a gesture saying, *well go on*.

"They are taking me to Greece this summer!"

"Shut up! You're not serious. Your parents? But they never go extravagant with their gifts."

"I know! Maybe because it's my eighteenth and I graduate? I don't know. I don't care. I get to go for a whole ten days! Oh, I can't wait."

"You lucky duck. I'll be stuck at Marshall's Books all summer wanting to die while my best friend goes to another country."

"Don't say that. We still have plenty of the summer to have fun."

She waved me off. "Yeah, yeah sure." She squinted at me. "But you have yet to say what Andrea did and knowing her, this was a doozy for your eighteenth."

I groaned. "Can't I bask in Greece glory for more than five minutes before you rain on my parade?"

"Nope," Sage said as she popped her p. "I need to know if I should order a hit out on her or not."

"Sage!"

"I'm kidding … mostly."

I shook my head. While I loved her fierceness and intense loyalty, I did not need someone to hear her and take her threat seriously. "Fine she bought me a book."

"Well, there's no way it was a good present with that expression. So, what's with the book?"

"It might be …" I took a deep breath and raced out the next set of words. "A book for couples to spice up your relationship. Y'know, go on adventurous dates and love each other more type of thing."

Her jaw dropped. Literally dropped. "That's no good—"

"Sage. I don't need you to fight her for me. I told her I'd complete it with my boyfriend by graduation."

"Mar, have you completely lost it? What boyfriend? Last I checked, you are single and *not* interested in mingling."

I twisted my fingers around the tassels from my favorite teal pillow.

"Why do you let Andrea get you down? So what if she's boy crazy? You don't have to be."

"I know, I know," I huffed. "It's my eighteenth birthday, you know? I didn't want her to win anymore."

"Who cares if *she* thinks she wins? You and I both know you are winning by attending your dream college while she gets into nowhere."

I grimaced. "So?"

Sage and I were so similar but she didn't understand this part. Andrea's opinion of me had always gotten its way into my brain. It didn't matter that I knew she was probably jealous and just projecting. She could beat me with boys, so she worked that angle. I knew that somewhere, but it didn't help when it was true.

I never had a secret admirer, never had someone want my number to get to know me. No one wanted to follow my social media to know what I was up to. There had to be *something* wrong with me to have been single all eighteen years of my life.

Even Sage with her I-don't-give-a-damn-attitude had kissed a few boys in high school and was only single of her own choosing. If she had agreed she could have had a boyfriend by now. So what was it that turned guys away from me?

"Oh, Mar. I'm sorry." She exhaled loudly, letting the silence hang between us. A heavy door shut on her end, reminding us both she was still at work. "Well, I'll think of some options. I don't want that twit to win."

"You're the best, Sage!"

"Obviously. I'm sorry again I missed your party."

My bed creaked as I shifted my weight to my stomach. "It's not a big deal. Your dad needed help at the store. That's more important."

"I guess. They always need help though."

When she was little she would sweep or organize some of the shelves by the cash register, but now it felt like every weekend she had to slave away there. I missed my best friend, but I wouldn't tell her. She would feel more guilty for bailing on me lately.

"And you're a dutiful daughter helping out."

"Ryan doesn't have to help, *ever*."

Ryan was Sage's brother. "Well, Ryan is practically a delinquent anyway, right?"

"Not the point." Sage's voice was filled with tension.

Ryan had always been a sore subject. He was three years older than us, but never finished high school. He had decided to party and smoke pot instead of go to class.

"You're right, but soon we'll be at college and that won't be your problem anymore."

Shouting emanated from Sage's side of the phone call. "Hey, I got to go. Dad wants me back out front, pronto! We should brainstorm, then come together tomorrow morning before class and figure out what to do. We'll come up with a solution. Okay?"

"Okay."

Sage hung up and I tossed my phone on my bed. Hugging my teal pillow to my chest, I stared out my bedroom window. Smaller kids in the neighborhood were using the remaining daylight hours to play a hockey game in the middle of the street.

Even *they* had more of a social life than I did. I sagged farther into my bed. What could I do to fix this? Telling Andrea the truth was not an option. I wouldn't let her win, not this time.

I leaned over my bed and pulled the book from underneath, my hand brushing the white and black rug that my bed rested on.

The book felt substantial. It's cover, glossy and black, was smooth in my hands. I flipped through a few of the pages, glancing at the dates. Nothing seemed too crazy. Maybe Sage had a guy friend I could steal to do the dates?

What was I saying? Sage and I were each other's *only* friends and most guys she gave a chance wouldn't be interested in me.

There had to be a solution I couldn't see. So like with everything else, I decided to let it go and wait for the moment to strike. Anytime I would get stuck studying, I let it go. I did something else, then came back and things were clearer. I hoped that it would work with this too.

Chapter Two

When I awoke the next morning, I had no inspiration for how to fix this no boyfriend problem. In fact, I felt worse about the whole thing because of how bad my nightmares had been. I had dreamt that it was graduation night and Andrea showed up to meet me, saw the empty date book and cackled in my face, lightning and the witch sound effects and all. I couldn't let that come true.

The whole drive to West End High, I tried to clear my thoughts. I turned up the music, I turned it off. Nothing changed the fact that I knew no guys that would be willing to do the dates.

Not a single one.

Sage better have brilliant ideas or I'd be screwed.

I parked in my designated spot. As a senior, we could park in the front few rows, so at least I never had a huge walk inside. Our high school was pretty big. There were over five hundred students in the senior class alone, making us the largest group. The West End Warriors were well known in our county. The only high school we ever lost to was Rosewood High.

I grabbed my bookbag from the backseat of my silver Honda Fit. My gaze blurred as I tried to focus on the building. It was hard to believe that I would graduate in a month or so.

The beautiful stone façade had invited me in with open arms from day one. It almost reminded me of a castle, with its large front exterior. Inside it boasted four floors. Many of the rooms were luxurious, paid for by the lovely sponsors of our organization.

We had a huge gym for spectators and all our sports teams. We had a state-of-the-art green room, technology lab, and a makerspace.

My favorite room was of course the library.

"Marley, let's go!" Sage shouted a few cars down.

I shook my head, trying to clear my thoughts. I had to focus and I didn't want to be tardy. I had a perfect record to maintain after all.

"Coming." I locked my car and jogged beside her, surveying her mood.

Today she wore vibrant pink capris and a white shirt that clung to her and merely kissed the top of her pants. I wouldn't be surprised if she didn't get a warning for the outfit. Her light brown hair was braided into two sections, making pigtail braids.

Sage always pushed the dress code. I on the other hand stayed well within the lines, which is why I settled on flare jeans without holes, of course, and my favorite cotton T-shirt in my favorite color—salmon.

"So good news or bad news first?"

I groaned. "Surprise me."

"Well, bad news is I couldn't think of any ideas to get you out of this."

"And good news?"

"I'll keep thinking. Or you could get a boyfriend?"

I rolled my eyes as I strolled past her toward the front

door. "Yeah, because if I couldn't find a boyfriend the first almost four years of high school, I'll manage to find one in the last month? Sage, get real."

"I am! Andrea deserves to eat her words."

"I agree, but I equally came up with nada."

She tapped a finger to her chin. "We are both smart, capable women. We can do this. A dating app?"

"Ugh, no."

"It could be fun. Do a date with each new person?"

"Andrea might be boy crazy and ditzy at times, but I think she'd figure out they were different people each time."

"Okay, so not the best plan, but we have time."

"Not really. A month is hard as it is."

She patted my hand. "It will work out. I know it."

We pushed open the front doors and walked past the office at the entrance.

She waved as she headed to her locker and I headed toward mine. The hallways bustled with students walking to homeroom and their lockers—a sea of red and black, our school colors.

My locker was the last one in the hallway, right at an intersection of classrooms in the history department. I hurried and shoved my books from the weekend inside, grabbed what I needed and headed to class. I would have to think about options later. Now it was more important to focus on my class schedule.

By the end of the day, as I headed toward my locker a few minutes before the final bell, I understood one truth: I was in over my head. What had I been thinking? I didn't have a boyfriend and Andrea knew it couldn't be done within her ridiculous timeline. I was foolish enough thinking I could come up with a plan to beat her. If only I had thrown it back in her face, but then I wouldn't have witnessed that wonderful view of her smug expression melting off her features. I had never pulled one over on Andrea and if I managed to succeed, it would be an accomplishment.

Each class I surveyed boys I thought could be a good option, but what had I noticed? Not *one* of them looked in my direction or acted like I even existed.

I leaned my forehead against my red locker door. I needed to find a way out of this or the next time I saw Andrea at graduation, she would rub it in my face.

Footsteps scuffled down the hallway.

I froze.

"Wyatt, you're failing my class. You need to turn in your homework and write those essays."

Someone cleared their throat. "Mr. Andrews, I just need more time."

I tiptoed toward the voices and peered around the corner.

Wyatt Shaw stood in front of Mr. Andrews, a history teacher. Wyatt wasn't in any of my classes, although in freshman year I thought I had one or two with him. Even with such a large senior class, I tended to know at least the names of all the students. And at this point in the year, word around school was that Wyatt barely showed up for class and truant officers were on a first name basis with him. How could someone ditch school *so* much? What could he really find more important?

"You've had all semester. You have one month until the semester is over, Wyatt. If you don't turn in all the work and pass your final, you will fail. I've talked to your other teachers. You aren't doing well. Do you really want to redo your senior year? I can't imagine that fits into your life plan."

Wyatt shifted his weight and adjusted his bookbag. "No. I don't want to repeat the year. I'll get you the work. I promise."

"See that you do."

The bell rang and students exited their final class. Wyatt turned the corner and walked by.

At least I wasn't in that predicament. I could fix poor grades. I was the best tutor in the school. How to do an adventure book with a boyfriend I didn't have? Well, that was another matter entirely.

Wait a minute!

That was it. That was perfect.

I shut my locker, threw my bag over my shoulder and sprinted after Wyatt.

He exited the outer doors and walked toward the parking lot.

I surveyed the lot, hoping no one saw me, then shouted, "Wyatt, wait up!"

He stopped and turned. He looked through me, as if I didn't exist, then turned around.

My stomach clenched. That didn't bode well for my plan. I hurried along, until I was next to him. I lightly tapped his shoulder and tried again. "Wyatt, wait."

His nose scrunched. "Who ... How do you know my name?"

Well, that was perfect.

I outstretched my hand. "I'm Marley."

He eyed my hand but made no movement to shake it. "And why are you talking to me, Marley?"

Ouch. Clearly I knew my classmate's names, but they didn't all know mine.

"I have a proposition for you."

He arched an eyebrow, eyed me up and down, then laughed.

He actually *laughed*!

"Look whatever you're selling, I'm not interested. I have somewhere to be."

"You haven't even heard what I want."

"Let me guess. Goody two shoes wants to take a ride on the wild side. Figured Wyatt Shaw was the perfect one to do that with."

My mouth gaped.

"I'm not interested in someone who sees me as a label to check off before college."

"Woah, woah, wait. Instead of being so presumptuous, how about you listen first?"

He crossed his arms.

"I-I heard your conversation with Mr. Andrews."

His smug demeanor cracked. "Eavesdropping on me? Even better." He turned away.

I grabbed his arm and stood in front of him.

He eyed my hand and I released him.

"Please just stop interrupting. I could have said it already. I heard about your situation. I'm a really good tutor. I could help you get your grades up."

"If I wanted a tutor, I could go to guidance for one."

"You have a month. You need serious help if you plan to turn around your grades. My methods work. Faster than most. I'm the *only* one who could help you."

"And why would you waste your time on that? I don't have money."

"I'll tutor you for free."

He eyed me warily. "And again, what do you get out of the deal?"

"I need help."

He snorted. "With what?"

"You ... uh. You seem adventurous and I need help with an adventure book."

"An adventure book?"

"Yeah, like those books couples get to amp up their dates.

They have all kinds, but one version is adventure themed dates."

Wyatt stared and then broke out into a sudden fit of laughter. He held his sides as he continued to laugh.

When I didn't start laughing too, he pulled himself together. "Wait you're serious. You want me to go on *dates* with you, while you tutor me? I thought I was being presumptuous when I said you were looking to take a trip on the wild side. What do you call this?"

"Okay, fine. I heard what it sounded like when I said it. I'm crazy, I get it. Just pretend I didn't say anything." I turned and headed for the other side of the parking lot.

He waited until I was at my car door before he called my name. "Marley, was it? I didn't tell you what I thought."

"If you walked all the way over here to tell me I'm insane, I didn't need the reminder."

He chuckled. "Actually, no. I haven't made any decision yet. I think I need more information. Exactly what do these dates entail?"

"Uh ... dates? I don't remember them all. There's a list of them, we complete it, take a picture, put it in the book, and move on."

"Move on, huh?"

"Yeah. I don't need any actual boyfriend perks. No kissing or PDA, no touching required."

He arched a perfect manicured brow. *Did he happen to get those done?* What was I thinking? I was worried about his brow when I clearly needed to be admitted to the hospital for a mandatory seventy-two-hour hold.

"I don't know. That still seems like you get a better bargain than I do."

My eyes widened. "Graduating isn't a big enough lure to you? Mmmkay, well thanks for your time." I turned to my car door.

"Sure, I guess it is, but to turn you adventurous will be a lot harder than digging my grades out of the hole."

I crossed my arms and glared. "Based on what? You didn't even know my name. How do you pretend to know so much about me?"

"You just have an air about you."

"An air? That's made up bologna. No one has an air about them."

"Of course they do," he said deadly serious, then moved close to me, our bodies almost touching, until I backed up against my car. "And yours says you have no idea how to be adventurous, date book ideas, or not."

I hadn't expected to be so close to him, the closeness overtook my brain and I hated that a stupid boy had caused this reaction. I didn't get all crazy over boys, but I also wasn't used to anyone this close to my personal space before.

"I don't have to become adventurous. I just need to complete the dates, adventure guaranteed."

He chuckled, sending his brown hair moving under his knitted beanie. It poked out under the edges and covered his ears and some of his forehead. "That's not guaranteed if I have to drag you through the dates."

"If you don't want my tutoring help, then just say so. I'm not here for your amusement."

"So, to summarize, you tutor me, I go on dates with you to be your fake boyfriend and there's no PDA or touching?"

At least he knew how to summarize. "Yes."

"And how long do I have to do these dates?"

"The book is due by graduation, same time you have until you fail."

He stuck out his hand. "Then you have a deal."

I shook it as reality settled in. I would *fake date* Wyatt Shaw. Sage would never believe me.

"Cool, so are you driving with me or following me?"

"What?"

He checked his phone. "I have a gig and you're the one who made it seem like now or never. So, are you getting in my truck or following me to my gig?"

"Do you even have your books?"

He shifted his bag to the front. "Obviously."

"Um, a gig for what? And where?"

"Marley for being such a fantastic tutor, you sure don't follow logic. Gigs are for musically inclined people like me. I'm the guitarist and lead singer in a band. I have to go there and you need to help me learn stuff, so in between our sets you can help."

A band? He had a gig on a school night? No wonder he couldn't keep up with his studies.

"Yes or no, Marley?" He smirked and I hesitated to answer. "See ... no adventure. You can't even break your routine and it's been two minutes since you started this plan."

I scoffed. "It's not about being adventurous!"

He outstretched his hand, palm up. "Then show me."

I placed my hand over his and let him lead me toward his truck—a black Chevy Silverado.

He walked to the passenger side, shifted a few things around from the sounds, and then held the door open and held his hand out for me to get inside.

I gulped. *Marley, what have you gotten yourself into?* I used his hand to steady myself as I jumped in then settled onto the seat, while he closed the door and walked around.

Before he pulled away, I wracked my brain. Could I actually do this? It was Monday so I didn't have any after school responsibilities, but I usually went to the bookstore with Sage, then home for dinner. I didn't know much about gigs, but I couldn't imagine they would get me home in time for dinner.

The driver's side door slammed shut. Wyatt shifted his bag on the floor between us, then got in the parking lot's line.

I was in Wyatt Shaw's truck. This was ludicrous. What was I thinking? What did I really know about him?

I pulled my phone from my bag and texted Sage first.

> I propositioned Wyatt Shaw to be my fake boyfriend. If I disappear, I went with him to a gig.

Then I texted my mom.

> Hey, Mom. I'm going to Sage's house after the bookstore. I'll be home after dinner, don't wait for me.

> Okay, honey. Be safe. Love you.

"I must admit, I'm intrigued why Marley Wix would want to associate with me."

I narrowed my gaze and turned to face him. "How'd you know my last name? I didn't mention that when I told you who I was."

He shrugged.

"You *knew* who I was. How rude! You pretended you had no idea when you knew."

"So, what if I did? Not a crime."

"Maybe not, but it's not sociable either."

"Well, last time I checked, I'm not known for being sociable. Which is why I'm intrigued. Of all the people you could pick to complete this so-called book, why me?"

"Because it was a mutually beneficial arrangement."

He chuckled. "I reserve my opinion for later when we actually do some tutoring."

"Well, while we're stuck together in this truck, we might as well iron out details of our schedule."

"You really are a goody two shoes. Syncing up schedules? Is that seriously necessary?"

"Yes. I only have you on my schedule for tutoring, so at least that frees up some time, but I'm in National Honor Society and SADD, you know Students Against Destructive Decisions."

"Yeah, I'm aware of what it stands for."

I leaned closer to him. "And you? What can I expect will interrupt our tutoring and the dates?"

We finally left the parking lot for West End High. Wyatt turned right toward the highway.

I crinkled my nose. "Where is this gig?"

"Outside of Rosewood County." He peered at me for the first time since we started to drive. "Someone isn't worried about crossing county lines are they?"

"No." I was, but I didn't want to tell him that. I pulled out my planner and pen from my bag. "Seriously, though. We need a schedule."

He closed my planner. "Okay, rule number one. If you want adventure, you *can't* plan it."

I sighed. "Is this going to work out? I don't actually need to be adventurous to do these dates. Are you sure you can take it seriously? Because if not, let me know now. I have until graduation to finish those dates and document them with my boyfriend. That leaves very little wiggle room."

"Fine then rule number one for fake dating *me*. I don't do planners and syncing schedules."

"Okay, then how else do you propose we pick days to tutor and date?"

"Wing it?"

"Well, I can't do that. I'll try to compromise. You don't have to tell me your whole schedule. If we're tutoring today, then how about tomorrow we do a date after school, if that works?"

He nodded. "Fine, but I'll pick the date. Do you have the book?"

"At home. I'll bring it to you tomorrow and you can hold onto it."

He grinned. "Relinquishing control? Look at you!"

"Don't get too cocky about it."

"I would never."

My phone chirped. I pulled it out to check my texts. One from Sage scrolled along the top.

> Wyatt Shaw?! Have you lost your mind?

> I need details. I need photos. He's hot!

My stomach lurched at the words. I shoved the phone back in my bag and glanced at Wyatt. Had he seen the texts?

No. He barely took his eyes off the road.

But I had to be more careful. This was strictly business. I could help him and he could help me. Okay, sure, Sage was right, and I had eyes. He was cute in that unkempt, bad boy kind of way, I supposed.

Even though it was getting warmer, he still wore jeans and that beanie over his mahogany-brown hair. And his eyelashes could have landed a plane. I mean, if he was a girl, I would have thought he used fake eyelashes. I honestly didn't realize someone's eyelashes could be so long.

I wrinkled my nose. What was I doing? As if sizing him up would help this situation. His attractiveness did nothing for me. It was *fake*. "What kind of band are you in?"

"Ouch." Wyatt grabbed his chest and glanced toward me. "Are you telling me you really don't know?"

I shook my head.

"Hmm, well, we're the Honkey Tonks, so I'm sure you can guess what we play."

I eyed him warily. Was he serious? I searched his car for any clues. He didn't wear cowboy boots or have a hat anywhere that would resemble what I pictured a country band to dress in, but I also knew I shouldn't judge someone by their looks for their taste in music.

"Oh, cool."

Wyatt's gaze connected with mine.

Was he studying my expression to see if I was judging him?

A smirk spread across his face, then he burst out laughing. "Seriously, Marley, the Honkey Tonks? You really fell for that?"

Words escaped me. I didn't want to fall into a trap, I honestly had no idea what kind of music he'd play. Guitars were versatile, so it could have been anything. "No?"

"You could have fooled me. You looked deathly serious. Honestly, we're a cover band right now. We do all kinds of songs, depends on the crowd, sometimes we shift the genre of the original, too."

"That's cool. I could never play an instrument."

He shrugged.

Wyatt drove over a rough patch in the road, sending me almost into the roof of the truck, as he turned right and parked.

I peered through the window to see the name of the place. The sign said LUCY'S BAR and GRILL. "We're going into a bar? Don't you have to be twenty-one?"

"At just a plain bar, yes you do. This is a bar *and* grill, which makes it family friendly, but they also book live bands throughout the week."

"Oh, gotcha. Okay."

Wyatt opened the door behind his seat and grabbed a guitar case and his bookbag. Then he sauntered toward the door like he owned the place.

I hastened toward him. The place was at least well lit, but I still felt uncomfortable being outside of the county.

Rosewood had everything I needed in a county. I never had much of a need to leave it.

"Are you coming or are you staying out here and gawking?"

I knitted my eyebrows. "I'm following. I've just never been here before."

He snorted. "That doesn't surprise me in the slightest, Ms. I'm-So-Adventurous." He pulled the door open and waited as I slipped inside.

The place was well lit. The walls were a dark beige and a bar was placed off toward the left side, while the rest had booths and tables for the restaurant end. A stage was perfectly centered, which at least was smart on their part.

Wyatt paused shortly, then strolled over to a table closest to the bar, but out of the way and off to the side. He plopped his bookbag down on the table, pointed to a chair and said, "Sit."

I began to protest but stopped short. It would have fallen on deaf ears anyway. So, I sat, even if it made me feel like a dog. He disappeared behind a fake wall by the stage, which was the exact moment my nerves kicked up another notch.

This was insane. I barely knew Wyatt and yet I was at his gig and somehow would tutor him? It made no sense.

A waitress strolled by the table and asked for a drink order. I asked for a Coke, then shifted uncomfortably on the leather upholstered chair. Thankfully, Wyatt reemerged from behind the wall and sat on a chair opposite me.

"We're the third band to play tonight, so we should have about forty-five minutes before I have to go back again." He yanked open his bookbag and started stacking textbooks on the table.

"You seriously did bring them all. I suppose that's a start, I guess."

He shrugged. "So, you know about Mr. Andrews, but I

also have math homework, an English paper, and the outline for my science research project."

My eyes widened. "What's the most pressing?"

"All of it? Everything except the math homework is late."

For more times than I could even count at this point, I had to wonder about my line of thinking. Even with my methods, that was a serious hole to dig someone out of. "Is any of it partway complete?"

"Yes and no."

"That's not a real answer. It either is started or it isn't."

"Okay, yes, but probably not the best quality."

I shifted the books around the table as the waitress dropped off my soda. "Here's what I'm thinking. Let's do the math homework while I review what you've started. Do you have questions about the math homework?"

"No."

"Good, now do that and hand over the rest."

He obliged, which was another good sign. I skimmed his assignments from Mr. Andrews that were due and they needed some work. It wasn't that they were bad, so much as incomplete and clearly not organized. His topics shifted too many times and had no evidence to back them up. As for his English and science assignments, he had little more than a skeletal outline completed.

"You sure you still want to do this arrangement?"

I squinted. "Are you trying to pile it on in hopes of scaring me out of the deal?"

"Why would I do that? You're helping me pass."

"Just checking, and yes, I do."

He held up both hands, then continued to stare at his textbook. "What I can't figure out is why."

I leaned over, looking at the problem he was on. "It's the same as finding x, doesn't matter what the variable is."

He chuckled. "I don't mean I can't find the letter y. I mean why someone would give *you* this book? Maybe even who would go along with it when they don't have a boyfriend."

"No wasn't an option."

"No is always an option."

I sighed. "Not with my cousin it's not."

"Our next band will be Broken Axles after a short intermission," said someone through the microphone.

Wyatt swiveled in his chair and stood. "Gotta go." He walked behind the stage as the crowd began to get louder. People shoved closer to the bar. It was barely five o' clock, but more and more people milled around. Were they here for Wyatt's band or for the bar in general? Five seemed early to be at the bar, but what would I know? I had never been to a party in my life. I had never had alcohol either, so my knowledge of parties in high school were limited to TV shows and movies.

Wyatt peered from behind the wall, followed by two other people, one guy I thought I recognized from school and the other a girl I had never seen before in my life.

Wyatt approached the microphone, looked around the audience and smiled.

His smile hit me right in the stomach, sending it careening to my feet. He was gorgeous when he smiled. His lashes bounced as he blinked, and he eyed the crowd like they were his best friend. "How're we doing tonight, Lucy's?"

The crowd raised a few glasses and a few people at the bar cheered, although I suspected they would have cheered for anything. Two girls were barely sitting on their stools from how wasted they already were.

I shook my head and sipped more of my soda. Why did people get that out of control? All it led to was regret and poor decisions.

"We are the Broken Axles and we hope you like our set!" Wyatt took a few steps backward from the microphone, whispered something to his bandmates, then began strumming his guitar.

Attending a concert? Check. I was already having more adventures. I took a picture with my phone and texted it to Sage with the caption:

Andrea's going down!

So hot!

I'm only tutoring him Sage, no PDA.

Well, change the deal.

No and I have to go.

I recognized their first song as a cover of *Counting Stars* by One Republic. The next two I didn't know, but they performed well. I found myself bouncing to the beat and Wyatt's voice was good. He definitely had a range. I had no idea he was so good at his music. And his presence on stage was there, too. He really connected with the crowd, even though it was clear most didn't know him.

By the final song, people had moved closer to the stage and many of the women waved and were watching the set. Wyatt looked over at me and winked, then went into his final song.

Had he winked at me on purpose? Was it for his stage act? Otherwise, why would he wink at me?

Then just like that he thanked the crowd and disappeared behind the stage. The crowd clapped and a few people shouted nice job, then he was back out by the table like nothing had even happened.

"Ready to go?"

"Yeah, sure."

He packed up his books into his bookbag, then threw a few dollar bills on the table before he led me back out to his truck.

"That was fast."

He shrugged. "That's how it goes when you aren't well known."

"Oh, well we didn't do much for tutoring."

"We will, but Lucy's isn't the best place to study or write papers."

"True. You're pretty good."

"Just pretty good? Not Earth shattering or life altering?"

I giggled. "I only heard five songs."

"And? A few notes is all you really need to make a decision."

"Not for me."

He frowned. "Do you make any spontaneous decisions?"

"Not generally." I looked around. "Except this one."

He chuckled. "Well, I guess on that note, there's hope for you yet."

We headed back to school to get my car and I was still in denial that this afternoon had even happened. If this was hard to believe, what would I do when it came to the dates? Tutoring was one thing; *dating* was something entirely different.

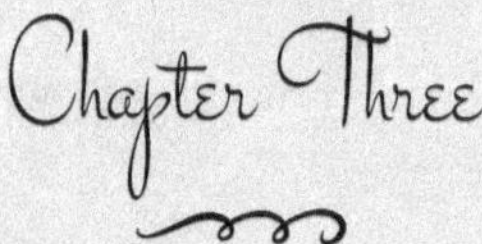# Chapter Three

age practically assaulted me at my locker. "You didn't
think a call was imperative?"

"No. Why?"

Sage rolled her eyes. "You went to a *bar* with Wyatt Shaw!
Marley, that's not a little out of your comfort zone. That's a
new solar system out of your comfort zone."

"It's not a big deal." I lied.

It *was* a big deal. It had been such a big deal that I had
barely slept.

I didn't know what was worse, the fact I wanted to back
out of the deal or that Andrea would have won. So instead of
doing what I would normally do, I decided that Andrea
winning was the greater of two evils and trudged forward.

But how would I do this? PDA aside, I had to *date* him
and get his grades up to pass senior year. Talk about pressure.

I peeked at Sage's face.

She haughtily stared at me, waiting for me to crack and
look her way.

When I did, she smirked. "You may be able to somehow
twist the truth around in your head, but I'm your best friend

and I know you. This is *huge*. And the fact you're in denial just proves my point more."

"What is that supposed to mean?"

"You always deny hard things. It's your thing."

"It is not."

"You denied taking Latin was hard. You denied the difficulty of AP Calc." She listed a few more as she ticked them off on each finger.

I raised my hand toward her. "Okay. I get it."

"See? If something feels really hard to you, you pretend it's easy. I mean it's a genius mind hack but does nothing for admitting the truth."

"Fine. I'm terrified. I don't understand why he *really* wants to help me, and I'm worried about my success rate. I don't want him to fail."

Sage looped her arm with mine and shut my locker door. "The first step to any problem is admitting you have one. You are now free to brainstorm."

I sighed. "That's not helpful. I need ideas." I shifted the book between hands. Wyatt would be here any minute to peruse it and my stomach had vacated my body. My brain could find no current location for it anymore.

Sage grabbed the book. "Stop fiddling. My goodness, Marley. It's a book. It isn't filled with magical potions and spells." Sage cackled. "Actually, that'd be better. You could use it to curse Andrea."

"Sage!"

"What?" She shrugged. "You know you'd be tempted."

Wyatt's face peeked around the corner. "Tempted? Ooh, goody-two shoes being tempted? Now that is something I'd want to see."

Sage raised an eyebrow.

"Uh ..."

Wyatt looked between us. "What are you tempted by?"

"Marley would be tempted to get back at her cousin, if given the chance."

I snatched the book from Sage and glared. "She doesn't know what she's talking about. No temptation here."

"Now that sounds more like you." Wyatt smiled. How was it so carefree as if he wasn't on the verge of flunking high school? I would have been a nervous wreck.

But no. He batted those beautifully long lashes and waited for me to eventually respond.

Ugh, my IQ was higher than this! Why was I being so dumb?

"Sage, don't you have *class* to get to?"

She crossed her arms then pointed to her phone.

I knew I would hear about it in texts, but I didn't care. It was a million times harder talking to Wyatt with everyone around and the careful scrutiny from my best friend.

Wyatt eyed the black bound *cursed* book. "Is that it?"

I nodded and proffered it to him.

He flipped through a few pages, his eyes widened on a few, but otherwise his face never creased with worry or disgust.

That was a good sign, right?

"Cool. So, what's your first class?"

I twisted my wrist to see my watch. We had ten minutes until the bell rang. "Actually, I have a free first period today. So, I'll probably go to the library and work on a plan for helping you. You have Andrews?"

He nodded. "Already memorizing my schedule, huh?"

I stuttered. "What? No. It just makes sense that you would since I saw you yesterday at the end of the day with him. That *is* how our schedules work."

Wyatt chuckled. "Relax, would you? I was joking, although seeing that reaction made it even more fun. You're too tense. Second rule, if you're going to fake date me, you have to be flexible. And being flexible means taking a joke and not letting it fluster you."

"I'm not flustered."

He leaned in. "Could have fooled me." He poked my right cheek, his skin brushing mine. "Your rosy cheeks tell me that you *are* in fact flustered."

My jaw tensed. "Well, anything I should know about your work before I devise a tutoring plan?"

"Nope. Just what I told you last night."

"Okay. Then I'll go from there. You have to make sure you let me know if you get other projects and all new homework has to be completed."

"Aye, aye."

I rolled my eyes. "Can you take this seriously?"

He pulled his smile into a thin line. "Absolutely. Completely serious."

"Right, okay. Where should I meet you for the date then?"

He took out his phone. "Why don't you put your number in my contacts and then I'll text you. If we're sticking with the plan, I think it'd make sense, don't you?"

Of course he was right, but why did he have to seem so smug about it? I took the phone and entered my digits and name then passed it back. Who knew this is how I would tick a boy asking me for my number off my list?

"Great. I'll see you later," he said then took off down the hallway, my cursed little adventure book tucked beneath his arm.

Focus, Marley. It's just a tutor session. You've done them a hundred times before.

My phone buzzed in my hand. I didn't have to look to know it was Sage.

Don't think you're off the hook for dismissing me. I saw through your scheme. I won't snatch Wyatt Shaw from you, but girl, you need to rearrange your deal. Put PDA on the table. He's cuter up close!

I put her on read, then shoved the phone back in my pocket. She was crazy and I was in no mood to consider PDA with Wyatt.

The library was centrally located on the second floor of our building. If I was being honest, it rivaled bookstores, let alone a school library. I strolled past Mrs. Swanson at her desk.

She smiled at me, then refocused on her tasks. She was a sweet older lady. Before I went to school at West End, she had taught science classes, but decided to *retire* as the school librarian.

I couldn't picture her as a science person. Her love of books was inspiring. She tended to find me new reads more than I did, and *I* was the teenager.

In the middle of the library were many tables grouped together for partner work or study sessions. Then bookcases surrounded those tables with smaller cubby type seating on the outskirts.

Since freshmen year, I always sat at the same place. The back right corner on the upper platform of the library, because, of course, we had two floors in one room. For the most part, I never caught anyone in my seat, and today was no different.

My bag thudded on the floor as I dropped it, then pulled out a legal pad to jot down ideas. A month was no easy feat to have a one hundred and eighty degree turn for Wyatt's grades. I needed clear and precise steps to get him on track.

I placed my phone face up on the corner of the desk and then wrote out all his assignments he informed me of. Staring at the list was daunting, especially with their delinquency.

My first step was to get his main idea or theses for each paper cemented so he could look for support afterward.

I tapped the pen to my chin. He wouldn't like ironing the details out, so I had to find an alternative way to get him to focus, without shutting him down.

My phone buzzed from a text.

WYATT

Testing, testing. Marley?

Yep. It's me.

Maybe if we worked on his paper *during* the date, one could be done. I sighed; he surely wouldn't go for that. I could hear him now. *This is a date, not studying.* Except he was out of time. Part of my job as a tutor was to bolster the person's confidence in their abilities. They had to know they could do it. Once that light clicked on, they took my structure and ran with it.

How's the library?

Fine.

You know, you can text in the library, there's only a rule about talking.

What are you talking about?

Your one word texts. You talk faster than a cheetah runs in person, there's no way you're a one word texter.

I scowled. Why was he dissecting me? That wasn't the deal.

I sent him a rolling eyes emoji and faced the phone down. I only had twenty-five minutes left of free period and barely a timeline. It was time to concentrate.

I shifted uncomfortably from foot to foot at my car. Wyatt had texted me to wait for him at my vehicle. I had no idea how he would start the dates and now that it had actually arrived, my stomach knotted up more than a toddler's hair with gum stuck in it.

Sage made a drum roll on my car's hood. "You got this and girl, *text me* when you get home. Or I will stalk your house."

I giggled. "Get out of here!"

She waved and strolled to her VW bug—lime green to match her wild personality.

Wyatt's black Chevy Silverado pulled up next to me. He

leaned out the open window. "Hop in your car and follow me."

I scrunched my nose. "Where are we going?"

"Rule two. Gotta be flexible." He gestured toward my car.

I growled. I hated this being a surprise. I wanted a warning. The dates in that book ranged from easy to hard and I couldn't tell how he'd start. I put the key in the ignition and started the engine. My radio blasted, almost giving me a heart attack.

I really needed to adjust my radio volume back to normal decibels before I got out. I pulled behind his truck and waited in the ridiculously long line.

Seniors should have had a fast pass. Like EZPASS or fast passes at amusement parks so we didn't have to wait in traffic for the last year of high school. I pulled my phone from my bag while I waited. I had barely moved an inch.

I already had two texts.

SAGE

Send me the picture you two take after the date. Oh, and I want ideas for your couple name. Has to be a good one. Nothing like Warley or Wyley.

WYATT

Stop scowling. It'll be fine.

I peered up and tried to see his gaze in his rearview mirror.

He waved and his lips moved, but I had no idea what he said. I was tragically awful at reading lips.

I texted back.

I am not.

I can see your face. You are.

Thankfully, traffic moved, and I had to put the phone down. I followed him on the main road leading away from school. He turned down several back roads that didn't even feel large enough to be a two-way street, until he turned down a gravel road. The sign said, WEST END CREAMERY.

He was taking me for ice cream?

After several bumps in the gravel road that I was pretty sure would require my car to need a new alignment, we parked. Then I grabbed my clutch wallet from my bookbag and locked the car.

Wyatt outstretched his arms wide and turned. "Welcome to the Creamery."

I arched a brow. "What date does this fulfill?"

"Try something new."

"I've been here like a hundred times."

"Not with me. Dating me is trying something new, so you're welcome." He leaned closer. "Plus, this would let us start easy. I perused the dates and you are not ready for some of those yet."

I wrinkled my nose. "Like what?"

He patted my arm; contact I hadn't expected. "You just let me worry about that." He rubbed his hands together quickly. "Okay, hit me with your favorite. Are you a cone or cup person?" He eyed me closely. "You like ice cream in a cup, don't you?"

My mouth opened wide. No words left.

"You are. I knew it, probably some silly excuse about it melting. So, to add a double layer, how about you get a cone?"

I crossed my arms. "Done."

"And I'll get mine in a cup, even though I think it's a travesty to the poor ice cream cone."

"The cone doesn't have feelings."

He gasped and placed his hands over his ears. "Do *not* say

that in there." He chuckled. "Kidding. Anyway, what's your favorite flavor?"

"Strawberry."

He nodded. "Classic. Okay." He led us toward the front door, then kept it open for me.

I hadn't expected chivalry from Wyatt. Although, what did I really know about him besides rumors and gossip? He appeared unapproachable and yesterday's meeting had certainly confirmed that, but today felt totally different. Was this how he really was or was he pretending for my benefit?

The line was short and before I knew it, we were at the front. He ordered a plain cone with two scoops of strawberry for me and two scoops of rocky road in a cup for him.

He reached for his wallet.

I placed my hand over his and shook my head. "It's the least I can do. The dates were my idea."

The cashier eyed us curiously but stayed silent.

Wyatt almost looked like he wanted to argue, but I handed my card over already.

We grabbed a seat at a picnic table outside. It had the perfect view of the rest of the property. There was a small petting zoo and I meant small. It only had three goats and a pig. Around the back was playground equipment for younger kids and in the front had two sets of cornhole.

Wyatt took out his phone and placed it in view of us. "Smile."

I had just licked the cone when he snapped the picture. "Wyatt, let me see!"

He held the phone in front of me, but far enough away I couldn't touch it. "I can't tell how I look."

"Good, you don't need to. It's evidence enough for the book."

I harrumphed. "Well, send it to me so I can print it."

He smiled. "Later. I don't want you calling re-do."

"Fine."

He scooped a large bite of rocky road on his spoon and shoved it in his mouth.

We sat in silence as we ate. I used the time to calm my nerves, which were ridiculous. It meant nothing that I was eating ice cream with Wyatt. This was a business arrangement of epic proportions and I knew that. Completely. Zero doubts.

But if it hadn't been, then wow, could I get lost in that smile. His best smile was the one that came naturally. His straight, white teeth, added to those long lashes over his brown eyes were easily swoon worthy.

I would be dead if I didn't notice. Not to mention this was an experiment. Observations were part of experiments, and they made a good scientist. So, I was merely being studious.

"Were you successful with my plan?" Wyatt asked.

"I think so. It will take work, though."

"I expected that."

"Well, good. We could do some work now ..."

"Nope. I'm instituting the rule that there is no tutoring talk, unless initiated by me on a date."

"Oh, really? Why?"

"Spontaneity. You'll slip back into your normal mode otherwise."

"Okay, well, then what?"

He tilted his head toward the cornhole game. "We play a game of cornhole after ice cream."

I groaned. "I'm not athletic."

"So? It's a low stakes backyard game."

"Yeah, but if I completely miss the board, isn't that like a foul?"

He chuckled. "Cornhole has no referees. I think you'll be safe."

I finished my cone slowly. The longer I took, the less time I had to embarrass myself in cornhole.

"Today, Marley. No matter what, you have to play, so let's get a move on." He squinted toward my cone. "And you wouldn't want it to drip down your fingers, making them all sticky would you?"

I twisted the cone and sure enough, a stray drip was closer to my finger. "Fine."

He tossed his paper cup into the trashcan, then headed to the nearest cornhole game. He checked the bags, but I had no idea what for. I barely understood how to play. It wasn't like my parents had a bunch of time to spend with me outside playing backyard games.

"Purple or green?" Wyatt asked.

"Huh?"

"The bean bags?" He arched a brow. "Do you know how to play?"

"Not really?"

His eyes widened. "But this is a classic game. How are you a senior and have no clue how to play?"

I crossed my arms. "How about you just tell me, instead of judging?"

"There's no judgment. It was an honest question." He shook his head, his gaze had somehow deflated.

Had I caused that?

I tossed my napkin in the trash and trudged toward where he waited.

He handed over the green ones. "You stand at one end and I stand at the other. When it's your turn, you toss the bean bag and try to get it to land in the hole or on the board. Our points cancel each other's. So, if we both get our bag in the hole, no one gets the point. Three points in the hole, one on the board. Okay?"

I nodded.

He stood behind the board, angled his wrist, then released at the top of his arc.

The bag lofted into the air, then fell a little short right at the foot of the board.

Had he done that purposefully to make me feel better about my athletic ability? Or was that just a warm-up throw?

I shifted the bags in my hand. "How often do you play a gig?"

"Depends on the week I suppose. It will happen more often as we get closer to the summer. More festivals, music programs, things like that."

"That makes sense. How do you know the other band members?"

"Jack goes to school at West End. Claire graduated two years ago. Jack and I met her at some party sophomore year. We ended up fooling around on the tops of tables and on my guitar that I had brought. We realized we meshed really well."

"That's cool. Does Claire go to college?"

"Yeah, for music. She's halfway through a music business degree."

"That's impressive."

Wyatt finished his turn. He had landed one on the board, but that was it.

I exhaled and tried to relax. I could do this. I just had to toss the bags to the board. I tried to aim as he watched me. Just as I released it, the bag soared into the air and veered way off to the left. I groaned.

He stifled a chuckle. Clearly I was terrible.

I threw the remainder and as with the first, none came close to the board.

We picked up each other's bags and walked them to the middle.

"Thanks," he murmured.

I nodded and walked back to my side. Maybe he would beat me quickly to put me out of my misery.

"What about you? Where are you headed to college?"

"UPenn for finance."

He nodded as if he expected that answer.

I pushed my unruly brown hair from my face as I watched him take his turn. This time he landed each bag on the board.

"What's your favorite song to play?"

"With the band or just in general?"

"Both."

"With the band, I love playing *Piano Man*. It always gets the crowd hyped and vibing with us."

"And alone?"

"Alone I love playing *Sweet Child O' Mine*."

Sweet Child O' Mine? That was not what I had expected at all.

"I know what you're thinking."

I doubted that.

"How could Wyatt Shaw play *Sweet Child O' Mine*? But my mom loved the song, and it always reminded me of her."

Reminded? As in past tense? Did that mean ...?

As predicted, my turn had been horrible again. I was a little closer to the board, but nothing close enough to give me a point.

Wyatt concentrated and landed two in the hole. "That makes eleven, which would mean I win if we played the shortened version."

I dropped the bags. "Fine by me."

He chuckled. "I think you did fine."

I placed my hands on my hips. "Really? We may be *fake* dating, but it doesn't mean you have to give me *fake* compliments. I'm perfectly okay knowing my strengths lie elsewhere."

"Fair enough." He peered toward the petting zoo. "Want to pet the animals?"

"Sure."

He walked toward the pig first, then stopped in front. He tentatively stuck his hand toward the pig's snout. When the pig responded kindly, he rubbed it more.

I on the other hand went for the goats. They were babies after all, and quite cute. I stopped in front of the black and white one.

The other goats tried to climb over to get my attention, but I ignored them the best I could.

"They like you," Wyatt said.

"They like attention and probably can smell I had ice cream."

"I don't know. They're watching you."

"So do I get to see the picture yet?"

"You really do have a hard time letting go." He sighed and pulled out his phone.

Mine dinged in response and I pulled up the message. There it was: our first *date* picture. His smile was relaxed, and I had thought I'd look horrible from the timing, but it wasn't bad. I looked at the ice cream cone, almost about to open my mouth and lick it, but I hadn't done so yet.

"And?"

"It's not bad."

He clutched his chest. "A compliment? From goody-two-shoes. Wow! I'm shocked. I figured it would take longer to manage that."

I stifled a giggle. "Whatever. Now, how about a *little* tutoring talk?"

He shook his head. "Nope. Dates don't end until someone pulls away."

I groaned. "Really? It's fake though."

"I take my fake dating duties seriously, as you should take the tutoring. So, nope."

"Ugh, fine." I crossed my arms and headed toward our parked cars.

Wyatt followed behind, giving me some room, but he was still close enough I could sense him. He stopped at his truck and leaned against the passenger door as I stood at my driver's side. "I have something to do after school tomorrow. So, I can't do tutoring."

I groaned. "Wyatt, we have to get busy. Each day that goes by is not helping the situation."

He put up both hands like a crossing guard. "I wasn't done. It's right after school, *but* I could meet you later around six."

I frowned. "The library is closed by five."

"There isn't anywhere else you can think of?"

"I mean my best friend's dad owns a bookstore. We could go there."

"Do they have drinks?"

I nodded. "And snacks."

"Perfect. I'll bring the books and meet you at six then."

"Okay. It's Marshall's Books on Creed Street."

He nodded. "See you at school, Marley."

I waved and got in my car.

He stayed put until I pulled away. One date down, too many to go.

Chapter Four

S age had screamed so loud when I told her what we did and saw the picture that I was pretty sure I needed hearing aids for the next two hours. Thankfully, she calmed down after the initial shock wore off.

I had printed it out when I got home and placed two-sided tape near it for when I would tutor Wyatt. I hadn't realized that it would be hard for me to place the pictures if he kept the book all the time.

Luckily, he promised to bring it when I tutored him.

My parents hadn't questioned much when I told them I'd be home later. I had let them know I was tutoring and that was that.

I guessed it helped that this week they were busy at work. My mom had a big case and my dad was ushering other colleagues around the hospital for tours and schmoozing as he called it.

Either way, I was home free.

I checked the time. It was five minutes past six and I still hadn't heard from Wyatt. I smoothed down my blouse for the fifth time and checked my phone for messages once more.

It wasn't like communication devices hadn't been invented. Technology made it possible to keep in touch with the world at the snap of my fingers. He couldn't text me he'd be late?

The bookstore wasn't super busy for a weeknight. I had chosen a table that angled itself toward the door but also away from the cash register and snack counter. I didn't want him to be occupied when he needed to concentrate on the tutoring.

My fingers tapped on the table, as if the faster they went, it would summon his presence.

Finally, the bell over the door rang and in strolled Wyatt.

His expression was strained and the carefree Wyatt from yesterday had been replaced by a sullen and brooding teenager. What was that about?

"I wish you would have told me you were going to be late."

His jaw tensed. "I didn't know." He piled his books from his bag on the table. "I'll be right back."

I sat there, mouth agape. He was late and now he was disappearing again? I seriously hoped he brought his will to work because otherwise this would be a *long* tutoring session.

After a few minutes, he sat with his hands clutching a to-go mug from the bookstore. He took several long drinks before he looked at me.

"Everything okay?"

"Fine. Let's just get this over with."

Fine. Grouchy Wyatt it is.

"I want to work on your thesis for each paper. Once we nail down those, you can separately work on finding support and then we meet to go over what you found."

"Sure. What do you need?"

"Do you have the original papers that show the requirements?"

He pulled several packets from different notebooks, then

handed them over. He sipped his drink while I skimmed them for the main prompts.

"Do you have to turn these in?"

"No."

"Perfect." I took a turquoise felt tip pen and underlined each packet for the main questions. "I underlined the point for each of your papers. Now we just have to answer them based on your opinions before we look for support."

He groaned. "We really have to do these today?"

"Yes. Papers don't write themselves the day before."

"No paper writes itself, but papers *can* be written the day before. I've done it plenty of times."

"And look at your grades."

His gaze narrowed. "Fine. Which one to start with?"

"Doesn't matter. You choose."

He ruffled through each one, until he landed on an English paper from his world literature class.

"Okay, so the question is how is pride involved in the novel *Things Fall Apart*?"

"Pride? Okonkwo falls victim to pride throughout the novel."

"Perfect. What are three examples of this?"

"He takes pride in his accomplishments, his pride gets in the way when he judges others, and his pride is damaged from his exile."

"Boom. That's basically your introduction. You have the graphic organizer for the other couple of sentences, but that is the main purpose of your paper. Use the organizer to write that down. Then we will do another one."

Wyatt dutifully started writing, while I surveyed the bookstore. Sage's dad wasn't at the cash register, but Sage had told me he had hired someone recently to work the weeknights she couldn't.

The ambience was peaceful. Small fairy lights were

wrapped around the tops of bookcases alighting the store in soft light. All sorts of things to sit on were littered throughout the space. There were several tables for moments like this, but there were also seats built into bookshelves near the edges of the rooms, large bean bag chairs, and soft rugs to warm up the dark hardwood floors. The walls were a slate blue, a nice contrast with the stain of the shelves.

I never failed to get lost in a book here.

"Okay, that's done."

"Which one next?"

"I guess I should do one for Mr. Andrews."

I nodded. "What about the most delinquent one?"

He pulled it from the bottom pile and read what I had underlined. "What is supply and demand? How does it impact a product of your choice?"

"Any idea on what product you want to choose?"

"No."

"Okay, well what do you like to learn about?"

He scrunched his nose. "Music?"

"Okay, so what about an instrument or songs?"

He sighed. "That feels dumb."

"Do you have any other hobbies or interests?"

"Fine. I'll just do a guitar."

"That works. Just write it next to the question, so you can come back to it."

Two done. I only hoped we could finish them all before it was too late.

"These look great."

Wyatt didn't quite smile, but he seemed to be at least somewhat proud of his work, which was a start.

I grabbed my mug of herbal tea and sipped as I watched

the patrons at the shop. Many seemed to be by themselves and older, around college age.

"Thanks for helping me. It was easier to concentrate with someone else around."

"No problem. That's the deal."

He nodded. "Right."

"So, have you figured out what we should do on the next date and when?" I pulled the photo from my bag. "I printed this for the book."

He twisted around and grabbed the adventure book from his bag.

I arched an eyebrow. "You brought it with you?"

"Never know when I'll need it." He grabbed the photo from me, our fingers gently brushing, and placed it in the spot for try something new. "I told you it was a good one."

"Yes, you were right."

He gaped. "I was right? Oh, man. I need to hear that again."

I averted my gaze and mumbled, "You were right."

He pumped a fist in the air like one of those eighties' movie love interests. "That makes the whole day so much better."

I scrunched my nose. There it was again, that feeling like something had happened. But even with the gut feeling that something seemed off, it wasn't my place to ask. I was his fake date, not his real one.

"What's your schedule like tomorrow?" he asked.

"I have our monthly National Honor Society meeting after school until four. Then nothing."

"Okay. So, meet you in the parking lot at four? I'll drive for this one."

I arched a brow. "Why?"

"Because and that's all the questions about that."

I sighed. "Will you ever give me a warning?"

He stroked his chin. "Probably not."

I crossed my arms. "Fine, but you'd tell me if I had to dress specifically for it, right?"

"Maybe."

"Fine. But you need to write out supporting details for one of these papers by tomorrow when I see you. Have you been keeping up with your homework?"

He nodded. "I just need the supporting details for one?"

"Yep."

"Easy peasy."

I huffed. "If it's so easy, why didn't you do it before?"

Wyatt leaned back in his chair, shifting his hair under a gray beanie. Something darker flitted through his gaze. I didn't know him well, so I had no idea what that was about.

"I'll make sure I do it."

"Thank you."

"So, what would you be doing if you weren't here with me?"

"Normally, I'd be home by now. Doing homework or reading I guess."

"Are you an only child?"

"Yep, and my parents usually have weird work schedules, so it's generally just me at home."

"What do they do?"

"Mom's a lawyer. My dad is a doctor."

"Wow. I'm surprised you didn't choose one of those professions then."

I wrinkled my nose. "I was never interested in arguing or needles."

He chuckled. "But finance does it for you?"

"I like the rationality of numbers."

"So, no pie then?"

My nose crinkled. "Huh?"

"Well pi is irrational ..."

Did he just make a math joke? I didn't even know what to say.

"Tough crowd."

"No. I mean that was a good one ..."

"Just didn't expect it from the dumb guitar player."

"Hey. I didn't say that."

He shook his head and closed the books spread out between us. "It's fine, Marley. I should head out."

Did he really think I thought that? I would never place myself above someone else just because they weren't a *school* person. I knew better.

Still, I couldn't help but watch him pack up and then leave, never turning around even as he reached the door.

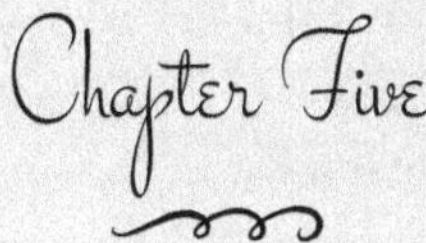

Chapter Five

I parked my Honda Fit in the driveway and sighed as I watched the house. The outside lights were on and my dad's car was in the driveway. At least I wouldn't be home alone.

Wyatt's mood nagged me. Something about it wasn't right but I couldn't figure out what could change his attitude in such a short time. It wasn't like I knew him that well, but it was unusual for anyone to change so much in that timeframe.

Something was happening in his life that I had no clue about.

The keys jangled as I shoved them into my bookbag and used the garage door to head inside. I placed my bag on the dining room chair and headed toward the scent of food sizzling in the kitchen.

"Hey, kiddo," my dad shouted.

"Hi, dad."

He jumped. "I didn't realize you were that close. Sorry I yelled."

"It's okay." I sniffed the air. "Whatcha making?"

"Cheesesteak. Want one?"

"Always."

He smiled and flipped the meat over again on the griddle.

My dad wasn't usually an unhealthy eater … unless his day went poorly. A bad outcome in a surgery or the loss of a patient usually meant fatty and fried foods for dinner.

I hopped up on the stool at the kitchen island, focusing on the marble designed counters. "What happened today?"

His shoulders slumped before he turned. "Patient died on the table."

"I'm sorry, Dad."

"I wish I could say it didn't happen, but unfortunately it does in my field. The patient's insides were all scrambled from the car accident. There wasn't much I could do."

I nodded. Variations of this story happened occasionally over the years, more as I got older. My dad tried to shield me when I was little, but I always noticed when we ended up with hamburgers or pizza for dinner instead of grilled chicken and broccoli.

"Is Mom coming home soon?"

"Maybe. She wasn't sure. More depositions to comb through."

"So, dinner for two."

He chuckled. "You got it, kiddo. How was your day? Mom said you had a tutoring session."

"My day was normal. I'm ready to graduate. The tutoring session was productive."

"I'm so proud of you sweetie. You give up your time so generously to help others."

My insides twisted. Usually, I would have beamed from that comment, but this time it was more of a quid pro quo instead of selflessness. I let a tight smile display across my features. "It's not a big deal."

He shifted more of the meat to a plate and layered more

onto the griddle. "Kids your age are more about partying and selfish motives. Just look at your cousin. No schools accepted her. I don't know what Steve is going to do with her. No colleges? I doubt even his money can squeeze her in somewhere. So, tutoring is a good thing. I'm proud of you."

I grimaced at the mention of Andrea. I didn't realize it had been that bad. I didn't even know where she had tried to apply to school. I couldn't imagine being rejected from everywhere. How bad could her grades have been? "Well, thanks."

He flipped over more meat, then glanced in my direction. "Your mom wouldn't tell me what she got you this year."

My stomach dropped. If I told him the truth, she would get in trouble and it would put a stop to the whole ordeal, which was kind of good, but I was invested now. And what if she had spoken to her dad? Although I doubted that too. They weren't anywhere near as close as I was with my parents. "Nothing worth mentioning." I shifted uncomfortably. "I'm going to go get changed. I'll be back."

"Okay." His gaze lingered before he began to hum while he continued to cook.

I hated lying to him, but it was for the best at this point. No good would come from him knowing the truth. I sauntered down the hallway to the last bedroom on the left. My room was tucked into the corner of the house with an attached bath. My bed was exactly how I had left it that morning—made and pristine. My floor was free of clothes or any dirt really. I couldn't help but wonder what Wyatt would think if he saw this room. No doubt he would assume it was more proof of me being a goody-two-shoes.

I plopped on the bed and kicked off my sandals, letting my bare feet sink into the plush white and black rug.

My phone's notification ringtone sounded. I leaned over the bed to pull it from my nightstand.

I'm sorry I was lousy company tonight.

My muscles tightened. I knew there had been something. But was it really my job to pry? We hadn't agreed to get deep, just to do the dates and tutor.

It's fine. We got the tutoring session completed regardless.

It isn't fine but thank you. I just couldn't shake the mood.

We all have our days. No worries.

Thanks, Marley. I really do appreciate your help.

No problem. How's the supporting details coming?

I have two of the three I need and page numbers for even more specific details.

My eyes widened. He went further than I had expected, which was good, but I had to admit I was impressed. It usually took a lot longer to get the ones I tutored to go above what they were used to.

That's great. It will put you in a good spot by the weekend.

Speaking of, what are your plans this weekend?

Why?

I have a few ideas for the adventure book but didn't know what your schedule was like. I have another gig on Friday. This one is longer though. We could do the date of Go to a concert and do some tutoring.

That should work for Friday. I have to do a service project for National Honor Society on Saturday, so unless you want to come with, I can't help with tutoring.

What's the project?

Rosewood Hospital for volunteering.

I could come with you if you didn't mind the company.

We would be happy to have you.

Okay, I'll see you tomorrow.

Goodnight.

Goodnight, Marley.

"Marley, cheesesteaks are done."

I placed the phone on the nightstand and plugged it in, then headed toward the kitchen.

Dad had already constructed the cheesesteak with lots of cheese and placed it on my plate, ready to eat.

"Thanks, Dad."

"No problem, kiddo." He took a big bite and chewed. "Want to watch a show together? I know it's a little late for a movie."

"Sure."

I plopped onto the sectional opposite him and ate while he scrolled through a couple of options. He settled on the newest episode of *Curse of Oak Island* and hit Play.

I nuzzled into the couch and released the tension in my body. This is what I needed—dinner with my dad and some yummy food.

Mr. McIntyre, our NHS moderator, stood at the front of the classroom. "If everyone can settle, this is our last thing on the agenda and then we can all dismiss."

Most stopped talking enough for him to continue.

"Our annual volunteer opportunity at Rosewood Hospital is Saturday. I expect to see you all dressed appropriately at eight a.m. sharp. We will meet at the front doors, check in with their volunteer program manager, then you will receive your tasks."

A few students from the back grumbled about the time.

"Alright, go ahead and skedaddle. I'll see you all on Saturday."

I packed up my bookbag and walked to the front. "Mr. McIntyre, I was wondering if I could bring one extra person on Saturday?"

His brows scrunched together. "Who?"

"Wyatt Shaw. I'm tutoring him and he wanted to come along. I promise I'll stay focused on my volunteering responsibilities."

He stroked his chin. "I know you will, Marley. Wyatt Shaw, huh? Okay, just make sure you keep an eye on him."

Keep an eye on him? He said it like Wyatt was some kind of criminal. "Of course."

"Then I say the more the merrier."

"Thank you. See you on Saturday."

He nodded and shuffled papers at the front desk.

I closed the classroom door on my way out and headed for the school parking lot. The building was eerie this late after school. The hallways that usually were filled with raucous noises, were quiet and darker than normal. Random papers littered the floor and red and black lockers reflected the light that streamed in through open classroom windows.

I shivered and grabbed my bag tighter to my chest, then pushed through the main doors after I passed the office.

Wyatt's truck was parked near my car, and he leaned against the hood with his arms crossed. He wore light-wash jeans with holes around the knee and up by the pockets. These jeans were clearly well worn, and I didn't see him as the type of person to buy jeans that looked shredded. He wore a plain black fitted T-shirt.

Heat crawled over my skin. His arms protruded from the sleeves of his shirt, revealing toned muscles. And even with the near eighty-degree temperature, he still had on a dark gray beanie with his hair peeking out from underneath.

I had to admit, his relaxed musician's look was tempting ... if we were a real couple.

He raised his gaze to meet mine and smiled. "There you are."

Today was clearly a different mood than yesterday. "Yep, all set after my meeting. And I double checked with Mr. McIntyre, and you're all set for Saturday too."

He pulled open the passenger door. "Hop on in." He outstretched his hand for me to use as I got in.

Once I sat, I smoothed over my dark red pencil skirt and flowy short-sleeved shirt with red roses.

He walked around the other side, got in and started his truck.

"Want me to check your supporting details while you drive us to wherever this date is?"

He chuckled. "Really don't like surprises and being flexible do you?"

I scuffed my black Converse against the floorboard. "Not really, but I'll get over it I suppose."

"Should be on top in my bookbag in the backseat."

I twisted around and grabbed his bag from the back of the cab. Sure enough the papers sat on top of his other books. I grabbed them and then readjusted facing forward. I read through his details as he glanced my way.

I had to admit, I wasn't used to quality like this from someone who had such severe disparity in his grades. This was quite easily an A paper when he put it altogether. Guidance was all I had really provided so far, and yet this stood on its own.

What had happened to him when he wrote those other versions?

He tapped his thumb against the wheel. A sporadic rhythm, like the beat of a nervous heart. "I could rework a couple of them if you think it's too extraneous."

I shook my head. "I think this is perfect the way it is, Wyatt. This is easily an A paper. Color me seriously impressed."

His demeanor instantly shifted. His shoulders were more relaxed and his smile was lazy but enticing. The glimmer returned in those deep brown eyes. "Thanks. I really tried."

"Well, I can tell. Keep this up and Mr. Andrews and your other teachers will easily raise your grades."

"That'd be nice."

"When we talked about college you didn't mention anything about you. What are your after school plans?"

"You mean *if* I graduate?"

I playfully nudged his arm. "Not if. I don't let anyone fail, *ever*."

"I don't really want to go to college. I want to move to New York and try to get in the music scene."

"That's so cool. I guess you like big cities then?"

"They're alright. It's more just where I'd have greater opportunities. Music producers aren't just walking around the cities of West End."

"True. Won't you miss it here?"

"Not at all."

His answer was stern, as if he was trying to convince me as much as he was trying to convince himself. Wouldn't he miss people here?

He parked in a large gravel lot located on the side of the road in a field. I recognized the area as part of the Maryland State Parks.

My eyebrow arched. "What are we doing?"

"Playing hide and seek."

"Here?"

"It says in an unexpected place. Last time I checked, no one expects to play here. And besides, we're taking the gravel road back behind some of the trees. I know a location that will be perfect."

I shifted uncomfortably in my Converse sneakers. Hide and seek in the woods? Wasn't that a bit ... horror movie like? Was this where he killed me?

"I promise you will have service for the whole time and if you're uncomfortable we can leave."

My eyes widened. How did he know I thought that?

He chuckled. "Your look of terror kind of gave away what you were feeling."

"Oh, well, okay." I peered around. "Do you come here a lot?"

"I used to. It's a nice place to hike and stuff, but it's been a few years."

"You hike?"

"Not in a serious way. It's nice to be out in nature though. Helps me relax."

"Ah. Does it help with your music?"

He shrugged one shoulder as he waited for me to catch up to his pace. "I've written a song or two in nature, but I haven't written anything lately."

"You've written songs? That's still impressive. I'm not creative like that."

He eyed me carefully. "You could try to be. I'm sure you just don't let yourself relax enough to see if you could be. Creativity is about expression, not about anything else. As long as you're expressing yourself, it doesn't matter."

"Well, my expression is poorly done then."

"Only if you focus on someone else's value of your pieces."

"Isn't that the point if you want to be good?"

"In some respects. It depends on your goals, I suppose. I of course worry about what others think of my songs and singing, but I do other things only for myself. And the process is more important than the result."

The path wasn't as scary as I had thought. Sunlight filtered through the trees, lighting up the path. I could hear birds in the distance. I could see how this would be a nice walk. I wasn't exactly a poster child for the outdoors, but I could appreciate its beauty when there were only a few bugs and low humidity.

"Maybe."

He nudged my arm. "You don't have to put yourself in such a small box. I know I joked about you being a goody-two-shoes, but that's obviously not all of who you are."

"Ha. My cousin wouldn't agree with that. She'd probably love that assessment of me."

"Well, no offense, but if family is willing to treat you like that, then they aren't good family. She should build you up, not tear you down."

"That's never how we've been. I've always been the smart one and good at school, and she's always been about boys and her looks."

"You could always change it."

I snorted. "Andrea isn't likely to change just because I ask for it. We're eighteen and she *still* bought this book to showcase my insecurities. That's always how she's been."

I could feel his gaze on me, but he remained silent. The energy that wafted from him made me squirm, like he had more to say, but was thinking better of it. So instead of chatting we walked in silence, the noise of the animals in the trees, deafening in my ears.

My cheeks flamed and I had no idea why, other than that I had a weird want to know his opinion of me. What else did he think I was like? I had barely interacted with him; it hadn't even been a week and yet he saw more to me than my own cousin did.

But maybe that was because this didn't *matter* the way other interactions did. This was fake, so either way it would happen. If I showed other people who I was and they truly rejected that, then it would be different. That had to be it, right?

Wyatt outstretched his arms. "Tada!"

I stared at the scene before us. A stone structure that had honestly seen better days stood in the middle. It looked like the structure had been several levels, at least two of the windows were any indication.

"What is this place?"

"It's an old grist mill from the eighteen hundreds. Isn't it cool?"

"It's not haunted right?"

Wyatt twisted his lips to the side like he was seriously considering that. "I don't think so. I've never seen any stories about it, but who knows right?"

Did he think that was reassuring?

"So here are the rules."

"What? There are rules for hide and seek? Isn't it just go hide and the other person finds you?"

"Sure, when you play in a house. This space is a little big isn't it?"

I looked to where he pointed. "Okay, yes."

"So, the rules." He cleared his throat. "You must stay on this side of the bridge and you can't go past the grist mill in this direction. Otherwise hide anywhere in between."

I groaned. "What if we can't find the other person? Is there a time limit?"

He drew his brows together. "I mean I may not have played in several years, but I am positive I can find you."

"Okay, what if I can't find you?"

"How about we wait and see if it actually becomes a problem?"

I crossed my arms. "Fine, let's take the picture then."

He moved closer and stood behind me as he smiled. When we were in the shot and it looked reasonably okay, I snapped the photo with my phone. I moved it closer to make sure it was fine, then showed him.

He nodded.

"Who hides first?"

"You can if you want."

I wanted many things in this moment, but my decision on whether to hide first or not was not one of them. "Sure. How long are you counting?"

"To twenty?"

"Okay." I waited for him to cover his eyes and begin, then I tried to sprint away as fast as I could without making sounds to lead him right to me. The grist mill was much taller the closer I got to its foundation.

My hand skimmed over the rough surface as I walked to the inside and looked for a good place to hide. Wyatt was already at twelve. If I didn't try to hide somewhere this would be too easy.

A large boulder with a wagon wheel leaned against it was off in the corner. I launched myself behind the boulder and crouched as low as I could in a pencil skirt. This was so not the attire to play hide and seek in.

"Twenty. Ready or not here I come," Wyatt shouted.

The sounds of twigs snapping and leaves rustling got louder as he neared. Then his head peeked around the boulder and he smirked. "Gotcha."

"What? That was like two seconds."

"What can I say? I'm a hide and seek master."

"No way. You peeked."

"I would never!"

I crossed my arms. "So, then what?"

He chuckled. "You really want to know?"

I nodded.

"I can smell your perfume. It got stronger the closer I got."

"Wh-What? Well, that's no fair. You'll be able to find me anywhere."

"Maybe. Once you've been more places it'll be harder."

"That still feels rigged."

"I can't help that I can smell your perfume."

"Well, I didn't know we would be playing hide and seek."

He chuckled. "You can gripe about it after you walk back so I can hide."

I muttered a few choice words under my breath. It may have only been hide and seek but I didn't want to be outwitted by *perfume*. I trudged back to the hiding spot and counted to twenty just like he had.

My eyes opened and I waited as they adjusted to more light after having them closed. I listened to the sounds as I waited, but all I could hear were sounds typical of the area we were in—birds chirping in the distance and leaves rustling as the wind blew.

I started toward the bridge to get a different vantage point. Wyatt hadn't been wearing any cologne that I could tell. I didn't know if he ever did to be honest. I could never get past his eyelashes long enough to let my nose do its job.

Focus, Marley.

Wyatt's shirt would help him blend into the surroundings, but those light-wash jeans should be easier to see. He was taller than me, easily six foot, maybe six foot two, so where would I hide if I had been that tall?

I surveyed the grounds looking for something tall but not necessarily fat. He could stand and it wouldn't be difficult to keep the position.

Near the edges of our area, a tall but skinny rock stood proudly. I would bet my GPA that's where he was. I creeped toward the rock, trying not to give away my own position and peered around it.

Sure enough, there he was. "Gotcha."

Wyatt's cheek pulled to the side as a half-smile emerged. "You aren't so bad at this either."

I rested my hands on my hips. "I am an honors student. I deducted the most reasonable places you'd be."

He stroked his chin. "Ah, well, I'll just have to change my strategy then."

I frowned. "Well, go count. I have to figure out my spot."

He winked. "Good luck, Marley."

I waited until he was back at the starting position before I moved to my next spot. I decided that he would try to use my strategy so I would be in an unpredictable place based on my outfit. I doubted he would expect me to climb at all in my skirt.

In a tree near the edge of the grist mill, mostly blocked by the structure of the building and the leaves, I hopped up to a limb that was at least ten feet from the ground. The limb had many large branches stemming from it with large leaves. What wasn't protected by leaves was shielded by the grist mill. He would never expect me up here. I just had to not fall out.

"Twenty," he shouted. In no time at all, I could see and hear him walking around the grist mill. I caught a few glimpses of his clothes, a leg here and an arm there, but never his face. If I could see him, then he could see me and it would be game over.

"I know you're around here, Marley. I can smell your perfume."

I covered my mouth with my hand. I was so close to giggling and ruining the whole thing completely.

His footsteps eventually faded as he walked in the opposite direction.

I exhaled. I had been right. He didn't expect me to be in a tree.

"Marco," he shouted.

Oh no. I wasn't giving myself away.

"Were you toying with me the first round? Because I have checked everywhere, and you aren't there." His footsteps stopped. "Well, I guess not everywhere because then I would have found you. So, if you aren't on the ground, which clearly you aren't, then you have to be up *higher*."

I sucked in a breath and clenched my whole body in the tree.

His footsteps got louder. Then just as he became clear in my vision, he looked up. "Gotcha."

I smirked. "Wasn't so easy, was it?"

He adjusted his beanie. "I have to say, I didn't expect you to be in a tree."

"That was the point."

He arched a brow. "How are you getting out?"

"Easy." I shifted my body so that my back was toward him. I slowly placed my right foot on the branch below, then my left followed. The nub closer to halfway that I used to get up, was a little harder to stretch to, but my foot stuck to the nub, then I jumped the remaining distance.

Wyatt's expression was hard to read completely, but I could still tell he was a little impressed. "Maybe you are more flexible than I once thought."

I scrunched my eyebrows. "Because I climbed a tree?"

He shook his head. "Because you adjusted your game when I was using your perfume. That's being flexible. Others would have stayed rigidly to their strategy, even if it was a poor one."

"Oh."

He nudged my arm. "That's a good thing, Marley."

I rubbed my hands together. "Think the date has been fulfilled?"

He chuckled. "Scared you won't be able to find me on the next round?"

"No. Fine, you're on. Go hide."

He smirked and walked in the opposite direction as I went back to the start. I could find him no matter where he hid. I was *that* good.

And so, we competitively played hide and seek until we exhausted all the possible places in our small section of the park.

Wyatt held out his hand.

I eyed it warily.

"I won't bite."

I slipped my hand in his and resisted the urge to squirm as the heat from his fingers enveloped mine.

"A fellow hide and seek champion. Well, done."

"Champion? Can you really win at hide and seek at a champion level?"

"Of course you can."

My eyes squinted as I tried to determine if he was being sarcastic or not.

"I haven't had that much fun in a long time."

"Really? It was hide and seek."

"Exactly." He nudged my elbow as we walked back toward his truck.

"I had fun too. Sage will think I'm crazy that I went to play hide and seek in the woods."

He chuckled. "What's the story with you two?"

"What do you mean?"

"She doesn't seem ..."

"Ah. She doesn't seem goody-two shoes enough to hang out with me."

"Well, that's not how I would put it."

"No. I know what you mean. We just sort of meshed when we had the same first grade teacher and never stopped. She makes me braver, and I calm her down."

"I see." He opened the passenger door, then walked around to his side. Once on the road again he asked, "Are we still good for tomorrow?"

I nodded. "Can I know anything specific about this gig?"

"Just be prepared for loud music."

Definitely not my scene. "Okay. Anything else?"

"Nope. That should be enough. Oh, and should I pick you up at your house?"

My house? I could just picture how that would go. My parents wouldn't think he was just a kid I tutored if he showed at the house while they were there. "Ah, no. Let's do school."

"You sure?"

"Yes."

"Okay, school then."

We listened to the radio as he drove me back to my car. My brain swirled with thoughts of the gig. I had done more this week than I had done in the four years of high school. How I would keep my focus during classes the next day, I had no idea. Sage would know what to wear. She always had the answers when it came to fashion. And possibly about going to a concert too because I was in way over my head.

Chapter Six

As expected, it had been hard to concentrate at school. Sage and I tried to discuss logistics over lunch, but it was too hard without being able to see my clothing options. So instead she demanded I head to her house after school and get ready there. Who was I to argue with that?

Sage's bed sagged as I plopped on it. "Why can't you just go with me?"

"As much as I would *love* to watch you tutor someone and see Wyatt's band, I can't. Dad needs me to train the newbie at the store and then I have to babysit my cousin while my aunt and my uncle go to a late-night movie."

I groaned. "This is our last month together as seniors. When are we going to hang out?"

"We're hanging out right now."

"You know what I mean. This concert isn't my scene. What if I make a fool of myself?"

"Are you that worried about a fake date? You don't have to impress him. He will continue doing the dates, that's the point of a *fake* boyfriend."

"No. I know, obviously."

She tilted her head. "Then why don't I believe you?"

I sighed. "He said this concert was longer. I have to help tutor him too, but what am I supposed to do when he's singing? Like, I don't go to places like that."

Sage swatted at my arm. "That's the other point of this. You haven't done most adventurous things. So, you add one more to your list. That's a good thing, Mar. You need to get out of your box a little more. College will be many steps from your comfort zone and that is a good thing. This will help prepare you."

"I guess. I'd rather you go with me."

Sage's brother lumbered down the hall by her door.

Sage held up a finger and bolted from her room. "Ryan," she shouted half in the doorway. "Ryan, where's my twenty bucks?" She huffed. "I know you can hear me!" Sage shook her head and sat at her desk chair.

"What was up with that?"

"He came begging for cash the other day. I knew I shouldn't have given him money. I'll never see that twenty dollars."

"I'm sorry."

"Just be happy you're an only child."

"He will turn around someday, then you'll be happy to have him as a sibling."

She crossed her arms, my cue to shut up, so I did.

She stood and walked to her closet. "Now, what are you wearing?"

"Um, this?" I pointed to my current outfit of straight legged jeans that were relaxed fit, my white Converse and a red crop top shirt with a larger white button up shirt loosely over my top.

She shook her head. "No."

"What? Why? This is cute."

"Not for a concert, Mar."

I groaned. "Why do I have to change? You were the one who said we weren't really dating."

"Do you want Andrea to think you faked these dates? Because she takes one look at that outfit and she will absolutely think you did."

My stomach flipped. I didn't want to go through all this just to have her think it wasn't real. "Fine, what did you have in mind?"

Sage pulled a few things from her closet. "The pants should be these black wide leg jean capris. The holes at the knees are perfect for a concert vibe, especially if you don't know the overall concert theme." Then she held up a few shirts. One had flowy sleeves with a tight fit around the chest, another was a too bright crop top, and the third was an oversized graphic T.

"Uh, none of those look like they match."

Sage eyed them each closely, then passed me the oversized graphic T. "This one."

"This is way too big for me."

"That's the point. Use my bathroom and go put it on."

I sighed. I knew better than to argue. Not to mention, Sage's fashion sense was hands down better than mine. I trudged to the bathroom and quickly changed into both. The shirt was enormous, like I figured it would be. How was this attractive?

"See? This is too big."

Sage met me outside the door and fluffed the T. She tucked in a healthy portion in front, then spun me back into the bathroom to look in the mirror. "See? Tucked in and it is perfect. This is so cute. Wear your Converses and then I'm taking your picture. You need this as your new profile picture."

"I don't even have makeup on."

"I know. I'll fix that." She held up a hand. "And before you gripe, it'll be natural looking. Mostly eye makeup for those lashes and some eyeliner. I love your freckles so don't you dare cover them with foundation."

I tucked a floofy strand of my hair behind my ear. Today's humidity had destroyed it, making the curls more frizzy than cute.

"I have a few curly hair products I bought for you to try. I think we have to dampen your hair with a spray bottle, put it in, then scrunch. Those curls will tighten and lock out the frizz."

I snorted. "You have seen my hair, right? I mean we are talking about *my* hair. Your hair can do whatever you want it to. My hair just rebels and gets worse."

Sage rolled her eyes. "These are social media approved. I've watched videos. Trust me, okay?"

I sighed. "Why so much effort for something fake? Didn't you just say that I shouldn't worry?"

"I did, but you can still look dolled up. Wyatt Shaw won't know what hit him."

I rolled my eyes. "He'll think nothing because I'm his *tutor*."

She shoved me toward the bathroom. "Just hush and let me work my magic."

"Whatever."

She grinned, that mischievous glimmer in her eye and grabbed all the things she needed. I'd let her work her *magic* and when it wouldn't make a difference later, I'd be the first to tell her I was right.

I tugged the strand of hair swinging into my eyes for the hundredth time.

Sage had been right. Of course.

The products she used in my hair and then shoved into my hands before I left were magical. I had never gotten my curls to cooperate without being so frizzy before. I had to admit, it *almost* made me like my curls, *almost*. The products also made my hair shine, causing it to be less like a mud puddle, which I was happy about.

I drove the short distance from Sage's house back to school. With how nervous I was about the concert, I was glad I wouldn't get picked up at home. That would have only made my stomach hurt more than it already did. Surprisingly the parking lot to the school was devoid of cars. I hadn't thought I would beat Wyatt here, but obviously I had.

Fine, it was one last minute I could double check my face in the mirror. Sage had also kept her promise and focused on accentuating my brown eyes, which I thought resembled sawdust more than they resembled anything pretty like Wyatt's eyes.

His brown eyes had depth, promise, and mystery.

Mystery? What was I saying?

Wyatt's Silverado pulled into the space next to me, but the opposite way, letting our windows face each other.

I looked up to see his expression and he smiled.

My stomach clenched and my cheeks warmed as if I'd spent time in the sun. What was *that*? Clearly all the extra pampering had confused my body. I was not reacting to his smile, was I?

No. Definitely not.

I opened my car door and grabbed my wristlet from the backseat.

Wyatt had waited until my doors were closed before he hopped down.

My body stilled under his gaze. Could he tell I put effort into my appearance?

He wore black straight legged jeans with boots that were

shaped similar to cowboy boots and my favorite color—salmon—faded T-shirt. And, of course, atop his mahogany brown hair was his dark gray beanie.

I didn't think he went anywhere without some sort of beanie. Would he really still wear one when Maryland hit ninety degrees with eighty percent humidity?

He arched a brow. "Marley, wow."

I patted the front of my jeans. "What? Is something wrong?"

He shook his head. "N-no. Not at all. You look nice. Dressing up for me?"

My cheeks reddened and my head went fuzzy. "What? Um ..."

He chuckled. "I'm kidding. I'm sure it's for the adventure book, right?"

"Uh, yeah. Of course."

He nodded and pulled his phone from his back pocket.

I turned so my back would face him for the selfie.

He moved closer and rested his arm over my right shoulder as he leaned closer to the left side of my head.

I pinched the inside of my palm to focus my attention and forced my mouth to smile.

He pulled away after taking it, then texted it to me.

I ached to look at it, but I didn't want him to think something of it. I wasn't even sure why I was feeling this way, like if I didn't look now my lungs would ignite. What was the deal?

"Ready?" he asked.

I nodded, then waited as he pulled open the passenger door for me.

A paper was placed on my seat. I scrunched my nose as I tried to decipher what it was. I spun around when I read the title. "You finished it?"

He nodded, a smile extending across his features.

"But we only agreed for the support and all."

"Just take a read and let me know what you think."

"Okay." I grabbed the paper then hopped up, buckling myself in, then launched into the introduction. It was his English paper for *Things Fall Apart*. And damn if it wasn't amazing.

The thesis had been what we discussed, as well as the support that we had talked about, but Wyatt had gone through the book and picked apt quotes and relevant examples to support the theme of pride as both a positive and a negative for the main character Okonkwo.

Wyatt glanced in my direction several times as he waited for me to finish.

My smile grew and grew until I had finished every word. "This is a fabulous paper, Wyatt. I'm so proud of you. I knew you could do it."

"Yeah?"

"Yes. Are you turning it in on Monday?"

"As long as you like it, yeah."

"Well, let's check this off your list then, because I certainly approve."

He smiled and tossed it gingerly to the backseat.

"How's it feel to have one less thing to do?"

"Good."

I smiled. "I'm glad, Wyatt. You deserve to graduate."

He averted his gaze to start the truck and put it in gear.

"So, where's the concert? Lucy's?"

"Nah. That's our more regular clientele. This will be near White Marsh and is kind of like a battle of the bands."

"Battle of the ... like you're competing?"

"Yep. Local cover bands competing for a chance to talk to a music producer."

"Wow. That's huge."

He hummed quietly to the song on the radio and tapped on the steering wheel. "It could be."

"You guys will do well."

"You haven't seen the other bands yet."

"No, but I've heard yours."

He cocked his head. "I thought you hadn't made a decision yet?"

My eyes widened. I had said that, didn't I? *Dang it.* "Well, I'll listen and let you know for certain at the end of the night."

"You better. We need honest criticism. I know we aren't perfect."

"Check. I can do that."

"I never had any doubts."

I nudged his arm. "Hey!"

He chuckled. "What? I'm saying you have opinions, not a bad thing."

"Mm-hmm." We let the music filter between us. He sang a few songs on the radio, but not all out, more subdued, only chiming in on the hook or chorus.

There were a few I had wished I was alone for. I sang when I was alone in my car, but *never* in front of other people. Sage had never even heard me sing before.

I had no idea if I was good or not, but I had no plans to do anything with it. I sang when I wanted to, not for any other reason or any person.

Twenty minutes later, we had pulled into a parking lot. The building had no sign and honestly looked more like a commercial warehouse instead of a venue for a concert.

"I know this place looks sketchy, but I promise it's not. They changed the inside into a sick stage and performer's dream sound system."

"So, you've played here before?"

He nodded. "Once, but not in a while. I've come here more recently as a concert goer than as a performer."

"Do a lot of people come then?"

"A fair amount. This will be busier. I've seen lots of the bands plaster the date all over social media. Bands with any sort of fan base will come out, so it could be crazy."

"Who decides the best band?"

"A little bit of the crowd and then there are judges, but we don't know who they are. We aren't allowed to know so no one can influence someone."

I giggled. "Wouldn't it be obvious?"

"Not as much as you think. The judges are skilled at blending in and not appearing obvious. I couldn't pick them out at other competitions."

"Oh, that's cool, but hopefully they have more of a say than the audience. If a band has a huge following that wouldn't be fair to those who are less well-known. It would be a popularity contest."

"Yes and no. More popular bands show that they have promise for sales, but most music enthusiasts can't contain their reaction just because it isn't *the* band they came to see."

"I guess." I mean what did I know? This was my first concert, aside from Lucy's, but I still felt like that way of judging would turn into a popularity contest. The more fans, the higher the possibility of influencing the crowd.

He turned off the truck and put his keys in his pocket, then hopped out. After he collected his bookbag and separate guitar bag, we headed inside.

He wasn't lying. The large space had a stage in the middle, with a partitioned section behind it covered by a large black curtain. Lights were everywhere above us, some for the ambience of the room, but many more for the stage. Standing tables were along the outskirts of the room, with a makeshift bar to the right.

"So, we have a place in the back behind the stage to get ready if you want to come with." He looked around and leaned close. "I wouldn't want to leave you alone out here. It could get crazy."

I nodded. "Sure, in there is probably easier to hear anyway if we do any work."

"Okay." He led the way toward the curtain, then placed his hand on the small of my back as we got near a bouncer. "Broken Axles."

The light touch sent a shiver through my body.

Why did that keep happening? It was a boy. My fake boyfriend. It wasn't real, but my body didn't care.

The bouncer looked at his clipboard, then moved the curtain to the side for us to enter.

A drywalled hallway was located directly behind the curtain, with several doors on both sides. At the last door a handwritten dry erase board had the name Broken Axles written on it in black marker.

Wyatt opened the door and let me go first.

As soon as we were inside, the noise immediately subsided. Were the walls soundproofed to some degree? They had to be if the bands could rehearse in here too.

Both of Wyatt's bandmates were already in the room.

Jack stood with one foot on the table and one on the floor as he bent toward the sofa strumming his base guitar.

Claire sat on the sofa, drumming on the table.

They stopped when I walked through the doorway.

Jack smirked and angled his body toward us. He gave me an elevator stare, before Wyatt smacked his shoulder.

"This is Marley. Marley this is Jack and Claire."

While Jack was open and light, Claire's stare felt weighted and judgmental. Who did she see when she looked at me? Could she tell I was some nerd, dressing up for the night?

"A girl? Wyatt, you didn't tell us you had a date!" Jack clapped him on the back before taking my hand to shake it.

"She's tutoring me, man. Lay off."

My stomach dropped, not for long, but like a short drop in a roller coaster. I knew this as a fact, and yet, I felt ... disappointed? Why would I care? We weren't dating even if he had agreed to this ridiculous plan.

Jack's gaze narrowed slightly, before lightening again. "Sure, man."

Wyatt flipped him off, then walked to the back couch and placed his bag. When he was close enough so they couldn't hear, he said, "Ignore, Jack. He likes to place himself squarely in everyone else's business but gets none of the facts straight."

"Isn't he like your best friend?"

"Yeah but doesn't change his truth."

"Fair enough."

Claire approached us, twirling her drumsticks as she did so. "Nice to have some more estrogen in here. Maybe it'll balance those two out."

My eyes widened. Had I imagined her tight expression?

"Thanks, I don't know how much help I'll be though. I don't really have a say in anything."

"Of course you do." She put an arm around my shoulder and leaned near my ear so Wyatt could only stare at us bewildered. "Wyatt has *never* brought a girl here. He doesn't share his life much. If he brought you here, he cares about your opinion. Tutor or not."

Hmm, was that true? He had asked for straightforward criticism. He wanted honesty and did agree I had opinions. But that didn't make us anything more than maybe friends.

Which was fine, because we weren't dating, and I had no plans to make that official. Fake dating was enough. It was all I needed.

"Alright, enough hazing Marley. What's our position in the lineup?"

"Tenth," Claire said.

Holy crap, ten bands? He was serious when he said this would be longer.

"Did we finalize our song list?"

Jack shook his head. "We only have the first and last choice picked. We need to figure out the rest and we only have fifteen minutes. No exceptions. They said they will silence our mics if we go over."

Wyatt grimaced. "Okay, let's figure it out then." He walked toward me with a ten-dollar bill. "Go grab yourself a drink. I know they have nonalcoholic options at the bar, and they won't card you so not a big deal. Can you grab me a bottle of water?"

I stared at the bill. "I can pay for it. I don't mind."

He narrowed his gaze, like he was looking for the code to my expression. "I'm fine." He placed the ten in my hand and closed my fingers over it.

I sighed. "Okay. I'll be right back." I grabbed my wristlet, just in case and headed toward the makeshift bar. The bouncer stamped my hand before I left the backroom, so I wouldn't have any issues getting back there, then I realized how long the drink line was. It appeared like everyone else had the same plan.

Refreshments before entertainment.

After several minutes of absolutely no movement, I pulled out my phone to text Sage.

How's the training going?

Awful. This guy doesn't know anything about books. I doubt he even reads his name on documents.

Yikes. What about making drinks?

Oof. I'm sorry.

Not your fault … Why are you texting me?
Shouldn't you be having the time of your life
at a concert and staring helplessly at the
lead singer?

First off, it hasn't started yet. Secondly, I'm
in the longest freaking line ever. I sent her a
picture of the line, with me at the back in a
snap. Thirdly, I will not stare at Wyatt
helplessly.

Interesting.

What?

You inserted his name. I didn't. It's a
concert, everyone stares at the lead
singers. Do you want to stare at him?
Hmmmm???

I cringed. Dammit. Now she wouldn't let that go.

No. You always insert his name since I told
you about the arrangement. I just assumed.

Well, you know what they say about
assuming.

Yeah, yeah. Oh I moved an inch.

Ha! Well, the trainee just spilled a cup of
coffee. I have to go help him mop it up or
the floors will be sticky for weeks.

Good luck!

You too. Kiss him!

👀 Goodbye, Sage.

I closed our messages and switched to Wyatt's. The most recent text was the picture he took of us. I finally opened it and checked the quality. I had to admit it was a good one. With the way my hair had cooperated from all of Sage's hard work and his smile … if I didn't know better, I would have thought we were a real couple. Andrea would freak out when she saw it, and I'd be lying if I wasn't excited at that prospect. Proving her wrong felt better and better.

I texted out the message and hit Send.

Line is forever. I promise I'll be back.

You better. I'm parched. 😉

Was that …? No.

Ugh, I needed to get a grip!

I was tricking my brain into thinking there were signs when there weren't. He wanted a water, that's probably why he sent me out there anyway. I mean he would have gotten it himself if he didn't need to do the schedule. I was over analyzing it all and that would get me nowhere.

In almost three and a half weeks I would walk across the graduation stage and he would forget all about me.

Chapter Seven

The line felt like it moved slower than waiting on a social media following, but I did manage to get the water and a soda for me. I needed the caffeine which was embarrassing to admit. It was only seven o'clock on Friday night. Didn't other kids my age party to all hours of the night? And nerdy me couldn't even make it to ten on a weekend.

Claire and Jack were nowhere to be seen when I returned.

I shut the door, listening to the little click as it shut fully.

Wyatt raised his head from staring at some book when I entered. "Thanks."

I handed him his change and the water. "No problem."

He slugged down a lot of the water.

Was he nervous or just lubricating his pipes for the performance?

"Did you all figure out the song lineup?"

He nodded. "I lost on one vote, but it's whatever."

"Shouldn't you be the number one chooser since you sing lead?"

"Nah. We're a team. We agreed in the beginning to make

this work, we all had equal say, no outvoting someone based on band position."

"That's good as long as it works, I guess."

"It has so far." He tapped the sofa cushion next to him. "I wondered if we could talk about my supply and demand paper."

I nodded and sat where he asked me to. "Besides deciding the overall topic, have you made any progress on it?"

He shook his head. "I tried focusing on English first. Now that I have this, I'm not sure if my topic is a good one."

"Well, the only constraints were to think of the effect of supply and demand on a consumer product. You know a decent amount about guitars, I'd presume, right?"

He rubbed his hand at the back of his neck. "Yeah, but not research. I know the guitar information for how to use it and when to use it for the type of song or music I am playing, not how supply and demand impacts the product."

"Okay, fair enough. Think of it this way. You're a consumer because you buy products, in this case a guitar." I pointed to his guitar leaned against the side of the sofa. "What made you pick that guitar at a store?"

"I didn't. My mom bought it for me."

"Okay ..." I pinched the bridge of my nose. "If you lost that one and had to buy another one, what qualities would you look for in the guitar?"

"I guess the cost. I can't pay for an expensive one right now. So, it'd have to play decently and not be a million dollars."

"Exactly. So as a consumer you'd need a product that is decent, but cost isn't too high."

"Okay, so what?"

"So that's the point. How many high-end guitars are bought? Who buys them? What about the middle-class people? What's their likelihood of buying a more costly guitar? If it isn't expensive, what's a good price point for a store to make a profit, but also meet the demand of that group?"

Wyatt stroked his chin. "I focus on the prices of guitars based on how many people could afford it and what makes sense?"

"Exactly. And Mr. Andrews only asked for two sources minimum, so finding statistics on guitars will take care of those requirements. For the rest, just think as a consumer because you are one. We all are. Based on what we buy affects the market. That's all he is trying to get the class to understand."

Wyatt nodded. "I think I could do that."

A smile crept across my face. "Considering how good your English paper is? I'll say. I need to put that on some graphics and market it for my tutoring abilities."

Wyatt chuckled. "Please. I am far from your best success story."

"I don't know about that. That paper puts you pretty far up there. Although I didn't do as much hands on for that. Makes me wonder."

"Wonder what?"

"Why exactly you need help in the first place."

He rubbed the back of his neck. "Just got away from me I guess."

"But—"

Jack and Claire burst through the door carrying Claire's drums. The door smacked against the door stop, jolting me.

"Hey, Melissa's band is up next. Want to catch them live?"

Wyatt glanced from them to me. "Want to go check out the competition?" He proffered his hand once he stood.

I drug my hands over Sage's capris as I pulled them closer to my body. "Sure, I guess we should get to the concert part of the night."

Wyatt grinned as I placed my hand in his. "My thoughts exactly."

Once I stood, Wyatt slipped his hand from mine, but he did hover near me. I wasn't sure if he was just trying to keep the whole group together or if he was trying to be closer to me.

But just as quickly I dismissed that idea because why would he? I was the one who suggested fake dating. He didn't have a need to make it real. He pegged me from the first day as a goody-two-shoes. Guys like him didn't date girls like me for real.

Once we passed the bouncer, the sea of people had grown substantially. There was barely any room to move through the crowd of people.

Wyatt stopped several feet from the front of the stage, in a small pocket of room. He whispered something to Jack, while Claire stood on my other side.

Melissa's band was introducing their set. From what I could see it seemed like a mixed band like Broken Axles. The lead singer was a female, with a male drummer then male and female guitar players. They wore somewhat of a uniform. They had complimentary colors on and each band member had a similar style.

They seemed more cohesive on their appearance, but would that matter if they weren't good?

Claire leaned close to my ear. "This group is crazy competitive. When they see something we do, they copy it. It's ridiculous."

"That seems unnecessary."

"That's what you do to be seen. This is our career. We do what we have to. They just happen to do a little more."

The lead guitarist silenced the crowd with their first strum. I didn't recognize the song, but they played nicely. The lead singer had a beautiful voice, almost haunting. It suited their style and the crowd around us swayed with their playing.

The skin on my arm prickled. I could see why they were concerned. They had a decent stage act. The next song had country vibes, not that I recognized it either. I didn't listen to country often, despite living in a rural area. It wasn't my style.

By the final song, I could see the appeal. Each song they performed was versatile. None like the other and the lead singer's voice was matched with the abilities of the others and their playing. To an untrained ear, they had a good chance.

The crowd erupted in cheers and shouting. They bowed, then exited the stage.

Wyatt gestured to a quieter corner and led us in that direction, while Claire and Jack remained where they were.

Wyatt picked at the leather cord from his band around his wrist. "What do you think?"

"Honestly?"

He nodded.

"I can understand the competition. To me, they sounded good."

"Yeah, to me, too."

My brow arched. "When did you know you wanted to be in a band?"

"I don't think there was ever a conscious choice. I always knew music spoke to me."

"Spoke to you?"

"It just made sense. I could hear the melodies and rhythms in all kinds of things. And when I learned different instruments or practiced? Everything just clicked and felt ... I don't know. Like home I suppose? Like I was free to be anything or do anything." He adjusted his beanie. "That sounds cliché."

"Not at all. I feel that with numbers or schoolwork. I get excited to figure out a hard math problem or unlock the theme of a book."

He smiled lazily as something crossed his expression.

"What? I know I'm a nerd."

"I didn't say anything."

"Your face did. I'm sure it sounds ridiculous to you."

"Not at all. We all have our own interests, that's pretty standard as a high schooler."

"Well, at least yours is more socially acceptable. It's okay to lose yourself in music. Numbers is a little weird."

The next band took the stage. Claire and Jack had disappeared. "Do we need to go?"

He shook his head and reached for my hand.

My eyes couldn't look away from his gaze as our fingers touched. What was happening?

"I want to try something."

My eyes widened and my stomach plummeted. "Try what?"

He tugged on my hand, leading us back toward the middle, he placed me in front of him, then stood right behind me. His hands settled on my shoulders. "Close your eyes and when this band starts to play, keep them closed."

I gulped but did as he asked. His hands were warm, but the touch was soft. It didn't feel like he had put all of his weight on me, but I couldn't be sure. I sensed him lean closer before I felt his breath on my neck. My skin prickled.

The first note played; it was a slow song. "Rest into the melody. Let it drift you."

Drift me? Like move? Did he think I would dance? I was not talented in dancing.

The song continued and I tried to *drift* the best I could, until his hands turned me to face him. He placed my arms on his shoulders and settled his around my waist, then pulled us a little closer.

"Just relax a little."

"I'm terrible at dancing."

"So what? It's about the song, not about the talent."

"Is that your way of saying to let loose and express myself without worrying about other's judgment?"

"Maybe."

"What about Claire and Jack? Won't they need you before your set?"

He shifted my gaze to meet his. "We'll go back soon, but I figured you should enjoy a concert like a real date and not just dissect the competition."

Like a real date? My heart skipped a beat at the thought. It was incredibly kind to worry about that for me, even though our arrangement was fake. "But going to a concert is all it really said."

"Well, enjoying the music with someone is the best part."

We swayed to the beat, his hands still planted on my waist. When the song ended, he removed his hands, and moved through the crowd.

"Do you usually take dates to concerts?" I asked.

"Nope. You're the first."

My eyes widened, but he had already turned to the bouncer to tell him the band's name. The moment lost.

When we arrived back, Wyatt pulled out his notebook and began writing his paper for Mr. Andrews.

I should have brought a book or my own homework. The silence between us felt deafening. What did it mean that he never took anyone to a concert? Or that he wanted me to experience it firsthand?

My messages were empty. Sage was still probably too busy with the new hire to harass me any further. I had texted her the photo we took in the parking lot of school, but even that went unanswered.

Eventually, Jack and Claire arrived back in the room. Jack sat on the edge of the couch next to where I sat, waiting while Wyatt worked on his paper.

"So, Marley, how'd my boy Wyatt manage to get you as a

tutor?" He eyed Wyatt then a mischievous sparkle filtered in his eyes. "Did he pay you?"

Wyatt didn't even glance up. He either didn't hear him or had decided to ignore his comments.

"No. I actually offered to tutor him."

"Pretty girl like you wanted to tutor him?"

My eyes widened. "I ... uh."

"Jack!" Claire and Wyatt shouted in unison.

He grinned. "What? You want me to ignore the obvious? She is pretty, there's no way I believe a pretty girl like her wants to look at your mug all day."

Claire rolled her eyes.

Was he serious? Not that I was comparing, because really I wasn't, but Wyatt was like a nine, whereas Jack could be a seven, but that was more from his humor, at least when it wasn't directed to me.

"I really did approach Wyatt. I may have cornered him in the parking lot."

Jack whistled. "She cornered you? Man, how didn't I find you first?"

To this Wyatt glared at Jack. "Lay off, man. Marley isn't some object; she is sitting right there. And she didn't corner me. I don't think that's possible at her height, but she did ask to tutor me. Now can we lay off so I can concentrate maybe?"

Jack placed his hands up in surrender. "I concede." He glanced at me and winked before moving closer to Claire and strumming his guitar.

Wyatt eyed me carefully.

Was he worried that I took offense to Jack's comments or did he suspect that I hadn't expected a compliment like that?

Because I was a nerd. I was even sure I had a class at some point with Jack, maybe gym class sophomore year and I was even more certain I didn't garner that kind of attention from anyone, let alone someone as attractive as Wyatt was.

"Look, Jack can be ... intense. He means well but his filter settings aren't great."

"I'm fine."

"You sure?"

I nodded.

He searched my expression then went back to handwriting his paper. Next time, I'd bring a book.

After way too long staring at the walls and trying not to interrupt Wyatt's workflow, it was their turn to perform.

He managed to push his way through the crowd enough for me to get near the front before he took his place behind the curtain as they were announced. The speaker stated they were the next band and I could feel as the crowd around me took a step forward. At least that was a positive sign, right?

If they hated them, they wouldn't move closer.

As soon as Wyatt took his place in the center of the stage, his whole demeanor shifted. His smile cranked up the charm and he batted those eyelashes like he attempted to flirt with everyone in the crowd.

It was like he was a completely different person. When we did the dates or tutoring, I noticed a small flicker of that energy, but on that stage, guitar in hand, it was like someone cranked it all the way up.

He seemed lighter and much easier to talk to, which was crazy. How could he change so much?

"Good evening White Marsh! We are the Broken Axles and can't wait to play for you." He shifted his guitar strap on his shoulder, strummed a note or two, then launched into a rendition of *Fast Car*. The tempo was sped up from the original, but it's catchy tune and lyrics had the crowd clapping and swaying along.

Most of the crowd seemed pleased with smiles and moving with the beat. I couldn't blame them. With Wyatt eying the crowd and his own smile, it was infectious. I too found myself smiling and moving along, although, if anyone asked later I would deny it for eternity. I also didn't dance. Not alone, and certainly not *with* a partner.

Their transition into the next two songs were fluid. I supposed they had to be in order to use the time to their best advantage. Why waste the fifteen minutes on speaking in between?

The fourth song was *Carry on my Wayward Son* and was much slower compared to the other songs in the set but showcased Wyatt's range or at least I thought it did. And at least the crowd continued to respond, they swayed, danced, and sang along with them.

Claire and Jack also radiated energy into the crowd as they had solos or songs that showcased their abilities too. Overall, I could see how the song choice was important. It showed the judges their skills as a band, not just Wyatt as a lead.

"Okay, White Marsh! It has been a pleasure playing for you all tonight," Wyatt said through the mic. "Here's our last song. We hope we see you all real soon! Check us out on Instagram at Broken Axles."

The first few notes of Nickelback's *How You Remind Me* emanated from the speakers. My dad actually listened to Nickelback, so I had heard this song before, but their version was different. As Wyatt sang through the chorus, goosebumps erupted over my skin. His voice was harrowing.

I could feel his anguish through the song. It was unlike anything I had heard him sing so far. What connection did he have to it? Because while his presence seemed good, I couldn't imagine he could fake emotion like that.

While he sang, the crowd had stilled. But when he

finished? They erupted louder than with their competitors. With that thunderous reaction, I thought they had a chance.

Wyatt, Jack, and Claire waved as they exited the stage. I walked toward the bouncer and released a breath as he waved me through. I waited a few minutes before they bounded in.

Jack was first.

"That was electrifying!"

Claire high fived him. "That was our best yet."

They turned to Wyatt. "Could you feel the crowd's energy? They practically froze on the last song."

Wyatt nodded, but his demeanor was subdued compared to the others.

"That was so amazing," I said. "I had goosebumps on that last song."

Wyatt's gaze snapped to mine, but he still didn't say anything. He was figuring something out, that much I could tell after the past week around him, but past that? I had no idea what he was working through.

Claire came up and squeezed my shoulder. "She comes to the rest of the concerts. She was our good luck charm."

"Please, I'm the only good luck charm we need," Jack said as he puffed out his chest.

Wyatt chuckled, but the heavy energy draped over his shoulders, merely shifted, instead of releasing. "I don't think Marley wants to trail us around everywhere. She's too busy for that."

I laughed. "Marley Wix, roadie. I can't say I expected that to be an adjective to describe me."

Claire pouted. "Well, local shows?"

"I'll see what I can do."

She grinned. "I'll take that!"

Wyatt walked past and placed his guitar in the case, then piled up his books in the bookbag.

I checked the time on my phone—9:30.

"Ready to go?" he asked.

"If you are. I thought you had to stay for the results?"

"No, they won't tell anyone tonight."

"Oh. Sure then."

He nodded and slung his stuff over his shoulder. "See you guys later."

Claire waved and Jack fist-pounded Wyatt.

Instead of walking through the front crowd, we went out a backdoor on this side of the curtain. It was a longer walk to his truck, but it was certainly quieter.

Once he loaded all his stuff in the backseat, we left.

"That was really good tonight."

"Did you mean your comment about the goosebumps?"

"Of course, why would I lie?"

He glanced in my direction.

I picked at a string from the hole in the capris on my knee.

"What else did you think?"

My lips twisted to the side. "The crowd reacted to your energy. They felt alive with the music."

A small grin spread over his features. "Have you made your verdict on our band?"

I tapped a finger to my lips. "I think you're decent."

"Decent gets you goosebumps?"

I laughed. "Fine. I enjoyed the performance. You're like a completely different person up there ... so light and charming."

He arched a brow. "Charming, huh?"

Did I say that out loud? *Crap.* "Well, isn't that supposed to be a good adjective for lead singers?"

"Mm-hmm I suppose."

I hoped he bought that because I did *not* want him to think I thought he was attractive. "When will they announce the winners?"

"In a few days. We will see."

"Well, I'd pick you guys."

"You didn't even see all the bands."

I shrugged. "That's my opinion and I'm sticking to it."

He chuckled.

"Will you be awake enough to handle the hospital thing tomorrow?"

"You don't think I can wake up early? It's not even late yet."

"Well, we aren't home yet."

"Maybe not, but I'll be fine." He eyed me warily. "Will you be fine though? I'd suspect goody-two-shoes is usually in bed by nine."

"No."

He cocked his head. "Ten?"

I crossed my arms. "Not always."

"Ah, I see. Well, Miss Rulebreaker, I applaud the flexibility."

"Whatever, I can't help if I'm predictable. Some people find that to be a good quality."

"I never said it wasn't. Stability is comforting."

Comforting? What teenager said that?

"I merely mean that I don't see it as a negative thing, even if I tease you for it."

"Oh."

Silence settled between us, but I couldn't tell if he thought it was awkward or just me.

Chapter Eight

Surprisingly, I fell fast asleep once I had made it home. Wyatt had dropped me off at my car, then promised to meet me at school around seven-thirty to be on time for the hospital service project.

It was early for a Saturday morning. My normal morning routine flew by in a blur of sleepiness. Darn Wyatt for being right about my typical amount of sleep. I tightened my laces on my black sneakers. We were instructed to dress appropriately *and* comfortably, so that was my plan. I wore boyfriend jeans, but no holes, and a West End High spirit shirt. My red zip up lay across my desk chair, turning the seat as I took it.

My dad always complained about how cold the hospital was. I didn't want to be freezing all day even if it was supposed to be close to eighty outside. After I pulled up the top half of my hair and clipped it, I headed to my car.

It would only take a few minutes to get to the high school, but I wanted to be parked at least five minutes before seven-thirty. I needed to go over the placements for the hospital before Mr. McIntyre handed them out.

After locking the doors, I started my car and pulled from the driveway. The sun had already risen and I could already tell it would be warm. Having thick curly hair meant I was an instant meteorologist. My hair always warned me of the humidity based on the amount of frizz my curls attracted, and today, well, today would be a doozy.

The school's parking lot had a few cars in the teacher's lot, but the rest of the lot had none. I was the first to pull in. Checking my radio's clock, it was only 7:15—perfect timing.

My phone chirped. Who could be texting me this early? Sage definitely would still be in a comatose for at least a few more hours.

It was Wyatt.

Any food allergies?

My brow furrowed.

No.

I'll be there soon.

What was that about? Was he planning some adventure date for today? My paper with the placements had shifted to the bottom of my bag. I didn't have time to dwell on why he had asked me something so specific, so instead I finalized the list and then exited my car.

I had gone on this trip last year, and I knew that Mr. McIntyre would be inside the school sipping his hot tea reading the school newspaper until he had to come outside and make sure everyone had shown up.

As expected, he pored over a section of the newspaper, focused on whatever article he had chosen.

I cleared my throat. "Mr. McIntyre, I have the placements."

He briefly glanced in my direction before sitting straighter on the bench and outstretching his hand.

I handed him the list and shifted uncomfortably on my feet as I waited.

"Looks good, Marley." He placed the paper in his pocket and stood. "I suppose it is time."

We walked to the front of the school and waited as everyone else showed up. Once we all checked in, we would head to the hospital. I had even gotten approval for Wyatt to drive us there. Most were taking Steve's minivan. He was also a senior. He could hold just about everyone, but it had been easy to volunteer to take other arrangements.

Wyatt's truck pulled into the parking lot and parked near my car. He hopped down, in his typical outfit—jeans, a fitted T-shirt and his gray beanie.

I chuckled. Did he own any other clothes?

He leaned into his truck and pulled out two cups before shutting his door. Then he trailed toward me as more cars parked in the lot. He proffered one cup to me. "I wasn't sure what kind of coffee you drink. If you drink any, so I kind of guessed."

"Okay."

"It's a maple vanilla and brown sugar coffee."

I took the coffee from him. "Thanks."

He swiped his hand through the hair that peeked out the front of his beanie. "No problem. The barista said that this was a good coffee drink. If uh, you don't like it, then you don't have to drink it."

"No, it's fine, thank you. I appreciate the offer." I sipped the drink. It certainly wasn't something I would have ordered but I had to admit it was pretty good. I usually didn't drink coffee that much either, especially not this close to the summer, but I would never have said that after he took the time to get me something.

Wyatt watched me carefully. "Do you like it?"

"I think I do actually. What did you say this was again?"

"Maple vanilla and brown sugar."

"Nice. Where did you get it from?"

"I went to West End Beanery."

"I don't think I've ever been there but after trying this I might have to make it a habit."

Wyatt smiled and sipped from his own drink. "So, what's on the agenda today?"

"Well once we get to the hospital, there should be somebody on staff that greets us and then we'll be broken into our placements."

"Our placements?"

"Yes. Each volunteer has a certain part of the hospital they will help in."

He tucked his hand in his front pockets. "And where are we helping?"

"I got us assigned to read in the pediatric ward. They also will have us in deliveries."

"Deliveries?"

"Yup like flowers and balloons to patients. You know that kind of thing."

"Sounds easy enough."

"It should be and we should have some time to do some tutoring. What did you bring to work on?"

"I was thinking maybe we could work on the science research paper."

"Sure, sounds good. Did you finish the paper for Mr. Andrews?"

"Yep. I typed it up when I got home last night."

My eyebrow rose. "Wow. I'm impressed. That puts you at what two papers down?"

"Two papers down, ten million to go."

I giggled.

"Okay attention everyone it's time to do roll call. When you hear your name, please let me know."

We listened to the list of names until he finally reached us alphabetically.

"Shaw?"

"Present."

A few people in the group eyed him warily. No one knew I had added him in except for Mr. McIntyre.

"And last but not least, Wix."

"Here."

"Good, now let's head over. You will receive your partners if applicable and your placements."

The crowd shuffled away. Wyatt and I walked toward his truck. He opened the passenger door and placed his hand on the small of my back as I lifted in. First coffee and then the touch? I wasn't prepared for that. It felt too much like a real couple. Getting me coffee didn't equal a date. That was what normal couples did. I didn't think it would constitute an adventure.

Wyatt walked around his side then followed behind Steve's minivan as we drove the few miles from school to the hospital parking lot.

We stayed quiet in the car, sipping our drinks.

He finally parked and we hopped out.

I wrapped my red zip up around my waist for later and strode over to the main entrance doors, where everyone gathered from school.

An older woman with dark brown hair stood waiting off to the side with a clipboard. She cleared her throat. "Good morning West End High NHS members. My name is Cynthia and I am responsible for you today. Please make sure to stay with your partners if assigned one and do not change your placements. These areas are in need of help today and we greatly appreciate you volunteering." She gestured toward Mr. McIntyre.

"Listen up for your placements and partners."

I already knew them by heart, so instead I leaned closer to Wyatt. "Are you ready?"

He nodded.

Mr. McIntyre clapped his hands. "You're responsible for finding your way back to school, but we are volunteering until two. No one is cutting out early."

It was almost eight now, which meant I would have six hours of volunteering with Wyatt.

We waited until the rest of the group entered into the hospital.

Wyatt outstretched his hand in front of us, letting me lead the way.

I had spent a decent amount of time in this hospital. Not that I was allowed to go to all the places my dad did, but a few times he had to take me to work over the years.

"Marley Wix! Come give me a hug!" Mrs. Tulane said.

I smiled and obliged. "Mrs. Tulane this is Wyatt. Wyatt this is Mrs. Tulane my dad's favorite nurse." I winked at her.

"Oh, stop that. Your dad doesn't play favorites."

"Mm-hmm."

Wyatt proffered his hand.

"He is gorgeous, Marley. What a handsome boyfriend!"

My eyes widened and my voice sputtered. I couldn't get the words out.

"She's my tutor, but thank you," Wyatt said seamlessly.

Mrs. Tulane winked again then rubbed my arm. "I'll see you two later."

When she was out of earshot, I faced Wyatt. My cheeks felt sunburned. "I'm so sorry. She is a sweet lady; my dad really does prefer her even if she won't accept it."

Wyatt shoved a hand in his pocket. "So, he works at this hospital?"

I nodded. "He's a trauma surgeon."

"Wow, when you told me he was a doctor I didn't expect he was a surgeon. I thought maybe a family doctor."

"Nope. It's pretty cool but keeps him busy unfortunately."

"Long hours?"

"And at weird times." I rubbed my hand against my jeans. "Let's head up to the pediatric ward first. We are on deliveries starting around eleven."

He nodded.

From the main entrance, we walked toward the elevator and I pushed the button to wait. Pediatrics was on the third floor and it was much faster by elevator than by stairs. "Have you ever done anything like this before?"

"What? Volunteering? Or do you mean reading to sick kids?"

I winced. I didn't want him to think I was a snob or looking down on him, I was just curious. "Reading."

"No. I don't have that much free time to do volunteering, so reading to kids will be a first for me."

"I actually hadn't until last year's trip with National Honor Society. Now I try to go once a month to see the kids."

"Just on your own?"

I nodded. "Gives them something to look forward to and I like to remember how lucky I am and give that back."

"That's not what a lot of people our age would do."

"Maybe not, but it feels right."

The nurse's uniforms shifted from maroon to bright colors and playful cartoon characters.

"Hello, Marley! I was happy to see you on our list today."

I smiled and could see Nurse Linda standing at the

entrance of the nurse's station. "Hello, Nurse Linda. I'm happy to help with the kids."

"Well, they're going to be happy you're here again. Come on. I'll set you up in the normal room, then have you go around to some of the sicker kids' rooms." She eyed Wyatt warily. "And who did you bring with you?"

"Wyatt."

"Ever read to any of the kids before, Wyatt?"

He shook his head.

"Well, it's real simple. Read whatever book they ask for and try to keep things happy and calm. If you need help, Marley is a pro."

My cheeks reddened. I didn't like the attention, even if she was only saying that because of the frequency of my visits.

"Thank you."

She nodded and strolled toward the big room in the center of the less sick patient rooms. These children would only be in the hospital a few days and they tried to keep it light and airy.

The room was painted a light yellow, that felt more like the color of a popsicle, than it did mustard. Someone had painted a mural of the Chesapeake Bay and all the creatures on the wall, labeled for the kids who were older and could read. And off to the back corner was a bookcase with as many books as the nurses could get their hands on.

I recognized a few of the kids, but most were new since the last time I had been there.

I leaned closer to Wyatt so he could hear me. "You can either mingle with them or let them come to you."

He nodded and went to the bookshelf to peruse the titles. I found a light and airy place by the window to sit and watched as the littles ones grabbed books and flocked toward Wyatt.

His grin grew, almost to the point it was when he was on

stage at the competition. I didn't think I had ever witnessed him that carefree in any other way.

Two little blond haired and blue-eyed twin girls plopped in front of him with the Pout Pout Fish books.

I giggled silently to myself as I waited for his reaction. The Pout Pout Fish had several books, and were enormously adorable to read, but it rhymed and had so much flourish that if someone didn't make cute voices or read it with enthusiasm, it just wasn't as good.

He cleared his throat and began to read. He raised his voice for squeaky fish and made it deeper for big fish. It was the sweetest thing I had ever seen.

The girls giggled, clapped, and chanted, "Read it again!"

He obliged while his gaze slipped toward me. He smiled and then winked before focusing back on the characters.

My heart zinged. How sweet was he? I couldn't imagine a star singer being so good at reading children's stories to little kids, but he was and it was precious.

Wyatt's arm rested close to mine as we sat in a chair by a vending machine eating chips during our break. It was almost eleven, when we would have to switch to deliveries.

"I swear those kids loved you more than me. Nurse Linda will make you come back all the time. They couldn't get enough of your voices."

"What can I say? It's my stage presence I suppose."

"Nope. It was something else, but seriously, I think you made their day."

He shrugged as he crumpled his bag and tossed it into the trashcan. "So, where do we go to complete deliveries? It's time."

I crunched on my last Dorito, then threw away my trash.

"That is done on the first floor around the gift shop and front desk."

"Got it."

We walked toward the elevator.

"So, even though you're here so I can tutor you, how are you liking it?"

"It's not bad, although I haven't seen the delivery gig. I can see why you like coming to read to them."

I smiled. "They can be so sweet, but honestly, I have no idea what they'll say half the time."

"This one kid gave me statistics on heat stroke because of my beanie."

I laughed so hard that had I been drinking something I was sure it would have launched across the room.

His brow furrowed. "What?"

"Well, he has a point. Do you always wear it?"

"Pretty much."

"Doesn't it become too much? I mean I get it, we're inside, but outside like today? It would be crazy."

He shrugged. "When you always wear something, it doesn't really register anymore. I'd feel weirder if I didn't wear it."

"That makes sense, becomes your baseline."

The elevator door dinged and we both climbed in. Wyatt pushed the button for the first floor. After we exited and turned down a long hallway, the front desk loomed in front of us.

"Hi, I'm Marley and this is Wyatt. We're with West End High for the volunteering."

A man behind the desk, glanced in our direction, then nodded as he scooted to the back of the desk then stood. "You'll make deliveries to the rooms all over the hospital. Your first task is to take these flowers to the cardiac floor, room five hundred sixty five, a Ms. Daniels. Drop it off on a table in her room, then come back."

Wyatt reached for the flowers, then we walked back to the elevator. "They seriously just have us deliver whatever around the hospital?"

"Pretty much."

"How will we get anything done with making deliveries?"

"Easy. You said you wanted to do your research paper for science, right?"

"Yeah, it's my last big paper."

"If I remember correctly, you decided to do the effects of pollution on the Chesapeake Bay, right?

He nodded.

"Have you done any research past deciding on the main topic? I think I remembered you needed to have at least five sources, then discuss how you might solve the problem."

"Not really. Is that a bad thing?"

"Not at all, but might be difficult with us running around to actually find the research." The signs for the rooms were to the left of the elevator, once I figured out which direction the room would be on we continued. "Have you thought about contacting Rosewood College? I think I saw something about a new research study coming out of there on that topic. They may be able to help you."

"I hadn't but I will look into it."

"Good." We stopped just outside the door, then Wyatt knocked and walked inside to deliver the flowers.

I could hear an older lady say thank you, then he was right back next to me.

We walked back the same way we came. "So, if you can't do the research now, then let's think. Rosewood could be one source. I'd say by Monday, find research for the first three effects on the Chesapeake Bay like the syllabus asked. I think that will be fine."

Wyatt's eyebrow rose. "Ending tutoring early? Wow, goody-two shoes, I didn't think you had it in you."

"In me to do what?"

"To go easy on me. I figured I would still have to do more until the stroke of two."

"Ha ha. I'm not crazy or mean. There is only so much you can do as we walk the halls."

"Mm-hmm. I know that but didn't know you did."

I nudged his arm.

He smirked as he adjusted his beanie. "What will you be up to tomorrow?"

"Well, Sundays I usually try to spend with my parents. Most of the time they manage to get the morning off and we just have family time. Why? Did you have a date planned?"

"No, was just curious. What does one do during family time?"

"We play board games, have breakfast or brunch. Just sit and talk. A lot of the times my parents are like ships passing in the night. We are rarely together. So, we don't *do* so much as just spend time around each other."

"That sounds really nice."

I wrinkled my nose. There was that feeling again like he had no idea how that was. Could that be possible?

I supposed it could. What did I really know about his life? It wasn't like he was outgoing at school. Most of the rumors I had heard were in regard to his classwork or lack of paying attention, not about what he did at home.

We arrived back at the desk to find the man behind the desk gone. I unwrapped my red zip up and put it on then plopped into one of chairs near the entrance.

"What are your plans?"

"Well, work on my papers of course."

"The whole day? I doubt it."

He chuckled. "Maybe not, but a lot of it then rehearse with the band. Also get ready for the week I suppose."

"Do you have any gigs this weekend?"

"Nope, yesterday was it."

"Are you nervous about the results?"

He shifted in his chair. "I suppose?"

"What's that mean?"

"I guess to be nervous you have to expect it to go your way. If you don't expect anything, then it's hard to be nervous."

"You don't hope you win?"

"I would love it if we won, but out of all those bands, do I believe it will be our break? Maybe not."

I frowned. Why did he have no confidence in his performance? They had done so well, especially that final song. Weren't musicians supposed to believe in their bands the most?

"Ah, back already. Good." The desk man shuffled a few papers and packages, then waved us over. "Next package is room four hundred one. You'll deliver this box and card to Mr. Watkins."

We nodded and shared the items before heading off again.

"When will you find out the results? Do they send everyone an email or just the winners?"

"Winners receive a phone call, supposedly on Monday at nine a.m. Claire's number is what we entered, since her schedule is more flexible. The rest receive a post that says the winners are announced and who won. So, no special email. Either a call or nothing."

Once on the fourth floor, we walked toward the doorway.

"I hate coming on this floor."

Wyatt looked into my expression. "Why?"

"It's the cancer floor. It's always so sad."

Wyatt froze. He stopped moving forward and maybe even inched back.

I had to stop completely.

"What?"

"Uh. Um." He pushed the package toward me and backed up. "I have to go."

"What? We still have more deliveries. It's not two yet."

"Yeah I know, but I'm not really getting service hours and tutoring is over, right? S-so, I'll talk to you later."

He turned and left me standing in the middle of the hallway. He had already disappeared inside the elevator when I realized I'd have no way back to the school now. Not to mention, I had no idea why he bailed, something I would certainly rectify later.

Despite not having any clue why he bailed, I continued farther down the hallway toward the patient's room. Mr. Watkins was asleep, so I left it on the bedside table and darted back to the hallway.

It took until I reached the elevators to let my no ride really sink in. What would I do? Steve might have caravanned everyone here, but I knew for a fact that he wouldn't do the return trip. Some had parents pick them up from the hospital, while others would have friends drop them back off.

I supposed I could ask my dad, but what would he say when I told him Wyatt ran off?

We weren't supposed to use our phones during the day, but I couldn't imagine Mr. McIntyre really faulting me for this.

Clicking his contact card, I hit Call, then waited for him to pick up.

"What's up, kiddo?"

"How late are you working today?"

"Until five, why?"

I groaned. Did I want to stick around here for three extra hours? "I need a ride back to my car."

He chuckled. "West End ditching their students?"

"No, my ride just ... uh. He had to leave unexpectedly."

"Hmmph. That doesn't sound polite."

"It's not a big deal, Dad. Maybe I can get Sage to pick me up."

"Don't bother Sage. I'll take a quick break when you're done. What time again?"

"Two."

"Two it is. Meet you in the front lobby."

"Thanks, Dad. You're the best."

We hung up, just in time for me to turn the corner to the front desk. I still had hours of deliveries, but at least one problem was solved.

Chapter Nine

I kept expecting a text or a phone call from Wyatt with a better reason for bailing, but it never came, even though I obsessively checked it once I had gotten home and even this morning. If Sage knew, she'd yell at me, then say I should have called or texted him about it.

But Sage didn't know ... yet.

I got dressed and headed toward the kitchen.

"Good morning, my sunshine."

"Good morning, Mom."

She smiled then glanced back at her Sudoku app. It was tradition that she started every morning with a puzzle, and Sundays were no different.

"There!"

I giggled. "Beat your score?"

"No, but I beat the puzzle for the day so that's always an achievement."

I pulled out a chair at the table. "Where's Dad?"

"He should be right out. Was finishing up his shower."

Mom put her phone face down on the counter. "So, how was your week? How's the new person you're tutoring?"

"My week was good. I have a test this week in AP Calc though. He's nice."

Her eyebrow arched. "He? Does *he* have a name?"

"Yes. His name is Wyatt."

"Do we like this boy?"

"Mom!"

She laughed. "What? I'm allowed to be curious. You haven't dated so far in high school ... not that I know of. You didn't go to prom. When is that changing?"

"Mom!"

"Leave her alone, Erin. She can't date until she's married."

"Hank! That's ridiculous. Our daughter is eighteen. She can do whatever she wants to."

My dad gave her a knowing expression.

"Well, within reason."

I giggled. "No boyfriends or boys of interest."

"No? Mrs. Tulane had plenty to say of the fellow you brought to the hospital yesterday. Although, I can't say I'm over him leaving you at the hospital. What if you didn't have a wonderful trauma surgeon as your father?"

"He left you stranded?" Mom asked, her voice rising significantly at the end.

"Stranded is a harsh term. He had to run. I told him it was fine because you worked there."

Mom's expression turned into her lawyer face, as Dad and I called it. She used it when she was trying to grill someone. "You're sure?"

"Yes. No harm done."

She studied my expression, but then relented. "What do we want for breakfast?"

Dad and I exchanged glances before we both said, "Chocolate chip pancakes."

Mom shook her head. "We've had them the past two weekends in a row."

I shrugged. "You make them the best."

She stuck out her tongue, then piled the ingredients for pancakes onto the counter.

Dad sprayed cooking spray on the griddle pan, while Mom stirred the batter.

I sprinkled a hefty amount of chocolate chips in, before Mom poured several circles on the pan.

"Interested in a three-way game of Scrabble after breakfast?" Dad asked.

Mom groaned. "Scrabble? Why not Upwords?"

"Why not both?" I asked.

"Hmm. Maybe," Mom said as she eyed the pancakes carefully. No one else was allowed to flip them. She waited for the bubbles around the edges and when they puffed out a little, then she flipped.

I had tried once and I tore the whole thing in half. The next one I had burned. I had no idea how she did it, but her timing was perfect *every* time.

Dad pushed the K-cup down into the Keurig and then waited as the smell of brewing coffee circulated the room. He nudged my arm. "Getting excited to graduate?"

I shrugged. "I guess. I actually like school. Leaving to go to college just seems too strange."

He laughed. "You'll get past that quickly."

My mom tapped my arm. "It's okay if you don't, too. Your father is a social butterfly, he didn't mind going that far from home, but we can understand if you do."

"Thanks, we will just have to wait and see in the fall, when I move."

Mom scooped several pancakes onto a plate. "Why don't you get started? You can also get out Scrabble and Upwords so we can play once all the pancakes are done."

The games closet was to the left of the kitchen, but close enough that I could see the door when I sat at the table. I honestly thought we had more board games than movie cases in our house. After grabbing the games and placing them on the table, I grabbed my pancakes, syrup, and orange juice. Then took my place.

This was what Sundays were all about and I would really miss it when I left for UPenn in the fall.

~

After spending the morning with my parents, I had agreed to take my books and remaining homework and head to Marshall's Books.

Wyatt still hadn't texted me anything and at this point, I didn't care. Well, mostly didn't care.

My Honda ended up fitting perfectly in a spot near the front of the lot, then I gathered my bag and headed inside.

Sage waved from the front desk and pointed to a bean bag chair near the middle of the store.

Yes, she had to work, but I knew she would spend as much time with me as she could on her shift.

The purple bean bag sunk as I lounged on it. Then I pulled out my remaining homework and piled it up on the table next to me.

The store was busier than normal. From the looks of it there were several families around the stacks of books, but the usual college customers I'd see weren't as frequent.

Sage's fruity perfume floated in my direction as she crouched near the bag. "I brought you a carbonated watermelon water."

I smiled. "Thanks. How's the newbie?"

She rolled her eyes and sighed. "He's awful. Mar, I don't know how I'm going to survive this."

"Well, everyone takes time to get used to things."

She eyed me like I had ten heads. "This is not normal jitters. This is like, can't figure out coconut milk from almond even though they're clearly labeled. Drinks he makes always come back. It's awful."

"So, why is he still here?"

"Beats me! I've told my dad like ten times and he just repeats, *Beggars can't be choosers* at me like that makes a difference."

I giggled.

She nudged my arm. "Not funny. Seriously, watch him and you'll see." She stood and shook her head. "I'll be around if you need anything, but I have to make sure he doesn't burn anything down or himself... again."

I grimaced. Sage was a good teacher, but if it was that bad, then maybe he should have been let go. It was like Mr. Marshall to give people a chance, but he didn't usually take risks when it came to his business. He wanted this store around for decades. It was his legacy as he had told Sage and me numerous times before.

I sipped my water as I opened my AP Calc books to where I stopped on the review sheet. This was one of the final tests we would have this year before graduation. After this was the final and that was it. If I wanted to keep my class rank close to the top, I had to maintain my grades all the way to the last day.

My phone beeped alerting me to a new text message. My curiosity piqued; I checked the sender. It was Wyatt.

I finished my outline for science. Think I can email it to you? I want to type up some of it if it looks good.

Hmm. Nothing about his sudden disappearance. Besides, I thought he would be rehearsing by now. I mean don't get me wrong, I was happy he was taking these papers seriously and so far, he hadn't added anything to it, but why such a shift so quickly? We had only been doing this for a week. Most of the students I tutored took at least a month to see significant changes in their habits. It just didn't make sense.

> Sure, email me away. I will check it and let you know.

Not even a few minutes later, my phone alerted me to a new email. That had been fast. I opened the email and scrutinized the outline, but as far as I could tell he once again finished the outline and then some. His points were relevant, his support was sound. How did he have grades that could cause him not to pass if he could pull this off?

> This is really good, Wyatt. I think you have a solid outline to go ahead and type up the paper.

> Thanks. Maybe I'll have something for you to read tomorrow morning.

> Works for me.

> Meet at your locker?

> Okay.

> See you then, Marley.

Despite his disappearing act, I smiled. I was happy that he was changing his grades around. Truly I was, but something felt off and I couldn't put my finger on it.

I looked around for Mr. Marshall, then sauntered toward Sage at the coffee counter.

"What's wrong?"

"How do you do that?" I asked.

"You're my best friend obviously. So, what's wrong?"

"Wyatt just texted me that he finished his outline for his science paper."

She eyed me warily as she wiped down the counter. "Isn't that the goal?"

"Well, yes. But Sage, it's been a week! Isn't that a bit soon?"

"Maybe you're his muse."

I rolled my eyes. "Sage, get real. Isn't that a little suspicious?"

She stopped wiping to gage my expression. "You clearly think so. Why don't you tell me your reasons for why?"

I fiddled with the sugar packets. "His papers are good. Like A plus good, and yet he was almost failing the year. That doesn't happen. I am missing something. I can feel it."

Sage twisted the rag tighter. "Why would someone pretend to be terrible at something? I can't imagine anyone trying to fail their senior year."

"I'm not saying he did that. But how can he do this one eighty so fast? I mean he has finished three of his delinquent assignments this week. Isn't that a bit fast?"

"Are you doubting your ability here or questioning his?"

I dropped my head onto my arms. "I don't know."

"Well, for a second if we pretend that he can do it on his own, you still get to prove Andrea wrong and keep your tutoring record. He'll pass and it will require little work from you. I say don't be upset that this is easier than you figured it would be."

"I guess you're right."

"Of course I am. Now go study. I don't want to be the reason you fail your first test ever."

I smiled weakly. "Okay, fine. I'll let it go and study."

Maybe Sage was right. Why was I overanalyzing this? I was still winning in this situation and frankly I needed a win or two, so I would take it and stop whining.

Chapter Ten

There were only five minutes until the bell rang and Wyatt had yet to show up at my locker. What was his deal? I had to walk all the way across the building and up a flight of stairs. If he didn't arrive in the next minute, I was leaving.

I shut my locker door and watched my phone's time like a hawk, literally counting down the seconds. When the minute was over, I looked both ways in the hallway, then headed toward my class. He seriously couldn't bother to do what he said?

Maybe that was why he had such a hard time with his grades. He was unreliable. Great grades meant studying and paying attention ... always. Not whenever he felt like it.

The door to my classroom was in view. I managed to sneak in and grab a seat before the bell rang. My books for class were arranged to optimally take notes. I needed to listen to all the information on this review sheet. We had our AP Calc test in two days and that would be a large chunk of this quarter's grades.

Mr. Warren stood at the front of the board as he projected

the answer key for the review. He would show us the answers, then we could spend the class asking questions. I planned to ask about *all* the ones I got wrong, just to make sure I knew how to do them.

Thankfully, I figured out early on that Mr. Warren based his tests around his reviews. They were never the same exact questions; the numbers were always different. But I could count on the type of problems showing up on the test if they showed up on the review. He never surprised us with anything that wasn't on the review, so at least that had been helpful.

I might have really liked math and numbers, but it didn't mean that it always came easy to me. I still had to work hard for my grades.

Why didn't Wyatt understand that? He had to work hard too. Did he expect things to just appear for him? Even if he didn't want to go to college after this, what did he think he could do? Just skip the last part of his senior year and no one would bat an eye?

Thank goodness we were only fake dating. I couldn't handle being with someone who didn't take school seriously or their *job* seriously. Until we graduated, we had to do school. If I ever dated anyone for real, they had to take that seriously. Otherwise, they'd be wasting my time and theirs.

I physically shook my head to control my thoughts. I couldn't go down a spiral about Wyatt in AP Calc. I needed to pay attention. He needed to be relegated to the back burner of my mind. I was his tutor; he was my fake boyfriend. Our business arrangement was intact, and I needed it to remain that way, regardless of whether his eyelashes could land an aircraft carrier, or his teeth were white enough to blind you.

It didn't matter.

Not at all.

～

The rest of the day, I received no text messages from Wyatt. My temper flared so bad it was like a sunspot affecting radio waves. He couldn't text me? Did he have a lobotomy since we had last texted?

Because short of that or a car accident, I didn't know if I could contain my anger.

When the bell rang signaling the end of the day, I bolted to my locker and headed to my car. No after school activities today and since Wyatt wasn't keeping his word, I had no plans with him either.

Only, instead of the sun gleaming off my Honda Fit's windshield, a tall broody musician leaned against it, blocking out all the light.

The straps on my bookbag dug into my shoulder as I pulled it tighter. After nothing all day, he decided to wait for me at my car?

Well, I didn't have to listen.

I sidestepped around him to the driver's side.

"Marley," Wyatt said. "You can't ignore me forever. We're dating, remember?"

I huffed. "Fake dating and I'm not the one ignoring people."

He raised his palms facing out to me in surrender. "That is fair. Honestly, I deserve it, but hear me out?"

I crossed my arms. "Why should I?"

"Because I had every intention of meeting you at your locker this morning."

I glared but let him continue.

"I turned in my English paper and then went to see Mr. Andrews. He wanted to read it right then. I couldn't leave. I barely made it to my own class in time."

I hated that I was curious to know what both teachers said. It was easier to be angry.

"And what, your phone broke and shattered into a million pieces making it impossible to text me?"

He grimaced. "Okay, yes, I should have texted you when I had time, like at lunch to let you know, but I like explaining things in person."

My arms relaxed slightly. "And how did it go with your teachers?"

"Good. Mr. Andrews grilled me for a few minutes. I think he was trying to see if somehow I plagiarized. Which he ultimately realized I didn't."

I moved a little closer. "And?"

Wyatt half smiled. "I got an A, on both. My English teacher found me at lunch to let me know."

I whooped with glee, then remembered I was supposed to be mad. "That's great."

Wyatt moved closer to me. "Marley, I'm sorry. Honestly. I'm not used to checking in with other people."

My lips twisted. What did that mean?

"I didn't think about how you must have felt waiting for me at your locker, until I saw your face as you walked out here. I upset you when you've been so helpful with my school stuff."

"Well, make sure to text me next time."

He nodded. "I promise."

I reached for my car handle.

"What are you doing?"

I twisted. "Driving home?"

Wyatt's eyes widened. "You aren't coming with me to Lucy's? Claire requested you at every gig. You're our good luck charm."

I rolled my eyes. "I'm sure I'm not and I had no idea about the gig. We haven't exactly talked since Saturday when you left me high and dry there too."

Wyatt winced. "I'm sorry. I forgot about a responsibility I

had and left." He batted his eyelashes playfully. "Can you forgive me?"

"That won't work on me." Or at least it shouldn't have worked. Damn him. I stood firm, but the longer I gazed at his expression, the more I felt myself cracking. "Fine. I forgive you."

"So, you'll come to Lucy's?"

I sighed.

"I have a date planned for before we get there too."

My eyes squinted as I surveyed his expression. "Which one?"

"The actual name is kind of long, so I'm calling it Dessert Swap."

"Huh?"

"I'll explain if you get in my truck."

My door slammed as I pushed it with one hand, then clicked the lock button on my keys. Grumbling and shuffling my feet, I walked closer to him. As I neared him, a scent I wasn't used to filtered through my senses.

Had he put on cologne? He didn't usually smell like that. But it smelled so good, like pine trees and something else I couldn't name, but it suited him with his rugged musician vibe.

He held open his passenger door and waited until I was in completely before he walked around to his door.

I had been so mad before that I hadn't noticed the eyes, but now as I sat in the front seat, I couldn't help to notice many of the other seniors glancing in our direction as he walked to his driver's door. Then they would dip their heads and say something as they glanced back at us.

Were they gossiping about us?

The truck lurched as Wyatt hopped in and closed the door. He eyed my expression. "What's wrong?"

"Nothing."

"Really, Marley? I can tell something's up. If you really don't want to come, I'd understand. It's just—"

"It's not about that. Have you noticed people are staring?"

His expression immediately shifted and relaxed. "Oh, well, that comes with the territory."

"No, I mean staring at us. They're ogling at us."

He chuckled. "Is that a problem? Can goody-two shoes not be seen with me?"

"No. I just ... I've never had anyone gossip about me. It's weird to have all their eyes focused on me."

"Welcome to dating a musician."

My eyes widened. "You think *they* think we're together?"

"Probably. That's the goal, isn't it?"

"Well, I ... maybe?"

He patted my arm before putting the truck into drive. "Better get used to it. It's only been a week. The more people see us together around town, the more they're going to think it."

Did I care about that? I had started this to fool Andrea. To prove her wrong. But what if other people started to buy it too?

We joined the car line.

"So, what'd you mean by dessert swap?" I asked, trying to change the subject.

"The book says that we should buy our favorite dessert and then swap it to the other person."

"Oh."

"So, I figured we could go to West End Bakery, secretly buy our favorite dessert, then swap them." He glanced in my direction as we moved a car length or two. "Is that okay?"

"Yeah, sure. It's for the book."

An emotion flitted across his face, but I didn't know him well enough to figure it out before it disappeared again. Was he upset with what I said? It was true though. If it was in the date book, then it was what he had to do, so even if I didn't like it, it didn't change anything.

"Maybe it'll help me with my studying."

"You need help with studying?"

"Of course. I have an AP Calc test, I want to do well. Finish the year strong."

"When is it?"

"Wednesday."

"Oh. Well, Lucy's has a back room if you really wanted quiet."

"No, it's fine. I can work on problems while I wait for you to go on. I'm sure you have homework to do too. Oh, did you bring me the science paper?"

He nodded. "All in my bag. I'll let you take a look when we get to Lucy's."

"Sounds like a plan."

We finally escaped the parking lot and headed toward town. West End Bakery was a family shop and was in the center of Main Street. It had been decorated to make everyone feel like they stepped into a special place. Large display cases took over most of the storefront. Only a few chairs fit inside and outside of the store.

Photos of the family littered the walls. The floors were black and white checkerboard tiles. But the best part was the smell. The bakery had all kinds of desserts, ranging from pies and cakes to cannoli and cream puffs. Of course, they also made fresh bread daily. Bread bowls, baguettes, Italian bread, if it existed, they made it.

I had no idea how they had time to do it, but they did, and they easily had wait times out the door for fresh bread.

Wyatt parked his truck in the side parking lot. It would be easier to leave but made a little longer walk.

"So, we shouldn't show each other until we're back in the

truck. We could open them and take a picture at the same time?"

"That works for me. I already know what I'm getting."

He laughed. "Me too."

We walked up to the front door, which he held open for me. A bell rang as we entered, then we split to opposite cases.

My all-time favorite dessert, whether it was from West End Bakery or somewhere else was Boston cream pie. It was so decadent and delicious, that I couldn't help as my mouth watered just thinking about it.

I almost wanted to get two slices, just to ensure I had some, because West End made it right.

A woman in her mid-thirties and the granddaughter of the current owner, waited on me. Her name tag read Marsha. "What would you like?"

"A slice of Boston Cream Pie, please."

She smiled. "Coming right up." She took my card, then handed me a receipt. Before I knew it, she was back in front of me with a white and blue striped cardboard box. It reminded me of the poles outside of a barber shop. The twine was tied in a bow and there was a West End Bakery sticker right on top.

I thanked her again and headed back to Wyatt's truck. He had beat me back and was already sitting inside his truck.

The aromas of the bakery followed us. It smelled heavenly.

"All set?"

I nodded.

We traded packages and agreed to open them at the same time after counting down from three.

We pulled the twine, unwinding the bow, slid it off, then pried open the sticker at the same time, then we laughed so loud, I thought bystanders could hear us.

We pulled out the desserts at the same time and placed them near us. I swiped my eyes from the tears of laughing so hard, then smiled.

"Say Boston Cream!" Wyatt shouted.

I stifled my giggle until he snapped a picture, then we stared at each other, smiling wide that my cheeks would hurt later.

"I chose Boston cream pie."

"And I chose a Boston cream donut."

"What are the odds? That's seriously your favorite dessert?"

"Yes!"

"Are you sure you just didn't hear me?"

"Nope. I was gone before you got to the case."

"That's too funny. Well, bon appétit!"

It was strange that out of all the desserts in the world, we had the same favorite. Even with the strangeness, I was thankful because I had stared longingly at the slice of pie, and I desperately wanted to taste that filling and eat the icing on top. The two best parts of the dish, at least in my opinion.

I took my first part of the donut, careful not to dribble any of the filling down my chin. "Ugh, this is delicious. I could eat like ten of these."

Wyatt laughed. "I almost got myself a second one ... just in case."

I whipped around to face him. "Me too!"

"No way."

"Yes, huh. These are addicting. What if you had chosen like a double chocolate lava cake or something? I would have cried."

He wrinkled his nose. "No. *Way* too much chocolate. That is just too rich for me."

My mouth hung agape. "That's what I usually say."

"I always say, *can't trust someone who likes that much chocolate.*"

I giggled. "No, you don't."

He smiled and looked down. "No, I don't. But I'm not all

about the chocolate. Boston cream, cheesecakes, give me those all day."

"Me too."

"Can't go wrong with someone who has the same sweet tooth."

My stomach quivered at the implications. "Unless of course you have to share ..."

He tilted his head. "That's true. I suppose we'd have to share the same desserts, which could be a potential problem." He placed his balled-up box in the cupholder, then put the truck into gear. We eased out of the parking lot and toward Lucy's, while I slowly savored my delicious donut treat.

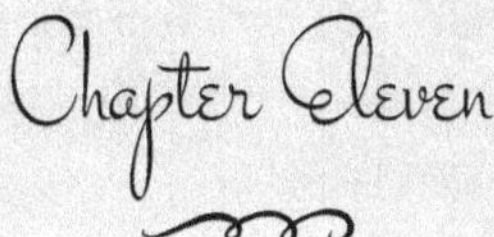

Chapter Eleven

Wyatt's hair peeked out from underneath his beanie as he stared at his homework.

I had been working on the same problem for the last ten minutes, trying desperately to concentrate to no avail. My brain circled with warring thoughts. How crazy was it that we had the same taste in dessert, but also how could he be so clueless as to text someone they couldn't make it?

It seemed at odds and no matter how hard I tried to focus on the math problem, all I kept thinking was that.

I placed my pencil in my notebook and closed it over the Calc book. "I'll be back. I'm going to grab a soda."

Wyatt nodded but didn't look up. He was focused on the second paper for Mr. Andrews now that his own math homework was finished.

And that was another thing. He received two As on papers I barely helped complete and his science paper was good too.

I had only a few grammar tips for him, which were minor at best. Could I really say I was tutoring if he seemed to be doing all the work himself?

I hopped up on one of the red topped stools with dark

wood stain for the legs and waited for the bartender to walk toward me.

Someone sat next to me. I sent a sideways glance and realized it was Claire.

Her dark red hair was cut in a short bob that angled toward her face. It made her light blue eyes pop as the light from the bar glinted against them.

"Hey," I said.

Recognition filtered through her expression before she launched at me in an embrace. "You came! I wasn't sure if you'd take it seriously that you're our good luck charm."

"Well, I have to admit I'm skeptical."

"Really? Even after knowing we got the call?"

My mouth dropped open. "You got the ... call? Wyatt didn't mention anything."

And how stupid was I that I didn't ask? I was absorbed in all the commotion about him ditching me that I hadn't even bothered to ask.

"Yep. They called at nine on the dot. It's not like a record label is signing us, but they liked our presence. They want to meet with us in a couple of weeks. We have to have an original ready to play for them."

"Wow. That's fast and intense."

Claire grinned from ear to ear. "And amazing. This is the break we've waited for." She nudged my elbow. "And you were there, so good luck charm."

I giggled. "I suppose."

The bartender sauntered my way. "What can I get you?"

"Pepsi please."

She nodded and fiddled around the back to make my drink.

"You know, Wyatt's a good guy."

My nose wrinkled. Why was she saying that?

"He doesn't open up much, but he has seemed happier

lately. I think that's because of you." She hopped off the chair and walked to a different table.

What did that mean? Why would he be happier with me? I wasn't doing anything.

I grabbed my drink and took it back to the table.

Wyatt dutifully wrote in his notebook and by looking alone it appeared he had gotten at least to the third paragraph.

My seat made a scuffing noise as I scooted closer to the table and placed my drink down. I waited until he glanced up before I asked, "Why didn't you tell me Broken Axles got the call?"

A slow smile splayed across his face.

My stomach lurched. It was sexy and endearing all at once.

"I planned to tell you."

"When?"

"At your car, but ..."

I sighed. "But I looked crazier than the Mad Hatter."

He tilted his head side to side. "Yes and no."

"Well, I'm an idiot for not asking. I'm sorry."

"No worries, Marley. It's no big deal."

I placed a hand over his. "It is and I'm sorry." Our gazes locked for a few seconds, before I released his hand and shifted my notebook. "Do you have any ideas on the song you'll perform? Claire said it has to be original."

Wyatt slouched in his seat as he leaned against the backing. "Nothing set in stone. Playing with a few melodies and lyrics."

"Do you write it or Jack or Claire?"

"Depends. We dabble here and there on different parts."

"That seems nice."

He nodded and bent his head back toward his work.

I took the cue to get back to work. Which I needed anyway. Calc was something I didn't mess with. No matter what.

~

The couch cushions had been pushed behind my back as I rested against the arm trying to study for AP Calc. Sage had agreed to come over after school on Tuesday to study and do practice problems together. This was our final test before we took the advance placement final. It would determine my grade in the class, while the final would determine if I could skip Calc in college.

Sage and I had the same teacher, Mr. Warren, but at different class periods, which in this case came in handy. It was easier to study with someone when they had the same teacher.

Sage tapped a pencil to her forehead as she laid on her stomach feet up behind her while hovering over her books. "Did you try number eight again? I keep getting a negative and I'm not sure how. I know it should be positive, but I can't figure it out."

I peered off the couch toward her notebook. "That line looks wrong."

She narrowed her gaze and nodded. "Thank you."

"Of course." I glanced toward my phone, face down on the end table. It was on silent, but even then I knew Wyatt hadn't texted me. I hadn't seen him at all since Lucy's last night when he dropped me off back at school.

I supposed I should be happy. He was using today to finish the two remaining papers he owed Mr. Andrews. Then all he had to do was study for finals and pull at least Bs on them all and he would be golden. Perfectly able to graduate.

It was an honest miracle. One I wasn't sure I could have actually pulled off, and yet ... it was happening, at least so far.

"If you want to talk to him that badly, just text him."

My gaze shifted away from the phone and toward Sage. "Who says I want to talk to him? Let alone *badly*?"

"You've been staring at it for five minutes."

My mouth opened and then closed. "I was not."

"You really were. What's the deal?" She scooted onto her bottom and sat crisscrossed awaiting my response.

"His band won from that contest the other day and he hadn't told me. Claire did."

"And?"

"And isn't that strange?"

"Aren't you his tutor?"

"Yes, but so what? It was a big deal for his band. You would have told me sooner."

Sage crossed her arms. "There's too many points wrong with that statement. I'm your best friend. Obviously, I'd tell you sooner. He also doesn't seem to be the person to spill his guts. And he didn't deny it, right?"

"Well, no."

"So, are you upset that he didn't tell you or that you thought he would and didn't?"

"I don't know. I've had other people I tutor tell me stuff before. I just expected he would have too."

"Maybe he didn't want to be too hopeful. He could be waiting until it's all a sure thing. Did you talk to him about it?"

"Of course not. We were at Lucy's and he was doing his work. It didn't seem to be the right moment."

"Maybe that's your answer right there. If you couldn't tell him something like that in that moment, maybe it wasn't how he wanted *you* to find out either."

Maybe she was right, but either way I didn't respond. Instead, I shifted my weight on the cream cushion and turned to the next page. I had at least ten more problems to practice in this set before it was a good time to break.

When I heard the rustling of Sage's notebook pages, I stole a glance. As I had figured, Sage had gotten back to practicing.

After a few more minutes the garage door closed. "Marley, I'm home," Dad called.

"Sage and I are in the family room."

No sooner than I had finished my statement, did my dad come around the corner.

He smiled. "Whatcha watching?" He scrunched his gaze at the TV, but frowned when he realized it was off. "No TV?" He leaned over to peer at the cover of my textbook. "Calc. Yuck. I hated Calc."

I giggled. "Well, soon I don't have to worry about it because it'll be done."

He ruffled my already curly monstrosity. "Very true. How about I make some dinner? Might help refuel you both."

I glanced at Sage who shrugged, then back to Dad. "Sure. Thanks, Dad."

He nodded and walked back toward the kitchen.

I strained to ignore the pots and pans banging and clanking as he prepared something for dinner. If I had any luck, I could get done the practice problems in time to eat, maybe Wyatt would text me, then curl up with a good book before bed.

I always told those I tutored that once preparation was complete, it was important to relax and set one's mind to something else. Cramming never worked long term and would only make the test more stressful.

And I had the perfect book to read on my shelf if I managed to succeed.

Chapter Twelve

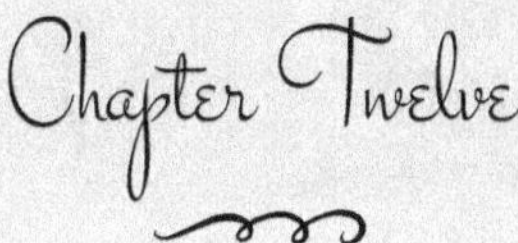

We parked in a gravel lot after school on Wednesday. I peered around, but the only thing I could see in each direction were trees and grass, and a singular porta potty. I shut the truck door. "Wyatt, why are we here? I thought we were studying today."

Wyatt shuffled a few things in the back of his truck, then strapped on his book bag. "I thought you had done enough studying for Calc. We needed a date."

My stomach fluttered. "Which date is this?"

He shrugged a shoulder and walked toward the trail. "Go on a hike."

I gasped and peered down at my worn sneakers, denim shorts and cotton T-shirt. His appearance finally registered— dark gray pants, boots, and a long-sleeve shirt, with of course, his beanie. "You didn't think to tell me that we would do that one today? I'm not exactly dressed for a hike."

Wyatt continued walking, without turning around. "You'll be fine."

I grumbled. If I broke an ankle, I would kill him. He

dressed up for the occasion, he could have at least warned me about it, too.

The trail entered into the trees, the temperature dropping several degrees. He hadn't looked back once to make sure I had even followed him. Did he not care that I was far from a girl who went hiking? Did he not care if I couldn't make it to wherever he planned to stop?

I cleared my throat. "Wyatt, can't you slow down? I'm not exactly in boots like you are. Besides, how long do we have to go on this hike to qualify meeting the date expectation?"

Wyatt stopped and swiveled toward me, brow arched. "Are you shirking on date responsibilities? That seems unlike you, goody-two shoes. Are you backing out on a date, Marley?"

"No ... I just. I really wish I had known about the hiking."

His lips twisted. "That's my bad. I guess I could have warned you about the shoes. But really this isn't Shenandoah Valley. Just a small part of the Maryland State Parks, we aren't going that far on the trail and it's fairly flat."

I harrumphed. Maybe it felt flat to him in his cushiony boots, but it didn't feel flat to me, not like a paved sidewalk or a concrete floor.

The woods were thick. I couldn't see anything besides trees in all directions. There was at least a clear path that had been well-maintained, but as the heat of May continued to rise, so did the bugs. After I had swatted away what was at least the tenth gnat, I groaned.

Curly unmanageable hair and bugs didn't mix. I hated that feeling. Hated it. "Shouldn't we take the picture for the book?"

Wyatt failed to look behind. "Not here. We will when we stop."

"Of course. Couldn't it be soon?" I muttered.

Many birds tweeted and cawed around us, fluttering through the trees. None got close enough for me to see what they were, but it at least sounded pretty and peaceful, if it weren't for the *freaking* bugs.

My focus stationed on the path, when I glanced up, Wyatt always seemed to get farther and farther away from me.

Was he unaware that I wasn't right behind him? Or did it not even occur to him to make sure I could keep up? What if I had asthma? He didn't know.

I huffed when a distant noise invaded my ears. What was that sound? Like a washboard or ... water. Were we by the water?

Of course. West End was surrounded by rivers and creeks that flowed into the Chesapeake Bay. It wasn't surprising that we could be by water, I just didn't realize this was the possible path he had chosen.

The trees thinned into a broad valley with a dirt path. Trees surrounded the area all around, but the more steps I took the louder the water sounds became.

When Wyatt reached the open valley, he finally turned and his eyes widened. "What are you doing all the way back there?"

"Dying from bugs."

Wyatt chuckled. "Not a hiker I presume?"

"Does that surprise you?"

"No."

"Well, a better equipped outfit would have eased some of the issues."

"I'll walk a little slower."

"That'd be nice."

He nodded and waited for me to set the pace before he continued forward.

"Where exactly are we headed?

"Rosewood Lighthouse."

My eyes widened. I hadn't expected him to take me there. I had never been. I had only ever seen it in postcards at shops around town or online for their social media pages as they requested donations for upkeep. "Have you done this trail before?"

"Yep, but—"

"When you were younger?"

"Mm-hmm."

"Does it look the same?"

He surveyed the area. "Mostly. The trees are taller, the path has been widened, but otherwise yes so far."

"Did you always go with both of your parents?"

"Yep. The three of us would go whenever we could to a new trail or to an old one. Took up most of our weekends."

"Why don't you go anymore?"

He shifted the strap of his bookbag uncomfortably. "I just don't."

And that was that. He didn't elaborate or mention anything more. His facial expression was clear that he had no intentions of explaining either.

What would make them stop going? Had they gotten divorced or separated?

Something had happened, but I clearly wasn't allowed to know yet.

For a long stretch we remained silent. I tried to focus on my breathing instead of on my thoughts, but that proved to be more difficult than I had imagined.

Eventually, the trail went back through the trees and I was forced to follow behind him, which somehow seemed easier. He couldn't see me struggle through the tree branches and narrowly avoid the roots on the path.

I had been staring at the ground trying not to trip when he had stopped suddenly. I ran straight into his backpack.

"Ouch!" I said as I rubbed my forehead. The buckles and straps were sure to leave an impression.

Wyatt turned, a grin he tried to stifle. "You know you

should really look where you're going and not at your feet. That is the worst thing to do while hiking."

I folded my arms over my chest. "Yeah? Well, I don't hike."

He chuckled. "Clearly."

I narrowed my gaze. "Maybe you shouldn't just *stop* with a beginner hiker."

"I stopped because we're here." He stepped to the side.

Sure enough there was the Rosewood Lighthouse. It was painted in dark green and white stripes circling diagonally all the way to the top, like a ribbon winding around a bottle.

At the base of the lighthouse was a placard stating when it was built and who had built it, then of course its name.

"First time?"

I nodded as I continued to stare at our surroundings.

Tall cattails stood at guard on the other side of the lighthouse. Past a thicket of cattails and tall grass, was the Rosewood River. It emptied into the Chesapeake Bay, but it was beautiful. An oasis.

"Worth the hike?"

I huffed, not willing to let go of my dislike for the surprise hike. "Maybe."

Wyatt smirked. "You know, I can tell when you're lying."

"Who says I'm lying?"

"You do. You scrunch your nose ever so slightly, like telling a lie is a smelly shoe."

"I do not!"

"Do too." He poked me in the side.

I screeched.

Wyatt took that as a signal to chase me around the lighthouse.

I sprinted toward the cattails and around the placard. I tried desperately to lose him, but I was no match for his long strides and proper attire.

He easily caught me and launched into a full-scale embrace, keeping me from escaping.

A laugh escaped my lips, followed by the realization of how close his mouth was to my ear. I could feel his breath on my neck, sending goosebumps across my body.

Despite my annoyance at his disappearances lately and this hike, the few seconds that his arms stayed around me felt like magic. Alighting nerves I didn't know could feel that way.

I imagined someone tolling a bell, an alert across my skin. And then he released me and took a few steps away.

My arms felt cold from the sudden change and lack of his body heat on me. What was that about? I had never noticed someone touching me like that.

Wyatt coughed and swiped the back of his neck with his hand. "Want to take the picture in front of the lighthouse with the water in the back?"

"Yeah, that will be pretty."

We walked farther from the lighthouse in hopes to get more of it in the picture behind us.

I stood in front of him, with his arm resting on my shoulder and then stretching to catch us both in the picture.

The scent of his shampoo and a minty smell wafted into my nose. He smelled so good, even though we went on this walk.

Marley, snap out of it.

What was I doing? Was I really focusing on his *smell*?

He pulled his arm away, then held it in front of us so I could see the picture.

When I smiled, he tapped a few buttons on his screen and I felt my phone vibrate in my pocket. I would bet that he had texted it to me already.

"It's too bad we can't see all the way from the top," I said.

He arched a brow. "We *could*."

"I'm not breaking into the lighthouse. No thanks."

He smirked. "What if it was for a date?"

I glowered in his direction. "I know there are no law breaking dates in that book, but nice try."

"Well, we can at least get closer to the water. There's a trail that leads down the embankment some. You can't touch the water from here, but we could at least get closer."

"Okay."

"And I promise to go slower this time. It can be a little rocky."

I tossed my arms into the air. "Just great."

"I've got you don't worry." He reached for my hand, squeezed gently, then released it.

My heart fluttered at the touch.

What was happening?

He went first, but this time, he waited for me to be at least within arm's reach of him. The first few steps down were fine. It was when we reached the gravelly part that someone clearly tried to use to keep the sandy soil from eroding, but only made the trek down worse.

My foot tried to grip the gravel when it slipped on vegetation.

"Woah, there." Wyatt reached for my arms, gripping my hands as he steadied me. "I've got you."

Which was at least honest. He didn't let me fall, but he continued to grip my hands as he walked down the pathway sideways and then waited as I followed. When the path flattened out again, we paused.

We were still at least ten feet above the water, but the crash of the river against the rocks drowned out everything else. It was peaceful and beautiful.

"It's so easy to get lost in the rhythm of the waves here. I forgot how much I liked to just sit and watch the boats come and go."

I found a large, flat stone and sat, pulling my knees to my chest. "I could watch this for hours."

Wyatt sat next to me, but leaned onto his hands as his legs were stretched out before him. "Me too."

And so we sat in silence and just listened to the waves and watched as boats moved down the river. Clouds shifted over the sky and the water's waves came and went, but the stillness was more peaceful than I could have described. It wasn't awkward that we sat there together without speaking. It was a comfortable silence, as if we had spent years around each other instead of almost two weeks.

How did that happen so quickly? Was it even normal? I hadn't dated before, fake or otherwise, but I couldn't imagine it was this easy this quickly for most people. But I wasn't about to ask and ruin the moment. So, we stayed as we were, until Wyatt slowly stretched, stood, and outstretched his hand to help me up—another date for the book done.

Chapter Thirteen

When we had gotten back to Wyatt's truck, he handed me his final two papers. They were good. Better than good, they rivaled something I would write and I prided myself on my eloquent way of writing a paper.

I had been so pleased with his progress that Wyatt proposed we spend all Saturday on a special date from the book.

Sage had wiggled her eyebrows at me suggestively and I had nearly hit her. Our situation wasn't like that, and all her ridiculous comments had messed with my head. That's at least what I had determined when I was safely in my room on Wednesday night.

I simply had Sage in my head and when he touched me, my body pretended to react and my brain went along with the trickery.

That was it.

Simple and logical.

Wyatt had texted me last night and insisted that we start

our date around nine in the morning and even asked for my address.

To say that my stomach was unsettled was an understatement. My parents weren't expected to be home, in fact, I checked that fact every two minutes with a constant watch out my bedroom window.

But what if they had forgotten something or had to come home for a quick minute? They would see Wyatt and I would have to explain.

Because neither of them knew that there was a dual purpose for our meetings.

And it wasn't that I thought they'd be mad. No, I figured they'd be thrilled ... at least my mom anyway.

Dad didn't want me to date, but Mom would eat it up and want to know every detail. But it was fake and *that* I didn't want to have to explain.

So, when Wyatt's truck pulled into my driveway, without my parents in sight, I sprinted to his truck and hopped in.

His eyes were wide. "Are you running away from a monster or just excited to see me?"

My jaw slackened, but words failed me.

"Relax, Marley. It was a joke, although, one might think it was the latter option with your lack of rebuttal."

Speak, Marley. "I was just thinking about whether or not I locked all the doors, that's all."

Wyatt cocked his eyebrow farther up but didn't respond to my statement.

In truth, I was more relaxed now that my parents weren't here, and Wyatt pulled from my driveway as quickly as he had pulled in.

I had no idea what we were doing today but decided to be casual and comfy. I wore my favorite stretchy high-waisted black denim shorts with the bottoms frayed from so many washes. As for my shirt, it was a light-colored salmon baby doll style blouse.

I shifted my attention to Wyatt who wore a hunter-green beanie, and a teal T-shirt with dark khaki shorts.

My eyes widened. "New beanie?"

Wyatt absentmindedly touched it, then replaced his hand on the steering wheel. "No, just haven't worn it in a while."

"I like the color."

As he glanced in my direction, he half-smiled. Then he rapidly tapped his hands on the steering wheel as he pulled over to the side. "So, before we go anywhere, I have to explain today's date."

"Okay."

"In the book it's called *Turn your date into a real life choose your adventure book.*"

My nose scrunched. "Choose your adventure book ...?" Then my eyes widened. "Like those Goosebumps books where you have to pick what happens next?"

"Exactly those."

"Oh my. Okay. Any ideas on how to enact it?"

"I figured we could take it step by step. As we get to stop signs or intersections, we decide which way to go. Then when places come into view we make a choice."

"That could work."

He pointed to the stop sign up ahead. "So that's our first choice. You ready?"

"Yes."

He pulled back onto the road and toward the stop sign. Once we stopped, I surveyed our choices. This was easy, either go straight or we could turn left.

"Go straight."

He nodded and followed my directions.

"This could take us anywhere."

"That's the idea."

"No wonder you wanted to start early."

"My thoughts exactly."

"I have to say the idea of this date might be my favorite so far."

"Just the idea of it?"

"Well, we haven't finished the date yet, so obviously I can't make a decision about that." I gasped. "How will we take a photo to prove it?"

"We could take several at the different stops we make."

"I don't think more than one will fit in the book."

"We could collage it?"

"Maybe."

The next time we stopped was at a red light. This time we could go left, straight, or to the right.

"Left," we said in unison, then laughed.

"Jinx," I said before he could.

As we headed down the road, we approached downtown West End. And the choices were a plenty.

"Okay, so first up we can decide on food. West End Bakery for breakfast or Rosie's for brunch?"

I searched his expression for a clue as to which one he wanted, but his expression remained passive. "Rosie's."

He flipped his blinker to the left and pulled into the parking lot.

"Inside or outside seating?"

"Outside," we said together.

I smiled, not expecting us to agree so seamlessly on two things already.

We seated ourselves at one of the bistro tables—a black iron wrought table and chairs with intricate leaf designs and a red umbrella over top of us.

Like most restaurants in West End, Rosie's was family owned and operated since its creation. They focused on breakfast and lunch every day of the week. Honestly, it was a miracle there were any tables open at all. Rosie's generally had a large crowd, especially during the summer months and on the weekend.

A young man a little older than us walked toward our table. His uniform was black pants, a white button up shirt and red bow tie. His name tag said Josh. "Welcome to Rosie's." He handed us both menus. "The special today is peach cobbler French toast and the Rosie's burger with a side of sweet potato wedges."

We nodded and then opened our menus.

I glanced at all the options, having no idea what I wanted.

Wyatt's brown eyes and forehead peeked over the top of his menu. "Want to make this even more adventurous?"

My stomach flopped, not sure what he was thinking. "Maybe? What's your idea?"

"We randomly choose our drink and food."

My eyes widened. "How?"

Wyatt placed his menu on the table, still open, and closed his eyes. Then he used his pointer finger to roam over the menu options. "Tell me when to stop."

"Uh ... what?"

"Tell me when to stop. Whatever I land on, I'll order."

I giggled. "What if you land on something horrible?"

"Then I'll figure it out." He peeked one eye open as he froze his movements. "Live a little, Marley."

I sighed. "Okay."

He picked up his speed and I squeezed my eyes and then said, "Stop."

His finger plopped onto the plastic menu with a thud, then he looked closer at what he had chosen.

I leaned in as well.

"Looks like it is the raspberry cream pancakes with a side of eggs and hashbrowns." He resumed his position of eyes closed and his finger roaming over the drink part of the menu. "Let me know when."

"Stop!"

His finger dropped. "Root beer." He laughed. "Nice. Your turn?" His eyebrow arched, his expression daring me to try it.

The ornery glint in his eyes sent shivers down my arms and a waffling feeling in my stomach like I was suddenly on a boat in the middle of the bay. I gulped, then sighed. "Okay."

I laid my menu like he had done, then closed my eyes and moved my hand over what I thought was the menu.

A light brush from Wyatt's fingers moved it over to the side, then he said, "Stop."

When I opened my eyes, my finger had indeed landed on food. "Spinach and feta omelet with bacon. Okay, I can live with that." Just like Wyatt, I closed my eyes after turning to the drink part of the menu.

"Stop."

After peaking at what I landed on, I said, "Orange juice."

Wyatt smiled. "See? Nothing to worry about."

"That was kind of fun, but just imagine if I had gotten something awful."

"Is that even possible at Rosie's?"

"Maybe not."

Josh returned after a few minutes. "Are we ready to order?"

"Yes," I said then proceeded to order what we had randomly chosen. Once he left to put the orders in with the kitchen, I leaned back against my chair, relaxing and letting the sun soak into my pores.

Summer was merely a breath away, getting closer and closer to graduation.

"You're a fall girl, aren't you?"

"A what?"

"A fall girl, as in the season. Yanno autumn?"

"What makes you say that?"

"Just a feeling I have. It was between that or winter, but watching you relax into the sun's rays, I went with fall."

"Okay. Well, yes, I enjoy fall. I don't know if I would call myself that."

"Why? Because you aren't into pumpkin spice?"

I crossed my legs and readjusted in my seat. "And what makes you sure of that?"

"Just a feeling." He fiddled with the sugar packets on the table. "Am I wrong?"

"No. I prefer the apple side of fall, instead of the pumpkin part. At least when it comes to food."

He smirked, clearly pleased that he had guessed correctly.

"Okay, well, I'd say you're actually a summer man, despite the fact you wear a beanie."

His lip pulled to the side, then readjusted.

Was I right?

"And your evidence?"

"Just a *feeling*."

He chuckled. "Touché."

Josh returned with our drinks and a few croissants that were complimentary.

My self-control had never been able to resist the flaky, buttery pieces of a croissant, let alone one from Rosie's which had the chance of secretly finding chocolate inside. I reached for a croissant at the same time he did.

Our fingers brushed, before we both pulled away.

"You go ahead, first," he said.

My cheeks warmed as I reached for one. When I moved my hand back to my side of the table, he grabbed one as well.

"If you could teleport anywhere in the world, where would you go?" he asked.

"Australia."

"Why?"

"My aunt went on a trip after she graduated high school for the summer. She said it changed her life forever."

He smiled. "That sounds nice."

I nodded. "And you?"

"Anywhere in Italy."

"Hmm, that would be nice too. Think of all the pasta."

"There's more to it than that."

"Well, of course, but I could be convinced on the food alone."

"Favorite color?"

I pointed to my shirt. "Salmon."

"That looks pink."

"No. There is a distinct difference. You?"

"No real favorite color."

"Really?"

He shook his head. "I suppose my clothing gravitates to certain colors, but no color makes me obsessed or anything."

I giggled. "That sounds funny to describe it like that."

"It's true. Some people hoard all things their favorite color. I don't have any need to do that."

"So, what do you hoard?"

"Who says I do?"

I shrugged. "No one, but I like to think everyone collects something."

He sipped his root beer. "I suppose you can say I collect journals."

"To write music?"

"Sometimes. I used to keep record of my days, like a diary, then it shifted into poetry or stories. Sometimes it is just ideas for songs."

"Any rhyme or reason to the type of journal? Like a certain way they are bound or anything goes?"

"It has to speak to me." He chuckled. "That probably sounds crazy."

"Not at all."

"What do you collect?"

"Books and pens."

"Pens?"

"Yes. Especially the ones that glide over the paper smooth as butter. It makes my heart beat faster just thinking about it."

Wyatt's expression was unreadable, but only because I had no idea what he was thinking. There was a glint in his eye, and then it was gone as Josh delivered our food.

He leaned over his food and breathed deeply. "This raspberry sauce smells so good."

I smiled, then unraveled my utensils from the cloth napkin, placing it over my lap.

He added butter and regular syrup with his pancakes before digging in.

We ate for a few minutes in comfortable silence. I tried not to drip or drop anything on myself. And the more I ate, the more I worried about eating in front of him, hoping I didn't look ridiculous, which only fueled my thoughts more.

Why did I care? And why couldn't I get those thoughts from my head?

"Smile," Wyatt said.

I quickly chewed my bite, then looked to see Wyatt had turned away and was readying to take our picture, the table of food in full display.

"A warning would have been nice."

"I said smile. I could have just taken the picture, with your scowling in full view."

"I wasn't scowling."

"Were too." He swiped his picture and, on the screen, displayed a picture of me scowling.

"Hey! Delete that."

He smirked. "Nope. I think that's my new screen saver photo."

"What? Why? I look awful."

He tapped his phone a few times. "Done."

Now I really did scowl.

When he glanced at my expression, his smile grew and his nose pinched in a stifled laugh. "It'll be more authentic. You want your cousin to believe you."

"Yeah, whatever," I grumbled.

"So, I've been thinking."

"About?"

"Your cousin."

I rolled my eyes and huffed. "Did you look her up and realize who she is?" I crossed my arms. "Figures."

His face contorted. "No. What do you mean, realize who she is? Is she some celebrity?"

"No, but her reputation certainly precedes her."

"Well, now I'm curious, but that's still not what I meant. I was thinking more about the believability of the arrangement."

"What do you mean? She will see the pictures then I don't have to deal with her anymore."

"You see, if it was me, I wouldn't just believe pictures. What if you photoshopped them all? How does it really prove you have a boyfriend?"

My stomach sunk, like an anchor for a yacht. Could that really happen? If we went through all these dates and Andrea ignored all the pictures, I would be even more upset. "So, then what should I do?"

"You're supposed to meet her to show her the book, right?"

"Yeah."

"Then bring me with."

My eyes widened. He was offering to meet her? "You think I should bring you to meet her?"

"Yep. That is if you want to really prove to her that you aren't lying and didn't fake it."

"But what if she doesn't believe that? I mean, photos are one thing, how would we make her really think it was real? I don't think she'd believe me. No offense, but I'm not in your league, Andrea would call it fake in two seconds."

His arms crossed as he eyed me warily. "What do you mean not in my league?"

I tucked a strand of my unruly hair behind my ear. "Wyatt, you don't have to pretend that I am. I'm a huge nerd and if I hadn't been so persistent in the parking lot almost two weeks ago, you wouldn't have even noticed me. Andrea is going to realize that in a heartbeat if she saw us together in person."

"If you remember, I did know who you were, so I think that is flawed, but I still stand by what I said. If you want to make it believable, she will have to see us together."

I hated that the moment he mentioned his doubt, I knew he was right. Andrea *would* insist on meeting him. I didn't have him on socials, I had no proof besides the pictures to say otherwise. She would call me out.

But how would we fake it in person? Andrea of all people would sniff out feelings or the lack thereof. She had a knack, which was why she was so successful with the men she had in her life.

My fork pushed around the food remaining on my plate. I needed to find a way to fix this problem, because as much as I didn't want to admit it ... Wyatt had poked holes in my plan and now all I could see was the instability.

Chapter Fourteen

After Rosie's, our adventure had taken us out of West End and into Chesapeake Hills to a thrift store I never knew existed. We each picked a random number and then in that aisle number we had to buy something.

I had ended up picking the candle aisle, which was a win for me, easily choosing a light and airy bamboo scented candle.

Wyatt had chosen the kitchen aisle and ended up walking out with a vegetable chopper. It had several attachments to adjust to different veggies and was actually pretty cool.

My dad would have been jealous.

"Okay, next adventure choice," Wyatt said as we waited to get to the front of the line at a four way stop sign intersection. "Straight, right, or left."

"Straight."

He saluted me, then at the stop sign, went straight.

We didn't get far down this road, before we were faced with more decisions. He pointed to his left. "That looks like a park and playground." Then he switched to the other side. "And over there is a farmer's market."

"Hmm. You pick."

"Park."

I nodded, and he signaled in that direction. Once we parked, I hopped out and waited for him in the front.

"Walk the trail or go to the playground equipment?" I asked.

"Hmm, walk then swing?"

I giggled. "Okay." The temperature had risen since our breakfast stop. I pulled the scrunchie off my wrist and tied my hair in a loose bun. It wouldn't crease if I took it out later, but it would keep it off my neck and be cooler from the weight of my curls.

Something flitted through Wyatt's expression as I did, but he didn't say anything.

I resisted the urge to squirm. It made me nervous not knowing what he thought when he looked like that. Was he annoyed? Although that didn't make much sense to me, but what else could he be feeling?

We set a slow pace, walking shoulder to shoulder around the circular trail on the outskirts of the park.

"Favorite band or artist?" Wyatt asked.

I groaned. "That is so hard and I feel like you'll judge it."

He placed his hands, palm outward. "Never. Music should speak to you. If it doesn't, then what is the point? I won't judge anyone for what speaks to them. It isn't fair."

My stomach twisted. "Billie Eilish." I stared at his expression, but true to his word, it didn't hold judgment. "What about you?"

"Favorites are hard for me. I have moments. Artists I like in certain moods I guess you could say. One Republic, Imagine Dragons, or The Weeknd. But I also like to dabble into older artists like Elvis and Johnny Cash. If it speaks to me, then I'll listen to it."

"That's cool. How do you have such an eclectic mix of music you like?"

"Just around. Not really sure actually. My mom and dad listened to some of the older stuff. As for the newerish stuff, just random playlists I stumble on or I hear it when we play covers at other places. All over. Claire is always bringing new music to practices too."

"How did Claire end up in the same circles as you and Jack? I just can't picture that happening."

He cleared his throat. "I saw her at a party, remember?"

"Yeah but seeing and becoming bandmates is a little different."

"Jack and I both flirted with her a bit. She pushed Jack away quickly, but we went on a date."

My brows rose. "You did?" My stomach lurched waiting for his response.

"Yeah, but it was clear we were supposed to be friends."

"Ah. Lucky that you all stayed close then."

"It could have gone south, probably would have if it was Jack's ex. He doesn't end things on good terms mostly. Either the girl leaves him high and dry or he ghosts."

I giggled. "I could picture that."

Wyatt's mouth pulled into a slow smile. "The worst case was this girl that followed our band in the early days. She liked our stuff and came to shows. He went out with her for a few weeks, then we did a slightly out of town show. He didn't know she was coming to surprise him. She caught him with his arm around another girl. She was so mad."

"I can imagine. She was probably hurt too."

"Yes, definitely. He shouldn't have done that, but I'll never forget his face. Claire and I mocked it mercilessly for weeks. Imitating it until we had it down perfectly."

"I can't imagine he enjoyed that very much."

He chuckled. "No, he didn't."

A family with two young children walked by us. The young boy and girl galloped around their parents, who looked exhausted.

Wyatt peered over to me. "How did you and Sage become friends?"

"In middle school we joined several of the same clubs and instantly clicked. We've been friends ever since."

"I wouldn't have expected her to be into the same things as you."

I laughed. "She would take that as a compliment. Her style changes so much. Something I like about her. I wish I didn't care what others thought."

"It's definitely not easy."

My brows scrunched. "But being a musician must feel good by their comments though, right?"

He adjusted his beanie. "Depends." He glanced at me then focused ahead. "You yourself had an opinion of me in the beginning."

My lips twisted to the side. "Only because of what Mr. Andrews had said."

"So, you never heard that I was a lazy musician or a free loader? Or even dumb?"

I shrugged my shoulder. "I may have heard it, but I didn't put much thought into it."

"Well, it goes both ways. People judging based on what they see never feels good when it contradicts what you see as who you are."

"But sometimes what they say is true."

Wyatt stopped walking.

My eyes widened realizing he thought I still meant him. "I don't mean about you. I meant about myself. I know I get called a nerd and prude and a geek. I do like school and math and those things make me a geek, so while I agree with those interests, they tend to be right about their comments."

Wyatt faced me, searching my gaze. "You don't really think that's all you are, do you?"

My neck tilted and I used my shoe to scuff the sidewalk. "I can't change the fact I'm a nerd, Wyatt. Even if they mean it negatively, it's not like I can deny it."

Wyatt gently lifted my chin to meet his gaze. "That's absurd. High school's job may be to put everyone in a neat box in order to label us, reform us, then ship us into adulthood, but just because you're given a box doesn't mean you have to stay in it." He exhaled loudly. "I mean, Marley, what the hell?"

"What? I'm not saying what they say about you is true. I don't believe them. You're not dumb or lazy. You work hard."

His hands balled into fists, then he released them, but his jaw ticked. "I don't just mean me, though. I mean you, too. You are *not* just some nerd. And it irritates me that you clearly believe that."

I crossed my arms. "What do you want me to say, Wyatt? I'm not adventurous. I'm not a cheerleader. I don't dance. I'm not musically inclined. I am suited for academics. I am logical. These are facts. Facts like the sky is blue and the grass is green. I can't change those facts, even if our classmates wanted to see other things, those are still *true*."

"But true doesn't make it bad. You say it like it's a badge of dishonor. We're about to graduate, who cares if the kid in the student body thinks you're one thing or even a cousin for that matter. We are eighteen. We get to write the next chapters of our lives. So, what do you want it to say?"

He faced the path again and walked ahead.

It took several seconds to process what he said before I could move again, but when I did things had felt like they shifted ... again. I didn't understand why he got so mad about a word describing *me*. It didn't affect him, so why did he take it personally? It made no sense.

After our walk, but before we got back in his truck, we swung on the playground. At least until real kids ran to the swing set forcing us out.

It was almost three o'clock. We hadn't eaten since Rosie's and my stomach gurgled so much it sounded like I was stashing a gremlin under my shirt.

"So, it may not be the most immediate question, but I say we detour towards food."

"Yes. Absolutely. I feel starved."

He laughed. "I guess our walking wore off brunch."

"I think so too."

Wyatt pulled up his map app on his phone and enabled restaurants. He merely used it to steer us in the right direction toward food places, then we used our eyes to make final decisions.

We ended up choosing a fast food chain.

As we waited in line to order, Wyatt turned to face me. "Want to have one last adventure?"

"In regard to what? Our food?"

"Yes."

"Like what?"

"We get whatever the car in front of us gets with a complete surprise."

"What if it isn't enough for us both?"

"We get back in line."

I laughed. "Really?"

He nodded. "It could be fun. If we really hate it, we could always use the second go round to get what we want."

"Okay, I'm down."

He rubbed his palms together quickly. "Okay. Here goes."

This was crazy. I had never left so many things up to chance at once.

Wyatt pulled up to the speaker.

"Hello, what can I get you?"

"Hi. I was wondering if we could get the exact order of the people in front of us? But don't tell me what it was."

"You want the same exact order?"

"Yes."

"Twenty-two dollars and nineteen cents at the first window."

Wyatt looked to me, then back at the drive-thru. "That at least sounds like it could be enough for us both."

I giggled.

When he pulled around to the window, I handed him my card, then he handed it to the lady at the window. At the second window, a man handed us a bag of food and two drinks. One was yellowish and the other a standard brown. We used the receipt to figure out the drinks were lemonade and a Coke.

"If you don't care, I'll drink the lemonade," I said.

"Sure."

He pulled over into a parking spot and then parked his truck, while I pulled out all the food items from within.

"Looks like two chicken sandwiches, two fries, one cookie, and then the drinks."

He nudged my elbow with his. "See? That worked out perfectly and you were stressed."

"Yes, adventure master. I was wrong."

He chuckled. "That killed you inside a little to say that, didn't it?"

"Maybe."

"Well, on occasion I can be right."

"I doubt that it is simply on occasion. You think I give myself little credit, you give yourself too little credit in your abilities."

He unwrapped one of the chicken sandwiches, while he

ignored my comment. So instead of preparing another rebuttal, I took a few fries and popped them into my mouth.

I couldn't believe that we had already done so much in one day for this date. Some activities I had never done, like going into a thrift store. At least at the end of this I could say I had gone out of my comfort zone, because even though I didn't have a real boyfriend, I had done those dates like they were real, well minus the PDA.

Wyatt pulled his phone from his pocket and snapped our picture while I was midbite into my chicken sandwich.

Why did he always choose the strangest times to snap a photo?

"I think that was quite an adventurous day."

I nodded. "One more date down."

"Another one to go ... tomorrow."

I raised an eyebrow. "Tomorrow? So soon?"

"Well, I figured you'll have me focusing on tutoring most of the week, so we have to get another date in this weekend. It'll be fun. I promise."

"Okay. Do I get to know anything about it, yet?"

"Only that you should wear clothes you don't mind getting dirty."

My eyes widened as I checked his expression. He was serious. "So old clothes that can be ruined?"

"Precisely."

"Okay, but can it be in the afternoon? My parents and I have our traditional morning breakfast then family time in the morning."

"Sure. I'll pick you up at three?"

"Sounds perfect."

We finished our meal, then he drove me back to the house. All the while, I couldn't help wondering what we could be possibly doing on this date. And how could I like it if I potentially could ruin clothes?

Chapter Fifteen

My morning with my parents resulted in French toast and several games of cards: Old Maid, Go Fish, and Liverpool Rummy. My parents separated into their Sunday tasks, including my dad having to go to the hospital for a few hours to cover another trauma surgeon.

I went to my room and made progress on flashcards for my classes, then when it was almost three o'clock, I changed into an old and almost too small pair of overalls with an old middle school shirt and beat up flip flops that really should have been retired long ago. My brown curly hair was up in a messy ponytail, with a headband to keep out my flyaways.

With my phone shoved in my pocket, I headed to the kitchen for a water.

Mom looked up from the kitchen table. "Where are you headed?" She did a double take. "Are those your old overalls?"

"Yep. I have a project for school to work on with Wyatt. Didn't want to mess up any good clothes."

She removed her reading glasses as she watched me. "With Wyatt, huh? Well, be careful."

"Always."

She nodded, but her gaze on me lingered.

It was unnerving, but then my phone beeped and I knew that meant he was here.

"See ya later, Mom."

She waved, then adjusted her reading glasses refocusing on the several folders spread out in front of her.

Wyatt was surprisingly right by my front door when I closed it.

"Hey," he said.

I twirled around. "This work?"

He nodded, then walked around to my side of the truck, and opened the door. Once I was in the seat, he walked around to the other side and started it.

"I set up the date before I got here so we're all good."

"And why did I have to wear clothes I could ruin?"

"We'll be creating something."

I groaned.

"Blindfolded."

I double groaned. "Blindfolded? Oh man. I can't create anything unless there are step by step directions, but blindfolded?" I sputtered.

He laughed. "You'll be fine, Marley. I'll guide you, then you'll guide me."

"Okay." He clearly didn't understand how badly I had done in art class. It was a requirement to take an art elective and theater was out of the question, so I had settled on art.

For someone who loved school and exceled in class, this was not that class. I had passed and I had managed an A but with strenuous effort. For many projects, I received a B, it was only by one project and the final that I managed to pull out the grade I wanted.

An afternoon doing art of any kind was not my idea of a fun time.

We pulled off the main road and onto a smaller dirt one. All around us were wheat plants. When Wyatt pulled off the road and finally parked, I could see that in a small clearing between the plants was a large canvas style covering laid out on the ground, then several bags of things, followed by an easel.

I gasped. "Are we *painting* blindfolded?"

He smiled, one of those lazy smiles, where his eyes were relaxed, but was sexy at the same time. "Yep."

Internally I screamed. Like a blood-curdling-running-from-the-bad-guy scream. Painting? That was as bad as I could get. My drawing abilities were limited to stick figures and squiggly lines.

And then another thought surfaced. "Did you buy all these supplies?"

He shrugged but avoided my gaze.

"You did! Wyatt, you shouldn't have done that. I could have gone and gotten them."

"You could have, but then you would have known what we were doing and that was the whole point of the surprise."

"But I feel bad you used your money. These dates are my fault."

"Fault is a bit strong, but I don't mind, Marley."

"Are you sure?"

"Yes, now get out and let's go."

The grass flattened as I jumped down, then sprang up around my toes, tickling my ankles and feet. I hastened my pace to get to the canvas before I was an itchy mess. I wasn't *actually* allergic to grass, but it never failed to make me itchy.

"I didn't have an actual blindfold, so I brought a tie."

"That's fine, I could close my eyes too."

"Oh no. You think I believe you won't cheat?"

"I wouldn't."

"You so would, you'd be stressed enough to look because it's painting."

I sighed. "Fine. So how am I going to paint?"

"I have a few colors. Pick the ones you want and we will put them on the paper plate. Then just tell me what color and I'll help you put it on the brush, then voila you use the canvas to paint."

"Voila, huh?"

"Yes." He brought the bag of paint colors to me, which had more colors than I expected: salmon, purple, teal, brown, cream, and red.

"Wow. Okay, these three," I said as I grabbed salmon, purple, and teal.

He grabbed those three tubes, put some on the plate, then let the bag plop to the ground.

When he searched for the brushes, I focused on what he had chosen to wear. His beanie was still present, but it wasn't one I normally saw. He had a white fitted T-shirt and light-washed jeans, with sneakers. As he stretched for the brushes, his muscles in his back rippled, sending heat over my cheeks.

Dang it, stop thinking about his body.

"Okay, we can just use this medium brush. You ready?"

"No, but something tells me that you won't accept that answer."

"That'd be correct." He picked up the tie: a satin powder-blue one. "Let me know if it is too tight." He approached me slowly, draping the tie over my eyes, then reached behind me to secure it. He was close enough that I could hear his breathing and his arms brushed my cheek. "How many fingers am I holding up?"

"I have no idea. This is darker than I thought."

I certainly hadn't expected to wear a blindfold, let alone with Wyatt Shaw so that we could *paint*.

"Good, that's perfect then. Okay, I'm putting the paintbrush in your hand." His fingers settled under my hand

and then with his other one, he placed the brush between the correct fingers for me to hold it.

My cheeks flamed from the touch.

"Okay, I'll help you put paint on it, which color first?"

"Teal."

He moved my hand until I could feel the brush scrape against the paper plate, then he shook it slightly, which I assumed was to get rid of excess paint.

"Okay, here's the canvas." He used my left hand to touch the canvas. "So, go ahead and have at it.

It felt absolutely ridiculous, but I swiped the brush up and down where I thought the canvas was. The bristles of the brush moved over the surface smoothly, giving that small rustling sound.

"Ready for more paint?"

"Yes."

Again, he guided my hand to the paper plate, then back to the canvas. And so we went, only speaking as I needed more paint or a different color. I found that one of his hands had a callus, was that from playing guitar? The skin was rough to the touch, but he only ever touched me gently.

What would it be like to be in his hands?

Where did that come from?

I needed to stop that. He was just being kind, nothing more. I certainly wouldn't be his type. Instead, I should be focusing on what the heck I was painting.

"Can I switch to the salmon?"

"Sure." He grabbed the paintbrush and wiped it off. Apparently, he had water in cups and paper towels to clean the brushes. Then he handed me the brush back.

"I put the paint on it for you."

I smiled and reached to the top of the canvas to put more of the color up there, but instead of feeling the brush touch the canvas, it resisted in a weird way, before my hand landed on someone's chest.

I gulped, not someone's, but Wyatt's.

"Woah!" Wyatt said before I could do anything. "I'm not the canvas, Marley. It's that way."

"Oh my gosh. I got paint on you?"

"Yeah, right here."

Suddenly a wet feeling engulfed my cheek.

"Hey! Did you put paint on me?"

"Oops," he said.

"Nuh uh. That wasn't an accident. I didn't do it on purpose. You got me on the cheek!" I reached for the blindfold.

"Oh no. You aren't done. Finish your painting. You can't see until you're finished."

"What? No! I don't trust you. You'll get paint on me again."

Hands reached out, but graced my arm, before I lifted the blindfold partially off my eyes, just in time to see Wyatt move closer.

I screamed and ripped the blindfold off and defended myself with the paintbrush. This time a long salmon stripe went down the front of his shirt.

He froze and his eyes widened. "Oh, that is a declaration of war." He lurched for the bag of paint.

As I realized what he was going to do, I ran to him, but too late. He had already uncapped the red and squirted it in my direction.

Had I remained where I was, almost nothing would have landed on me, but alas, I was closer, and a splotchy red streak went from my shoulder to my right knee.

Throwing the blindfold to the canvas, I went after the bag of paint too.

He was so dead. I would get him for that. I managed to

grab the brown but had at least three more squirts of paint over my arms and overalls.

Looking away, I uncapped the paint and launched it at him. Thankfully, my poor aim got him anyway.

He placed his hands up in surrender. "I'm out. You can't shoot an unarmed man.

"Wanna bet?" I smirked and sprayed him again.

A mischievous grin spread across his face. He moved closer as I aimed it steadily at his chest.

"Don't move any closer or I'll spray."

He arched a brow, then jumped toward my paint.

We wrestled for the ownership of the tube, neither of us letting go.

I tried to twist and turn to rip it from his fingers, but the more I moved, the bigger his smile was. My breathing was ragged and my arms were sore. I was gassing out, and he knew it.

I released only slightly from the paint, but that was enough for him to strike. He twisted it once, and it flew away from my fingers. The momentum pulled me close to his chest.

He raised the paint above my head and squeezed, keeping it out of reach. I tried to jump for it, but I couldn't maintain the stamina. I paused and so did he.

Our chests stayed together. I could feel him breathe against my own chest as it heaved to get my breathing under control.

His arms slowly lowered as did his chin as he met my gaze.

The air around us changed. It sparked with something I couldn't name. His pupils were big, despite being in the sun.

He leaned forward, our faces even closer. "Truce?"

I nodded. Words were too much at the moment.

Up this close, I could see his eyelashes, and they were even longer than I had thought they were. They fluttered over those gorgeous brown eyes as he blinked, until we took a breath and leaned toward each other. My eyes had closed.

Then our lips touched. My eyes flew open. Was I having my first kiss? Was this really happening?

His lips were soft and gentle as he lightly pressed them against mine. His hands had moved to my waist and all the sensations were enough to completely screw up my breathing again. He didn't rest all of his weight on my waist, but enough so that I could feel exactly where every finger laid over the top of my shirt. My skin erupted in goosebumps from the contact.

What would it have been like if his hand was on my bare skin? I couldn't imagine it. Our bodies were so close, my thoughts were stuttered. How was I having my first kiss? And why couldn't I just focus on it instead of thinking about it to death?

I laid a hand on his chest and leaned slightly back, but it was enough that he had stopped.

The moment broke and I had no idea how to even process that whole thing.

Wyatt's expression searched mine and then shifted. "I'm so sorry. I ... you. I should have asked. Are you okay?"

"I'm. Uh—"

He removed his beanie, his hair falling everywhere. "Marley, I'm so sorry. I shouldn't have. You said no PDA. I broke that rule."

I placed my hand to his arm, my stomach twirling. "No. It's okay. I think I wanted to."

"That's not the point." He shook his head. "I just couldn't help it. You looked so cute with that blue paint on your cheek and how hard you tried to keep the paint from me. But we had an agreement. I—" He coughed and took a few steps backward before replacing his beanie. "I'd understand if you want to go home."

"Wyatt, we're okay. Okay?" If my stomach was any

indication, I was more than okay. That kiss had been like nothing I could have imagined on my own. Sage had told me to expect the worst first kiss I could ever have, but that? If that was a bad first kiss, then I didn't think I was ready for a good one.

He searched my gaze warily. "You're sure?"

I nodded and reached for the blindfold. "Want to keep painting?" I smirked. "And on the actual canvas this time?"

A half smile returned. "Yes, I do have a painting to create too." He looked around at the cream canvas beneath us. "Although I think we had some color sacrifices."

I giggled. "I'd have to agree. You look nice in salmon and brown though."

"I'll remember that."

I held out the blindfold so he could help me put it back on.

He took a few steps to me and then replaced it over my eyes. "Good? Can you see anything?"

"Nope."

He placed his hands on my shoulders, my body leaned into the touch, before he guided me back to the painting. We kept the paint on the canvas, but only because we had kept a truce. And after that kiss? I had way more important things to think about than revenge for paint.

Because if I was being honest with myself, I liked it. And that truth? Well, it changed *everything*.

Chapter Sixteen

I removed my blindfold, when I felt like there was nothing else I could do to my painting. I tilted my head from side to side, but I still couldn't tell what I had done. The colors were blended well, although I hadn't done it purposefully.

"It looks terrible."

"Nah, it's just abstract."

"That's being too kind."

He chuckled. "So, did you have fun doing it?"

My thoughts swirled back to the kiss. "Yes."

"Then that's all that matters." He pulled a thin black sharpie from his pocket and held it out to me. "Now you have to sign it."

I groaned. "Really?"

"Yes. That's the rule."

"Fine." I signed the bottom corner with my name and date. I didn't have big plans for it, but I would remember this night and not just because I was covered in paint, including my hair.

"You ready to paint now?"

"Yes. I have just the thing in mind."

"And what's that?"

"You'll see." Instead of letting me get all the paint for him, he pulled out a fresh paper plate and put his colors of choice. When he was all set, he cleaned my brush, then started with cream paint. "You think you can manage the blindfold?"

"Yes, but you have to crouch down a little."

He did as I asked and just like he had, I placed the tie over his eyes, then tied it in the back. "How many fingers am I holding up?"

"No clue."

I turned his shoulders toward the brand new canvas and placed his left hand onto the canvas as he had done for me.

Each time I had to touch him it was torture. I had to avoid touching my lips before, but now that he couldn't see, nothing stopped me from doing it.

If I closed my eyes, it was like his lips were on mine again and my cheeks flushed. This was bad. How would I concentrate on our business arrangements and finish tutoring if I had these thoughts?

But what was more, was he had kissed me first. What did that mean? Did he have feelings? And while I think he truly was sorry for not asking, did that mean he wouldn't try again?

Did I want him to?

No matter how hard I tried to answer one question, ten more popped into my thoughts, confusing me even more. And would it change how he saw the situation?

I had been thinking about what he said yesterday about Andrea not believing it was real. And even in that moment I knew he was right but didn't want to admit it.

I would need to have her see us in person for it to work, but would he want to after that? Were we just swept up with everything?

I liked it, but that didn't mean I had feelings for him. Did it?

Focus on helping him.

"Want any more paint?"

"Do I have a lot moving around or minimal?"

"I'd say minimal."

"Then yes, but not a lot."

"Okay." I helped guide his hand to the cream paint, but only let him get a little before returning him to the canvas.

"So why did you settle on painting, instead of something else? It said to create, we could have baked cookies or something."

"Well, that would require a kitchen, which by the speed to which you bolted from your house yesterday, made me think you wouldn't want to use yours and we couldn't use mine, so that was out."

"Okay, well we could have colored."

"That feels like cheating. And I remember what you said about being creative. You were creative today and I think you secretly loved it."

I nibbled the bottom of my lip. Damn him for being right. It had been nice to paint without expectation.

"Fine. I did, but my painting is still far from good."

"So? Wasn't the point. You created something. I'd say that's a win. Okay, next color."

He switched to teal and used it mostly at the bottom of the canvas. I had no idea how he stayed within the sections of the canvas he wanted. It was almost like he could see it, but I kept checking if he could and he never reacted. I did the chicken dance, made goofy faces, everything I thought would cause a response and nothing happened, so he must have just intuitively known, which irritated me. Of course, he'd be good at instruments and singing and now painting too.

"I haven't seen the book in a few days, are we halfway

through the dates? We only have two weeks left before graduation."

"We're on track. I haven't sat and counted, but I'd say we're in a good place."

That was such a non-answer. How many more did we have? "So, I was thinking ..."

"Okay."

"I think you're right."

"Wow. About what?"

"About Andrea. I think she won't believe the pictures alone."

"Ah. So you have a plan?"

"Well, what if you go with me when I meet her to show her the adventure book? She can meet you, see that it's *real* then I win."

"And what if she wants us to kiss or prove it?"

I gulped. "I don't know. What do you think?"

"I think it's likely that she would expect something."

I frowned. "Then I have no idea. I'm not just going to kiss you for her benefit. She can imagine my first kiss anyway she pleases; she doesn't need to be privy to the truth."

"Wait, what?"

My hand clasped over my mouth. Did I just say that? *Yikes. I didn't want him to know that. Just act natural.* "More paint?"

"What? No, Marley." He reached out with his left hand as he held the brush in his right. Then he slipped the tie off his right eye. "Did you say your *first kiss*?"

My gaze averted to the ground. "Um."

This time he removed the whole thing. "Was that your first kiss?" His gaze searched my face.

"Yes." I picked at the red paint on my hand, trying to peel it off.

"I had no idea."

And now he really would understand that he had made a mistake and another kiss would surely be out of the cards.

"It's fine. You have to finish your painting."

He opened his mouth, and then closed it like a goldfish. He nodded once, then pushed the tie back over his eyes.

He didn't mention the kiss again, but I could feel it sitting between us—a weight on my chest.

Wyatt dropped me off two hours later and as soon as I crossed the threshold, I ran to my room. Luckily neither of my parents were in the family room because I needed to unpack it all with Sage.

Once my bedroom door was closed and my radio was turned on for background noise, I placed the painting against the wall then plopped on my bed and video chatted her.

It rang twice, before she picked up.

"Hey, what's ... Woah! What happened to you?"

I puffed out my breath, letting a piece of hair that had wiggled out of my hairband flutter. "My date with Wyatt."

"You're covered in paint." She gasped. "Was that a paint war? Oh my gosh, I need details."

My cheeks reddened.

"Something happened." Her phone waved around crazily, then settled back on her face, screams muddled by the movement.

"He decided today should be the create something blindfolded and he settled on painting. He drove me to this wheat field and had set it all up for us before picking me up. I painted blindfolded first."

"Wait. Blindfolded? That is so hot." Sage grinned. "Continue."

"And I guess I had gotten his cheek by accident and so he

retaliated and put it on my cheek. I might have retaliated back."

"Ooh, paint fight. Okay."

"And we ended up wrestling for one of the tubes of paint and it ended up against his chest." I covered my face with my free hand, unable to make eye contact with her when I said, "And we kissed."

Sage screamed again and again. "You had your first kiss! Ahh! Wait, how was it? Too much tongue or saliva or sweet and gentle and toe curling?"

"Woah. First of all, thank you for all those lovely mental images, but secondly, Sage, we kissed. This is colossally bad."

"Nope, stop. We aren't analyzing it yet. I want to know how he kissed you. God, I bet it was sexy as hell. His lips are so kissable anyway, but—"

"Sage, focus! I'm panicking here."

Sage pulled it together and switched her expression to one of composure and grace. "I'm listening."

I had to stifle a giggle. I didn't know how she could do that so quickly. "The kiss was magical. His lips were soft and I don't think it was even that fancy, but now ... well, now, I can't deny I liked it. I couldn't stop thinking about it."

"So? That's a good sign. Ah! Mar, I'm so proud of you. And with that hunk? Nicely done."

"But, no. It hasn't changed anything, if anything, it made it more impossible."

Sage frowned. "How?"

"Well, for a minute it seemed like he had really been into the kiss too, but then it all switched. He kept apologizing for not asking me if it was okay and that I had said no PDA, he literally put space between us." I glanced down. "And then, I accidentally let it slip it was my first kiss?"

Sage's eyes widened. "How does that just slip out?"

"I was rambling? I was nervous, it just popped out in one

long thought and then I couldn't take it back." I laid back on my bed. "This is bad, Sage."

"It is not, we just have to figure out a few things first, then I can help you get out of it."

"How?" I sighed. "I won't be able to look at him tomorrow."

"Yes, you can, but you have to be honest with yourself first."

"What do you mean?"

"How do you really feel about him? You said you liked it, but does that mean you'd want it to happen again?"

My insides flipped. "I don't know. Doesn't that seem a little too soon to decide on? There are so many factors that go against the possibility."

"So what? You have to figure out what you'd want, because until you do, then it's hard to pick a course of action."

I groaned. "I have no clue on what that answer would be."

"So, wait and see what happens. You still have lots of time together this week with studying for finals and the dates, right?"

I nodded.

"So, see how you feel about it. And if the moment presents itself, lean in and kiss him again." She winked at me.

I shook my head. "You just want us together."

"I want my best friend happy. If it happens to be with him, well, I can get behind that."

"Yeah, uh huh, sure. Well, I'm going to shower now. This paint will be murder getting out."

"Love you and good luck!"

"Love ya too," I said, then hit End.

I had hoped a phone call with Sage would make things clear, but they felt muddier. How was a kiss responsible for all these unanswered questions?

Chapter Seventeen

My butt had fallen asleep in the chair at Marshall's Books. When Wyatt had told me no Lucy's today, I had been excited to spend it studying for finals. Most of them were Monday through Wednesday of the next week, but advanced placement finals were sooner and my AP Calc one was *this* Wednesday.

"Need a refill?" I asked. I needed any reason to stand and shake out my limbs. This chair was uncomfortable after so long sitting still.

Wyatt's hair shifted as he glanced up. "Nah, I'm good."

"Okay."

I grabbed my cup and walked over to the boy behind the counter. Sage wasn't working tonight, and she didn't want to be trapped here any longer than she was already mandated, so I couldn't convince her to study with us.

"Can I have a caramel latte?"

The boy nodded and placed my mug on the counter, before preparing the ingredients and then dumping it in. I handed him my debit card, then took my receipt and hot cup of coffee back to the table.

I stood, gingerly sipping it. The heat raced down my throat, warming me from the inside out. It may have been an almost summer day outside, but inside Marshall's I was freezing.

Wyatt smirked. "Are you going to sit?"

"In a minute. My butt seriously hurts."

He chuckled. "Have to stretch."

I made a scrunched face. "I was thinking peruse the shelves for a minute or two."

"That works too."

I walked a few steps when I realized he stood too. My brow arched. "Whatcha doing?"

"Following along?" He spread out one arm in front of him, telling me to lead on.

I groaned. "You want to see what I read, don't you?"

"I must admit, I am curious."

I laughed. "Well, prepare to be underwhelmed. I'm sure it is exactly what you think I would read."

"And what do I think you'd read?"

I crossed my right arm over my chest and rested my left arm on top. "Romance."

"And do you?"

"Of course, but in lots of genres. YA romance, adult romance, fantasy romance. But also epic fantasy, magic, dragons, honestly anything that has a good cover and catches me in the blurb."

"Then I'm not underwhelmed at all."

I rolled my eyes but kept moving as I sipped my drink. A few shelves over, there was a table inspired by books popular on social media. I eyed the covers and titles, picking them up only when I was caught by the cover long enough to want more.

Wyatt floated around the shelves, running his hand over the spines, as he circled around me. I felt his gaze on me more than I caught him doing it.

When the feeling in my butt returned and I didn't feel so stiff anymore, I floated back to our table and stuff, then added the books I saw to my Goodreads TBR. Later I'd buy them when I had finished the stack in my room. But that was for summer and after finals, I had too much to do right now than read endlessly, because once I started, I had a hard time putting books down.

Wyatt joined me momentarily after I sat.

"Have you finished making flashcards for economics?" I asked.

"Somewhat. I don't usually use them, but for all the vocabulary this class has, I thought it was best to do something."

"That's a good strategy."

He leaned closer. "How's your studying coming?"

"It feels slow. Everything at once, my brain feels crowded. I'll be happy when it's over."

"Won't we all."

"Have you gotten grades on all the papers you turned in?"

"Yep. All A's."

I smiled. "Wyatt that's amazing. Seriously."

He averted his gaze. "Thanks."

"I have to ask ... how did you get in such a big hole? You turned this around so quickly. I have never had someone I had to tutor do that before."

He blushed. "It wasn't much."

"That's not true. You wrote those papers. I may have focused you and made a list of tasks, but you did the work. You spent the time. I'm enormously proud of you for that."

"I guess I just needed a little push."

"But how didn't you have that before? Little ol' me couldn't have changed you that much. Not in two weeks."

"You just did. And I'm really grateful, Marley. If I had

been going to college, you certainly would have helped push me in a better direction."

Now my cheeks reddened. Did he mean that? I still didn't know how someone had shifted so drastically in such a short time period, but if I had really done that, then I was a better tutor than I realized.

He tapped a few flashcards on the table. "There's something I wanted to say to you."

"Sure."

"I haven't forgotten about the kiss or what you said, but I wanted you to know there's no judgment from me. For whatever reason you haven't kissed anyone, that's only your business. I just wish I hadn't been so presumptuous. It feels like I stole it."

"I wouldn't say stole. Honestly, Wyatt, I'm fine."

"You're sure?"

"One hundred percent. A girl could have had worse first kisses."

The one side of his mouth tugged up, widening his smile. "So, you're saying it was good then?"

My eyes widened as I was positive my cheeks reddened deeper and deeper. "I'm saying I don't regret it."

"Okay." His gaze lingered, before it ultimately shifted back to the books in front of us.

Which was good for me. I needed to calm my emotions and at least discussing it put it out in the open. Now we could move past it, and I could focus solely on finals.

But the gnawing curiosity of what he thought about the kiss wouldn't go away, even after I wrote it on my paper then scribbled it out trying to ignore the thought.

I cleared my throat and fidgeted in my chair.

Without glancing up once, he asked, "What's wrong?"

"Who says there is?"

"You are usually still while studying or have been for a

while, but you're wiggling in that chair more than an earthquake shakes a house."

"Well, I was just curious."

At this he did meet my gaze. "About?"

"Um."

He arched a brow.

"Well, obviously, you have ... I mean it wasn't ..."

Wyatt chuckled. "What are you trying to say?"

My cheeks inflamed and I covered my face with my hands. "What did you think of the kiss?" I sharply inhaled hoping his answer was positive, but also not believing I had even asked that question.

When he didn't respond I snuck a peek.

Wyatt had leaned against the back of his chair and smirked. Clearly, he was enjoying my pain and agony from his silence.

"Well?"

He leaned forward slowly, drawing out the moment. "I'm saying I don't regret it."

I stifled my smile as he parroted back my same response. It hadn't been a no, so at least that was a step in the right direction, but did he really believe that or was he being nice about it?

"Is that so?"

He shrugged then winked at me.

And even though I needed to focus on my finals, the majority of my thoughts were trying to decipher whether he believed that or not.

Chapter Eighteen

It was officially Wednesday morning and as I walked to my locker, my stomach was twisted in knots. Today was my AP Calculus final and regardless of having taken other advance placement tests in the past, this one felt different.

I was going into finance. This felt personal if for no other reason than I liked numbers. If I didn't do well, not only would I have to take it in college, but I'd feel ridiculous.

None of which helped soothe my anxieties. As I approached my red locker, Wyatt turned the corner.

He stopped, clearly waiting around for me. I hadn't expected to see him during school.

I stopped in front of my locker door and watched as he smiled and kept his arms behind his back. "Did I forget about a meeting today?"

"Nope." He rocked on his feet. "I know you have your AP Calc test today and I wanted to wish you luck."

I smiled. "That's so sweet."

He pulled his hands to the front and held a stuffed animal of a fish. "I don't know much about what kind of soothing foods you like, but you told me that salmon is your favorite color. So, I got you a salmon."

My eyes widened. He had bought me something? And not only that but he had remembered my favorite color? What did that mean?

"Thank you." I peered into his gaze. "Wyatt, this is the sweetest thing anyone has ever done for me."

He smiled, the one I usually saw as he was on top of a stage, serenading the crowd. It was a genuine smile and it made my stomach do backflips.

"It's nothing. I just knew how nervous you were. And I know how awesome you are at school and studying, so I wanted you to feel confident."

I grazed his arm with my fingers. "Thank you."

He nodded. "And then after school be prepared for memories."

I arched an eyebrow. "What?"

He laughed. "It's the name of the date, *Go down memory lane.*"

I shivered. "Oh, yours or mine?"

He shrugged. "Not specific, so I planned for mine."

He was going to share something of his past with me? Other than his family hiking a lot when he was younger, I knew nothing of his family, past or present. "Okay, sounds good." I squeezed the salmon to my chest. "Thank you for this. Really."

Our gazes met in the crowded hallway. The warning bell tolled over the PA system and as much as I didn't want it to happen, it was our cue to get to class.

Except the pull his luscious brown eyes had on me was intoxicating. It reminded me of our kiss and I wasn't sure I could separate from him if I wanted to.

He tucked a piece of my unruly hair behind my ear. "I'll see you later."

I nodded because words were useless in my present condition. Having to study for one of the biggest tests in my life was doing a good job distracting me from what that kiss had meant and what was happening, but after today, that distraction was gone.

Wyatt turned left at the end of the hallway, and I forced myself to go to class. I had no idea what memories I would have to think about later, but if it helped me understand Wyatt more, I was all ready for it.

The day went surprisingly quick. My AP Calc test was over and while I had no idea how well I did, it couldn't be changed at this point. I had to let it go. Besides, I had other things to worry about for the afternoon.

I shoved my books in my bag from my locker and I listened to Sage continue to drone on. "Marley, are you listening? I'm not sure how I did on the AP Calc test."

"You'll be fine, Sage. We studied, now we just have to wait for the results.

Sage pinned me with her stare. "What's with you?" She studied me harder. "This is about Wyatt, isn't it? He has officially gooified your brain."

"What? He has not."

"Totally has. You aren't even focused on the test anymore. You're focused on something else. And normally you'd be stressed about the results with me until we received them, but you have that faraway look in your eyes. Why?"

I sighed. "We have a going down memory lane date today."

She arched a brow. "Have you two talked about the kiss?"

"Not more than what I told you happened at the bookstore."

"So, this is the first time without your AP Calc test in the way?"

I nodded.

"No wonder. You're overanalyzing that instead."

"What if I am?"

"What are you worried about with the date?"

I shifted my bookbag on my shoulder. "I wouldn't say worried. I am just nervous-excited to find out about his past. He doesn't really talk about it."

"And that's all? Have you thought about what I asked you?"

"No. Yes. But I don't have an answer."

"Mm-hmm."

"Don't mm-hmm me like that."

"I think you do, but you're avoiding it."

Most of our classmates had filtered out of the hallway. "Sage, I need to go. He's waiting."

She waved me away. "Text me later."

"I always do." I waved behind me then headed for the parking lot. Wyatt wasn't telling me where the date was, but at least I knew what to expect the theme to be.

The late May heat soaked through my thin shirt. It was a humid one today. Wyatt leaned against the front of his truck's grill on his phone while he waited. I hadn't noticed earlier but for once he wasn't wearing jeans. He actually had on *shorts*. He always wore jeans or at least pants, so I couldn't help myself when I could finally see his legs, which were lean and muscular.

Was it weird that I thought his legs looked good? Did people actually think that? Or were legs a weird thing to be obsessed with?

I shook my head. This was ridiculous. He had a fit body, of course his legs would be too. I shouldn't have been surprised.

"Hey," he said.

I had been so engrossed in my thoughts I didn't realize he had put away his phone. "Hey."

"*So*, how do you think it went?"

"No idea."

He chuckled. "Well, I'm certain you did well. Probably got a five."

My laugh was choked. "I doubt that, but as long as the score is acceptable to college, then I don't care."

"Fair enough. Are you ready?"

I nodded.

He walked around to the passenger side and helped me up. I threw my bookbag in the back while he walked around and started it up. We coasted toward the parking lot line.

"I will not miss waiting in this line," Wyatt said.

I giggled. "It *is* the worst."

"Only thing that tops it are the lines at the mall during the Christmas season."

I shuddered. "Those are terrible, I waited for two hours once just to get to the cash register."

Wyatt shook his head. "Oh no. I would have put down whatever I was buying and left. The thought of waiting in that long line makes my skin crawl."

"Really? Even if it was what you *really* wanted? Like a special edition guitar?"

"Yep, really. Nothing is worth wasting two hours of my life."

Wasting? It was boring sure, but I never saw it as wasting. I had the chance to watch others in line and scroll on my phone. This time I used the book I was reading to pass the time. And no matter what, time was never wasted reading.

"No long lines, got it."

He glanced in my direction. "What were you waiting for in line?"

"Oh, I don't remember now. It wasn't anything special, but I read while I waited so it went faster than it could have."

"I could see you doing that."

We finally made it to the front of the car line and left the school parking lot.

"Where are we going for today?"

"Close to where we went hiking, but in a different section."

"Your memory lane is in the wilderness?"

He smiled. "Of course."

Internally my stomach knotted. At least this time I wasn't dressed too inappropriately in my denim shorts and T-shirt. "Like hiking or a leisurely stroll?"

"More of a leisurely stroll this time."

"Okay. I think I can handle that."

"If not, I'll help you along. No major exercise today."

"Good, because the humidity increase is more than I can handle. My hair has already grown like eight inches from the short walk to your truck."

He chuckled. "I like your curly hair."

My eyes widened. Did he just compliment me? I didn't think he had ever complimented me like that before. "Well, only you do, because it drives me crazy. Other than the one time Sage tamed it with products, it never does what I want."

He tugged a loose strand by my left ear. "I still like it."

I searched his expression. Was he flirting with me? Or was he just being honest? And oh, how I hated the fact that I was almost graduating and couldn't tell if he was flirting with me. How messed up was that?

I listened as Wyatt sang several of the songs from the radio.

"You know, we haven't really talked about the whole winning the battle of the bands thing."

Wyatt shifted his gaze to me momentarily, then back to the road. "Oh?"

"Yeah. Other than you confirming that Claire had said they called. You really haven't said much. How is it going with the demo for the label?"

"Okay, I guess."

"That doesn't sound very confident."

"We can't decide on what to do for one of the sections. It makes the creative process more annoying."

"Oh."

"We will figure it out."

"It's due soon, right?"

He nodded as the truck bumped over a gravel road. "Sunday after graduation."

"Really? Everything all at once then."

He tapped a steady beat on the steering wheel. "Generally, that's how it goes."

"Still. Do you think you'll all be ready by then?"

"I mean we have to be. Once finals are over, we have more time to finalize everything, but yeah, I guess."

"What genre are you making the demo in?"

"Kind of pop and rock."

"Can I hear it when it's done?"

Wyatt glanced at me then back to the road. "You want to hear it?"

I tucked my hands under my legs. "If that's okay with everyone."

"I think that can be arranged." Wyatt smiled, then focused on his driving. We had veered off the main road, passing several pastures and loads of trees.

"I can't believe I've never been to these places. I've lived here my whole life and not once have I gone and explored them."

"That's honestly a tragedy."

"Well, until now. Thanks to you."

Our gaze met briefly, until he broke it to refocus. We

finally parked. There were several dirt trails leading to and from the lot.

"Wow."

"Just wait until you see the main event."

I arched a brow. "Main event?"

"It's a short walk up that path." He pointed to the trail directly in front of his truck, but behind the railing that framed in the parking lot. "Then you'll see even more of a beautiful view."

What could be more beautiful? There were trees everywhere surrounding all the pathways to and from the parking lot. We weren't alone on the trails, based on the number of cars in the lot, but I couldn't see anyone.

Wyatt locked the truck and stood by me. "Ready?" he asked as he outstretched his hand.

He complimented me and now was asking to hold my hand? I placed my hand in his. My skin slipped over his fingers, sending bumps over my arm.

"The first time I came here, my mom brought me. We walked around this path; I think I was like five. And we just walked, laughed, and played. It was nice. The next time we brought my dad. We had walked just about every trail in this area. My mom liked to explore each one and bring us along."

I smiled. "That sounds nice."

"It really was. I miss going on the walks, it's been nice showing you around on them."

I squeezed his hand. "I am enjoying it too. As long as I am dressed properly."

He laughed. "You're not going to let me forget the lighthouse, are you?"

"No! I could have had some proper warning."

"Mm-hmm."

"Why don't you go on the walks anymore?"

Wyatt's expression clouded with an emotion I couldn't

name, except it was exactly what he showed when he showed up for a tutoring session grouchy. What was it about his family that caused him to feel those darker emotions?

"We just don't."

I wanted to ask more about it, but his tone had shifted and I didn't want to ruin this moment, so I dropped it. Even though this was the second time I had outright asked him about his past and he had avoided the answer. What was it that he wouldn't share with me?

"My parents aren't really outdoorsy people. They like to grill, but that's about as far as it goes."

"What's your favorite childhood memory?"

"Hmm. I guess if I had to choose, it would be when I was eight. My dad had taken off work the whole time I was off for Christmas. We had spent time baking bread and cookies, but then one day after Christmas, he took us to the movies. I don't even remember what we saw, but I had so much fun. It was just us."

Wyatt gazed into my eyes. "That sounds nice."

"It was. He always tries to do something special just the two of us around Christmas. It's always our time together, plus Sunday mornings of course, but that's with my mom too."

We walked around the corner and suddenly the path cleared, leading to a red covered bridge. I gasped.

"I told you the main event is worth it."

"A covered bridge? Really, these are so fun."

He nodded. "Let's go closer." He tugged gently on my hand as he led us forward. I had always wanted to take a picture near one. There were always photographers posting photos near the covered bridge during engagement sessions and weddings, but I hadn't realized there was one in our county on these trails.

"Did you come to this part?"

"Yep, we would come and swim in the creek."

My eyes widened. "Are we ...?"

He grinned with a mischievous glint in his eyes.

I crossed my arms. "Wyatt, I'm not going swimming."

"You don't have to, but you can wade into the water. It's not deep enough to fully swim here anyway."

I relaxed slightly. "Fine."

"But let's take our photo for the book up by the bridge first."

He led us to the opening and, angling it sideways, took a selfie with his phone.

My hair was sticking out everywhere from the humidity, but I loved the backdrop of the red covered bridge in the background. Wyatt had actually faced me the whole time and the way he looked at me in the picture made my stomach squirm.

What was happening?

I felt my phone vibrate from the photo coming through my messages, but all I could think about was the expression he continued to give me.

He took off his socks and shoes and placed them on the edge of the water, before he took a few steps in. "Get in, it feels so good."

"Is it cold?"

"Only at first."

I toed off my own shoes and put my socks inside. My left toe dipped below the surface. "That is cold! What are you talking about?"

"It won't even be noticeable once you submerged your whole foot."

I glared at him, but still ended up wading into the water up to my ankles. The chill took my breath as I inhaled sharply several times. "It still feels frigid."

He laughed. "You'll make it." He lifted his chin until he stared at the sky. "Isn't this the best?"

"Standing in freezing cold water?"

"No. Being in nature with good company."

"Oh."

He glanced toward me, sending shivers across my skin. How did a simple glance cause such a reaction? I never paid so much attention to his looks before we kissed. Now, I couldn't stop noticing it.

"Why aren't you dating someone?" Did that actually come out of my mouth? Did I actually utter that question?

His eyes widened.

"I'm sorry, I ... I shouldn't have asked that."

"I think we're past general etiquette here with all the *dates*. I was just surprised by the question." He fidgeted with his beanie. "There wasn't a conscious effort to not, if that's what you're asking."

"I'm not sure what I'm asking, but it doesn't seem like you would have a hard time finding someone to date." My mistake was looking at his expression when I said that. His expression betrayed nothing, but his eyes held amusement and curiosity. "I mean with you being in a band and all. Don't girls love a guy who can play guitar?"

He chuckled. "I don't know. Do they?"

I gulped. My words were officially stuck in my throat. Was he flirting? Or was he asking what I thought? I was a girl, so I should know the answer, shouldn't I? "I think it certainly helps."

"Helps?"

"Um." My cheeks heated. Now not only did my stomach keep doing somersaults, but my cheeks were warm, no doubt reddened like a toddler learning to put on blush while she played with her mother's makeup.

Wyatt moved closer to where I stood. "Helps what?"

I snapped my eyes shut, forcing the words to escape, but also safeguarding myself from his reaction. "Your eyes and smile?"

"Is that so? What about them?"

His hand settled on my bare arm.

I jolted, my eyes flying open. "This is nothing new. You know what I'm trying to say."

Feigning innocence he said, "I'm sorry, but it doesn't register."

"Your eyelashes are long. Like girls would kill to get their eyelashes that long with makeup, and yet, there you are with long beautiful eyelashes that flutter over your deep and rich brown eyes. And whether you ever went to an orthodontist doesn't matter because your smile is perfect. So yes, playing a guitar and serenading someone with your voice certainly *helps* with the other features you have going for you."

Once the words had escaped, I wanted to reel them back in. Wyatt was still, saying nothing, but his eyes roved over me. I had no idea what he was thinking, but I couldn't bite down the embarrassment from saying what I just did. Those were thoughts for private, for Sage even, but *not* for my fake dating boyfriend, who clearly only accepted our arrangement because of my desperation and his desperation to pass.

His hands reached up to cradle my face, then his right hand slipped into my hair. "For the record, any guy that doesn't recognize your beauty and your wit is the one missing out." Then just like that his hands were gone and he waded farther down the creek, leaving me in utter shock to eventually follow him through memory lane.

Chapter Nineteen

The smooth surface of my vocabulary cards lulled me to sleep as I reviewed them at the table of Marshall's books. It was a Friday night, a week from graduation and yet, I was spending it studying. Obsessively studying some may even say. Yet did I change my plans? No, I didn't.

Wyatt sat across from me with his head bent, nose in his economy notes, trying to ensure an A on his final on Monday.

So maybe, I wasn't *that* upset to be studying, because at least a very cute boy was across from me doing the same.

Sage would die if she could hear what I was thinking now. Up until the walk down memory lane, I had convinced myself that maybe I was the only one with possible feelings. Sparks were simply illusions from my overactive brain and therefore not real. But how could I deny that things had definitely shifted after Wyatt told me guys who didn't realize who I was were missing out?

So why, if I had realized the shift, was I not telling my best friend? This was best friend newsworthy. It should have been the first thing I did when I got home from our date on

Wednesday and yet, two days later, that information was still kept lodged in my brain.

I straightened my pile of notecards and went through them again. Maybe if I remained focused on studying, I could ignore the fact that I was unsettled. Feelings for Wyatt Shaw was a bad idea. He was leaving for the big city after graduation and he might find my studious tendencies endearing now since they would help him graduate. He surely wouldn't find them endearing when he was trying to become a big name music mogul and I was a freshman in college worried about midterms and projects.

"Your nervous energy is seeping into my body all the way over here. Want something from the counter?" Wyatt asked, never once looking up from his notes.

"My ... what? Who says I'm nervous?"

"No idea what you're nervous about when you're going to ace your finals, but you can't stop jiggling your leg, which has shaken the table, not to mention if you shuffle through those index cards any faster, I'm certain they will combust."

My brows rose. "I didn't realize." I settled my body. "I'm sorry, I distracted you."

See? I was already being a nag.

Wyatt finally glanced up to meet my gaze. "Didn't say I was distracted, just wanted to make sure I couldn't help calm your nerves with a nice drink."

"Oh, um, maybe a chai tea? I don't think coffee would exactly help me here."

He nodded then stood. "One chai coming up. I'll be right back."

I smiled, then waited as he walked away before I threw my head over my arms and pouted. I needed to get it together. If I was that readable while I said nothing, then what would he think when I tried to pretend I had no feelings for him?

Because somehow in almost three weeks, I had caught real feelings and that was not in the agreement.

The sound of his chair moving forced me to sit up and plaster a steady smile on my face. "Thanks."

He nodded then went back to his notes, like nothing was wrong.

Maybe I just needed to focus on the business part of our arrangement. He needed my help. When was the last time I asked him about his classes or how things were going? Did I even know what his current grades were?

"How's your studying going?"

He raised his head, meeting my gaze. "Good, I think. Economics feels solid, which is the only one I have Monday. Tuesday is Mr. Andrews and English. Wednesday is science and math."

"That's good. How about studying for Mr. Andrew's test? Do you feel ready?"

"I think I will once I review a little more this weekend, but it doesn't feel as impossible. I recognize it is more achievable now that I'm out of my hole."

"That's awesome, Wyatt."

He smiled so broadly it almost hurt my cheeks thinking about it.

"What about you?"

"Like you said, I shouldn't have anything to worry about."

He closed his notes after placing a pencil inside as a bookmark. "Good, then I was thinking."

I arched a brow. "About?"

"Graduation and meeting your cousin."

My stomach flopped. "Please don't remind me about that. I get nauseous every time I think about it. What if she sees us together and doesn't believe it?"

Wyatt's smile turned into more of a smirk. "You don't think we have chemistry and could pull it off?"

My mouth instantly dried up. Grappling for my chai tea, I sucked down a few sips before answering him. "No, just that Andrea is good at assessing a situation. She also knows me."

He crossed his arms. "Does she though? I mean if she did, why harass you about not dating? It's not her business."

He had a point there. "It's more about making me admit it, I think. But if you really think we could sell it."

"I do." He placed his hand over mine, then squeezed my fingers gently. "So, this is also a book date night."

"It is? I thought we were almost done and were waiting for finals to be over?"

"Well, mostly. We still have to teach each other something."

I groaned. "Really? That is really a date in there?"

"Yep."

"Well, I already did that, right? With tutoring?"

"Nope. No visual evidence, so it didn't happen."

"Well, I have no idea what I could teach you."

He chuckled. "Good thing I have an idea for what I can teach you."

"Oh, yeah? What's that?"

He stood and outstretched his hand for mine.

Reluctantly, I placed my fingers in his hand. His touch was warm, invigorating me more than I thought possible. He laced his fingers with mine, pulling us out into the balmy air. It was a typical May evening. The sun was still hanging on in the sky, setting off soothing blue tones and slight oranges as the sun descended.

Town was busy. People walked toward the ice cream parlor a few stores over, but Wyatt pulled us in the opposite direction toward his truck. We stopped at the back of his truck's bed, where he pulled down the tail gate, then went around to the front of his truck and opened the passenger door. He pulled out his guitar case and immediately my stomach dropped to my feet. He wasn't really going to teach me guitar, was he?

Didn't he know how astronomically bad I was at instruments? I didn't even attempt them.

He also grabbed a thick comforter and laid it in the truck bed, then jumped up into the back. Once he stood at the tailgate, he crouched down and proffered his hand to help me up next.

I placed my hand once again in his, then jumped as he pulled, until I was officially standing on the comforter. I criss crossed my legs and settled comfortably on the blanket.

I blinked rapidly at Wyatt as he pulled his guitar from the case, then placed it on my lap. "You can't be serious."

His smile grew and his lashes batted over those rich brown eyes before saying, "Deadly serious. You can do this. I'm a great teacher."

I scoffed. "I think you either overestimate your ability or overestimate mine, but either way a train wreck would go down better than this."

"I highly doubt that, and I think I'm offended. I'll have you know I can teach people to play the guitar."

Once the guitar rested on my leg, he pulled the strap over my body and across it, until it laid loosely in place. Then he sat next to me, our bodies grazing here and there, sending a shiver through me every time, despite the humidity.

"Any knowledge about a guitar?"

"Besides what I read in your research on how they are consumed in the economy? Not really. Oh, and I know you use a pick to strum the strings."

He stifled a laugh. "Okay, well, Marley, each string is used to play different notes. And notes have letters. Do you know the letters?"

I shook my head.

"That's okay. There are six strings on this guitar and there are sections we call frets down the neck of the guitar."

My eyes felt crossed as I focused on each part of the guitar he named and discussed with me. I couldn't even focus on all the words, they went in and out like in cartoons where they're squished between the character's ears, then forced out the other end.

"Does that make sense?"

I nodded, even though I had definitely zoned out. I had tried to warn him.

He spun around front so he could see my face. "Your eyes have this glazed over look." He chuckled. "Okay, maybe I don't explain the parts yet. How about you play a song with me?"

My brows furrowed. "If I can't even figure out what each string is and what notes it can play, how will that work?"

"Good old fashioned I'll help guide your hand and you can strum it and I'll make the other notes with my hand."

I giggled. "That seems like it goes against the point."

He shrugged. "It's still teaching you something."

"Fair enough. Okay. What are we playing?"

"You'll have to wait and see."

He sat back behind me and then scooted closer. Now his arms came around both sides of my body. I resisted the urge to squirm as people walked through town and glanced in our direction. But their glances weren't nearly as nervous making as the fact that Wyatt hadn't been this close to me since our kiss, and yet, it felt like that day had never happened and still did all at once.

My thoughts weren't even making sense.

He settled his hand over mine and rested them both on the side to strum the chords. His other hand sat on the neck of the guitar, at least that's what I thought he called it. My second hand rested under the guitar to help hold it off my leg.

As Wyatt took a breath, his chest grazed my back, sending warmth through my thin shirt. If it weren't for the jargon of musical instruments twisting my thoughts, this contact was certainly doing an even better job.

Without warning, Wyatt moved our hands to strum the guitar, while his other hand moved with speed and accuracy across the strings. The results were a beautiful sound emanating from his guitar. I felt mesmerized by the movements and then when he began to sing *Iris* from the Goo Goo Dolls, my heart felt like it was melting.

Damn him for picking this after what I had confessed.

Being a part of him making music was better than watching him on stage. I didn't even have to see his face to know how at peace he was and how moving his music made me feel. But this song? Was it on purpose? Or had he picked it because he knew it?

Either way, I couldn't help noticing that with each chord, my heart was dancing and swelling, and the feelings I had for Wyatt weren't going anywhere. If I thought I could deny them before, now there was no way that would work.

His body moved with every breath and even though his voice wasn't for everyone, in this moment he was singing only for me to hear, it felt like he was singing in the loudest microphone on a grand stage.

When the final note of the song rang out on the guitar and from his lips, I resisted the groan ready to explode. I didn't want this to end. I didn't want him to create space between us. I wanted it to start over and to feel this moment again for the first time.

Instead, he shifted to my right and helped lift the guitar over my head, then placed it between us.

"That was amazing, Wyatt."

His gaze searched my own, but I had no idea what he was looking for. "Well, I had a good helper."

"Oh, please. That had nothing to do with me and everything to do with you."

"I don't think so."

"How come you don't play that song in one of your sets? The girls would go crazy over that."

He snorted. "I don't think that would be true and I don't exactly want that attention either."

"Why not?"

"Not why I sing. I'm not trying to have girls fawning over me because of what I sing. I'd rather help someone through something or make them feel like a different person from my song."

"Well, couldn't that difference also be about romance? I mean if they're moved to stalk you, then wouldn't that still be *moving* them?"

"I'll admit, you almost had me." He adjusted his beanie. "Stalking, really?"

I giggled. "Okay, stalking may be a bridge too far, but Wyatt, you're so talented. You have to know you'd have groupies. And groupies *love* those kinds of songs."

"Maybe, so."

I focused on the sky before us. The sun had dipped even lower, mixing more oranges and purples into the sky than before, although still quite warm.

"Now it's your turn."

"What? I can't play by myself."

"No. I meant it's your turn to teach me something, but first we have to take our picture."

I nodded and scooted closer to him.

He settled his arm around me and pulled me even closer until my head fell on his shoulder. Then he snapped the photo.

The glimpse of it that I caught, before he pulled it back into his lap, enticed me.

What would I do with all these photos after next week? I would literally have a book full of photos with someone I fake dated. How crazy was that? And what was worse was that I secretly wished they were real.

He hopped down from the tail gate, then helped me down as well. He put his guitar back in its case, then placed it and the comforter in his truck before putting up the tail gate.

We walked back toward the bookstore to reclaim our seats.

"So, what am I to learn today?"

"I have no idea. What could I honestly teach you?"

"There has to be something."

"Um." I wracked my brain for something, until it wouldn't budge past one idea. "Okay, this is probably beyond ridiculous, but what about how to read fast?"

Wyatt laughed. Not even like a little chuckle, full on-no-holding-back-tears-spill-down-your-cheeks-kind of laugh.

"Why is that so funny?"

"Wait. You're serious?"

I crossed my arms. "Yes. I only know academic bookish things. So, I can teach you how to read faster."

"Aside from the fact that I never expected you to say that, I'm quite curious."

I plopped in the seat across from him at our table. Then I turned his economics notes so they would face me and him, perpendicularly to our sitting positions. "So, the trick is you have to focus on more than one word at a time. Like you focus on phrases or small simple sentences instead of word by word."

He squinted at the page. "On a whole sentence? That's a lot."

"Start only a little larger. Like instead of one word at a time, you focus on three words."

"Okay ..." His squint lessened slightly, but he still looked pained. "That's hard."

"It can be at first. It takes time. But just read this page and try to focus on three words at once as you read down the page."

He nodded and I grabbed my phone and opened the timer. I started the stopwatch and then waited for him to stop reading and look up, then stopped it.

"I think I know what I read. I'm not really sure."

I laugh. "Okay, now try to do it again, but do five words."

"Uh, I'll try."

Once again, I used the stopwatch to time him. This time when I stopped, I compared the speeds. "You were faster this time."

"Yeah, but I think I'm getting a headache." He lifted his chin to meet my gaze. "Is this what you do? Do you read like this?"

"Sometimes. Depends."

"What do you mean?"

"Reading new things that I really need to focus on, makes it almost impossible to read that fast, but I use it for novels or notes that I've written or am familiar with."

"That makes sense. I had no idea someone could even do that. I regret laughing."

"See? You can keep practicing it and eventually it gets even easier."

"Definitely would have come in handy earlier this year with all the reading Mr. Andrews gave us."

"Well, now you have it for the future."

I sipped my now mostly cold chai tea, then shuffled my index cards. It was time to get back to studying, no matter how much I didn't want to.

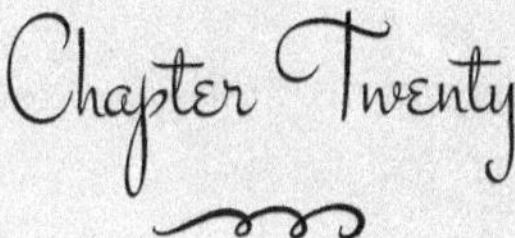

Chapter Twenty

I waited outside in my driveway. Wyatt would appear soon to whisk us off to the next adventure in our book. All I knew was that I had to bring a zip up in case it became chilly and that it would take a large portion of our day to complete.

My parents had asked why I was up so early on a Saturday, but once I said it was for school, they left it alone. I wasn't sure if my mom really believed me or not, but she didn't argue it at least.

Just like clockwork, Wyatt pulled into my driveway and idled while I hopped in.

I shifted my zip up over my legs and faced him. "Good morning."

"Morning."

His smile reached all the way to his eyes. Could he feel this energy between us?

After being so close to him when playing guitar, I couldn't help feeling like everything had shifted, even more now, than when he had kissed me.

"So, where is our destination?"

"Well, one of the adventure dates says we must explore a random point on a map. So, I got out a map of Maryland and my finger landed on Baylin. Have you ever been?"

I shook my head. "Where'd you get a map? *I* don't even own a paper map."

He shrugged. "My mom had some that we used to use. Okay, then Baylin it is. You ready?"

"Surprisingly, yes. Normally I would be spending every second studying for finals, but I don't feel stressed that I'm not chained to a book."

His eyes widened before shifting his attention back to the road. "Goody-two shoes doesn't care about studying? Who are you and what happened to Marley?"

"Ha. Ha. Very funny. I didn't say I don't care about studying. I just said that I don't feel like I need to be chained to the books. That's all."

Wyatt whistled. "We may just make you adventurous yet!"

I swatted his arm. "Quit that."

He chuckled. "No, honestly, I'm proud of you. You've come a long way."

"And so have you."

Our gazes snagged on each other's and we held it, until he was forced to look where he was driving.

"A week until graduation. Can you even believe it?" I asked.

"Not at all, especially considering the state of my grades three weeks ago."

He was right. We had struck our deal, not even quite three weeks ago. How could my life have changed so much in such a short amount of time?

"Well, you deserve to walk, just like the rest of us."

"Thank you." He gave me a side glance. "So, will you be giving the speech at graduation?"

I snorted. "No! Are you crazy. I'm not a speech person."

"I think you'd do an amazing job."

"Well, oh well. I'm not valedictorian. That spot has never been my goal. I pride myself on my goals, but they aren't that extreme. I'd have to take nothing but AP courses. My college doesn't even want us to come in with that many credits, so no. Not it. Not to mention, I really didn't take top courses in everything until Junior year. Standardized tests and me aren't really friends."

He chuckled. "Well, I wish I could hear the speech you'd give."

I feigned silence. I opened my mouth to speak, then closed it, repeating over and over like a goldfish.

"Are you okay? What's wrong?"

"You asked to hear my speech, so that's what I was doing."

He laughed.

"I'd be speechless. Way too many people for my abilities. No, thank you."

"That was actually pretty funny."

I crossed my arms. "What's that supposed to mean? I'm dorky, but not funny?"

"Not what I said at all. I just thought you were hurt or something. It was a good joke."

I gave a curt nod and slowly uncrossed my arms. "So, Baylin? Any ideas about it?"

"Not really. I know it's by the Chesapeake Bay. Like right on it, but otherwise, no." He winked. "That's the point. It's supposed to be random."

"Right, okay. Well, how far away is it?"

"About another thirty minutes. Then we can walk around aimlessly all day."

"As long as they have something for breakfast, I'm fine with that. I should have eaten before you got me. I am starving."

"Want me to stop now?"

"Nope, if the adventure is to explore a random point on the map, then that is what we shall do."

"Aye aye."

I fiddled with the zipper on my lap. "Do you really think I'll need this? It's almost Memorial Day, it's so warm already."

He shrugged. "All I know is that the breeze off the Chesapeake Bay can make the temperatures a little chilly. Didn't want you to be cold."

Was that another sign that things had shifted? When we had gone hiking he hadn't worried about what I wore at all, but now he was thinking ahead?

Get a grip, Marley. It's just a zip up.

"Can you believe we've almost finished these dates?"

I shook my head. "Absolutely not. I didn't think it was possible to pull myself out of that hole."

"It was a fine predicament. I guess you got lucky my grades were such a wreck. What would you have done otherwise?"

"Cried most likely."

"Now that I don't believe. You would have figured out something."

"Nothing that would have worked with Andrea. She's like a bloodhound. She would have sniffed out the truth any other way."

"Have you set up a time to meet about the book?"

"After graduation, around five."

"Where?"

"At Hal's in Chesapeake Hills. She lives closer there so it's easier."

He pursed his lips.

"What?"

"You. You have to stop giving in to her demands. She got you the gift, make her drive to West End."

"No thanks. I'd rather she stays out of town limits. It's honestly easier for everyone that way."

"You give her too much power."

I snorted. "She gives herself power."

"And everyone lets her."

He had a point. I supposed if I wanted to take back some of it, I could. She had deemed herself better at knowing about boys, clothes, and hair, but did I really care? Did I believe that made her better? I wasn't so sure. Being right didn't seem as important anymore. Would we really keep this competition going between us? We were eighteen. Adults. Shouldn't that stop now?

Wyatt's hand rested lazily on the steering wheel as we drove down the road. Signs for Baylin showed it getting closer and closer, until eventually we hit the town limits and saw the welcome sign. As soon as we passed it, the road opened and I could see the water from the road.

"Wow. This place is beautiful."

Wyatt's eyes had widened. "Yeah it is. Way to go random point on the map."

I eyed him suspiciously. "You've really never been here?"

He made a cross over his heart. "Not at all. I swear."

"How can Maryland's geography change so quickly? This place is stunning."

"The wonder of Maryland."

We passed many industrial buildings on the road, until a restaurant came into view.

Wyatt nodded toward the diner. "Want to try there for breakfast?"

"Sure, why not."

He grinned, put his blinker on, then pulled into the parking lot.

From the outside, a large sign with a big stack of pancakes was clearly visible at least three streets down. If they didn't have a good breakfast, then they needed to update their marketing.

Wyatt hovered by my side as we walked to the front door. Then he held it open for me, as I walked through the doorway. I couldn't tell if it was my imagination, or his glances were more nervous than usual.

The hostess ushered us toward a booth in the back, with a perfect view out to the water. I could have stared at that view all day and been satisfied. The water wasn't far from our town, but you had to really go looking for it. Baylin apparently had beautiful views no matter where you sat.

"Earth to Marley."

I startled. "Huh? What?"

"Are you going to look at your menu? I think I see drool from you staring out the window."

I giggled. "I don't drool."

"Could have fooled me."

"Well, for your information, I was admiring the view."

He reached for my hand, still rested on top of my menu. "We can explore the waterline as soon as we fill up your tank."

I nodded. "Much appreciated. I really am hungry."

I perused the menu and as expected, ninety percent of it was breakfast items. The last page of the menu had lunch items, but I didn't really want lunch foods. Once I settled on peaches and cream crepes, I closed my menu and watched Wyatt.

His gaze was trained on the menu, his hands reaching up to tug his beanie this way and that. When he caught me staring, he arched a brow. "What?"

"Nothing. You're just looking at your menu so intently."

"I take breakfast seriously. It is *the* most important meal of the day. A goody-two shoes should know that."

I rolled my eyes. "Haven't we established I am *not* a goody-two shoes?"

He twisted his lips to the side in contemplation. "I don't

know, have we? Can we really say we've broken that mold yet?"

"I think so. I've done more in these last few weeks than I dare say I have my whole life."

He chuckled. "Now that I believe, although I blame you for doing that to yourself."

My brows knitted. "How?"

"You had the ability to be adventurous if you wanted. I didn't have to twist your arm for these dates. You just didn't trust yourself to do it."

"Hmm. Maybe, but I doubt I would have attempted it on my own."

An older gentleman sauntered to our table. "Good morning, my name's Al. What can I start you two off with?"

Wyatt eyed me, letting me go first.

"I'll have a glass of orange juice and your peaches and cream crepes."

"A town favorite," Al said then winked at me. "And for you, sir?"

"I'll take the same."

"Two peaches coming right up." Then he walked to the kitchen to put in our order.

"The same thing?"

"Yeah, why not? You've proven you have good taste buds."

I laughed. "Is that so? Have I won an award since we like the same dessert?"

"It certainly helps." Wyatt pulled the dish with the sugar packs closer to him as he reorganized the different kinds.

"So, when will you have the song completed? You're running out of time, right?"

He shrugged one shoulder as he finished taking out all the sugar packets. "We see the producer the Sunday after graduation."

"That's next week. Do you have much left?"

"Not really."

I eyed him cautiously. "Why don't you still seem happy? I'm sure your family is excited about your talent."

An emotion I couldn't name filtered across his expression, then disappeared behind a strained smile. "Yeah."

Even after the last few weeks, I still knew so little about his family. Something had happened, but he was too tight lipped to tell me much. Did he not trust me? Or just didn't see it as relevant?

"Well, once it's over, I hope you tell me how it went."

He arched a brow and tilted his head. "Invested are we?"

"Well, I *am* the good luck charm."

He shook his head. "For someone so superstitious, I'm still surprised Claire named you that. The band does like you, for what it's worth."

"The *band*?"

He shuffled a few more packets in the dish. "Yeah."

How vague was that? Did that include him or did he just mean Jack and Claire? I fiddled with the hem of my shirt and avoided his glance. I wanted to ask what about him. How did he see me at this point? But the words were lodged in my throat, too swollen to move.

As the silence drowned on, with each of us glancing at the other, Al brought our food and drinks. "Can I get either of you anything else?"

I glanced up to meet his gaze. "No thank you."

He nodded and returned to the kitchen.

Once my napkin was placed on my lap, I unrolled the silverware so I could cut my crepes. They turned out to be three large crepes, with peaches and cream oozing out of the sides, drizzled with what smelled like peach syrup.

"We could have probably shared one of these. I have no idea how I'll eat all three."

Wyatt chuckled. "They are large. I don't think Rosie's portions are even this much."

"Definitely not." I used my fork to get my first bite and then hesitated before plopping it into my mouth. It was delicious. The cream was more from the buttercream frosting family instead of whipped, and the peaches were fresh and yummy.

When I glanced at Wyatt, I caught him watching me. I dotted my napkin on my face. "What?"

"Nothing. What do you think?"

"Delicious."

He nodded. "I think so too."

Our conversation continued to lull as we finished our food. It wasn't until we had both dropped our silverware on our plates before we discussed anything else.

"Ready to go down by the water?"

"Yes. I can't wait."

He threw cash on the table overtop the receipt, then stood and outstretched his hand as I scooted out of the booth.

Intertwining our fingers together, we walked out of the diner and jogged across the street. There was a large walkway that led to a dock and then a small beach.

"What are your plans for tomorrow?" I asked.

"Studying for finals. My tutor says I have to at least get a B."

I giggled. "Smart lady."

"Yes, she is." He made eye contact with me when he said it.

My cheeks flushed and tempted me to squirm, but our fingers were still connected. Was his brain focused on our fingers touching too? Or was it just me?

The sound of the water hitting the shore grew louder as we stepped off the concrete path and started down the wooden dock. The air had grown even warmer than before we left.

At the end of the dock, our hands slipped from each other. I toed off my shoes then pulled off my socks and stuffed them inside. The sand beneath my feet was warm, but not burning hot like it would be in July.

I squished my toes between the sand and lifted my chin into the air, soaking in the rays of the sun.

Wyatt's chuckle pulled me from my thoughts to open my eyes. "What?"

"Nothing, you look so peaceful."

"And that's funny?"

He shook his head. "No, it's nice to see you so relaxed. Who knew it would take the water?"

I rolled my eyes. "I can be relaxed at other times too."

"I know, like surrounded by books."

I scoffed and nudged his arm.

He bumped me back, until we both laughed. Then I grabbed my shoes and walked next to him on the shore. "What will you do this summer?"

"Honestly? Not sure. I didn't really expect to graduate on some level, I guess."

"Will you stay in West End until September?"

"Depends on how the producer meeting goes I guess."

My eyebrow rose. "If you get a deal, are you leaving sooner?"

Wyatt shoved his hands in his front pockets. "I don't know. I don't like to hope on things that aren't guaranteed."

I frowned. Once again his optimism was wounded. Why didn't he even believe they had a chance? Or even contemplate what it would be like if they did succeed?

"What about you? What awaits for you this summer?"

"Spending time in West End until I move to UPenn this fall. Probably hang out with Sage at her parent's bookstore."

"Ah, any particular books in mind?"

"Always."

He chuckled, then swiped a stray curly strand from my cheek and tucked it behind my ear. "Maybe we will have to take a few adventures too."

My brows rose. He wanted to make plans with me after graduation? "But all the adventure dates will be done by then."

"Is that a problem? I like spending time with you, Marley."

"You do?" The question left my lips before I had time to suck it back in.

"Why is that so hard for you to believe? You are a special person, Marley."

"I guess."

"No guessing." He lifted my chin with his fingers, to gaze into my eyes. "Stop doubting yourself. It may have begun because of that gift, but even without the dates, I would miss being around you."

"But I don't usually do these activities. I don't go on hikes and to concerts. I stay in and read."

"Then we read books together."

Was he serious? I had hoped he could see me as more than his tutor and the adventure girl book, but hearing it was different and harder to believe.

He grasped my hand and moved closer. "I don't have to fake feelings for you in front of your cousin. At this point I have genuine ones, maybe I always have, ever since you had enough courage to walk up to me and demand to be heard even though I had made it difficult."

"What are you saying?"

My brain focused on the pressure his fingers made on the palm of my hand as it swirled over my skin.

"I'm saying, can I kiss you again, Marley?"

When I looked into his gaze, he had moved ever so slightly closer. He wanted to kiss me? Again?

I nodded because words were stuck in my throat.

"Are you sure?"

I nodded harder.

His hands dropped mine and moved into my hair near my neck. Our bodies slammed together as he pulled us closer. His lips were soft and still tasted of sugar from breakfast. His hands roved in my hair and on my shoulder, until they shifted to just above my waist. Between the touch of his lips and his hands, my body was more than distracted.

I matched his kiss and soon my own hands were holding him closer, running over his shirt at his back. The soft cotton tickled as my hands moved.

When we finally broke apart, we both breathed heavily, trying to regain our breath.

My smile grew as I looked into his eyes and I could finally tell that he meant what he had said. He was just as affected by that kiss as I had been.

"That should have been our first kiss."

I shook my head. "No. I liked our first one."

He arched a brow and stood closer to me. His arms holding me against him, rested around my waist. "And this one?"

"Perfect, too."

He leaned his head down and gently kissed me, his touch feathery light.

I laid my head on his chest as he continued to hold us together. I didn't want to move from this spot for anything and I wouldn't forget it any time soon.

But of course, my brain was now overanalyzing everything. What did this mean? Did it turn our fake relationship into a real one?

"Why are you stressing?"

I lifted my head and gasped. "How?"

He chuckled, which shook me too. "I just do. So, what is it?"

"I." I sighed. "I was wondering what it meant."

"Well, I'd hope it means we could stop fake dating and do it for real."

"Oh."

He leaned back slightly, to see my face better. "That is, if you wanted to?"

"Yes. I'd like that."

He smiled, similar to his stage smile, but better, because this time it was because of me. "Me, too."

He shifted his arm, to hold me from the side as we continued to walk down the beach. This was my favorite date of them all.

Chapter Twenty-One

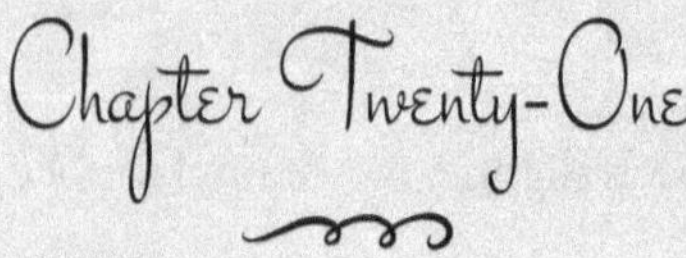

I didn't understand how I could feel such elation and stress simultaneously. The way to the guidance counselor's office was filled with seniors throwing papers from their locker and I was beyond excited to have finished my finals.

But now I had to wait for them to be graded.

Sage would yell at me for even worrying with it out of my control, but I couldn't help that I would worry a little bit.

I pushed open the guidance counselor's office doors and entered into a flurry of excitement and movement. I hadn't realized the counselors would be just as active as the seniors.

Wading through the crowd until I reached the final door on the left, I found Ms. Wasko sitting at her desk.

"Hello, Ms. Wasko," I said as I knocked.

She startled, then relaxed as she registered my voice. "Oh, Marley." She removed her reading glasses and gazed at me. "Why aren't you out celebrating with your class? You're free."

I giggled. "I will soon. I wanted to check in with you and return my key to the tutoring room. I meant to do it sooner, but I got caught up with my final tutoring student."

She arched a brow. "Who was that? I thought Cindy was your last one?"

"Oh, I picked up Wyatt Shaw." I shifted my bookbag to my other shoulder. "I heard about his grade situation and wanted to help him. I hope it's enough to let him graduate."

She tapped a finger to her chin. "Wyatt Shaw, huh? Such a shame. He had such potential until Junior year. Great grades, top classes." She waved a hand. "Anyway, thank you for the key. We will miss you."

Top classes? What was she talking about? He had been doing that well? What happened to get him to almost not graduate?

I passed the key over, trying to focus on the conversation in front of me. "Thank you. I'll miss you too."

She smiled. "Now go have fun. I'll see you at graduation."

I nodded and headed out of the offices and toward the front of the school. Her comment stuck with me. I needed to understand what she meant. How had he changed so much at the end of high school? And I couldn't help feeling like it had to do with his family.

But I didn't have time to dwell, because he was expecting to pick me up from my house for our final date.

I couldn't even believe we had completed all the dates in the adventure book or that this time it would be a *real* date. I would have never expected how much could change in three and a half weeks.

The parking lot was littered with my classmates celebrating the fact that we were free until graduation practice on Friday and then graduation Saturday. The rest of the school would get out in a week and a half, but we were officially done.

My Honda was parked in my usual spot and for once I didn't have much of an issue getting out of the parking lot and heading to my house.

Sage had lost her mind when I told her about the previous date we had, and of course I would owe her a longer explanation, but with finals, we had put it on hold until the next day when we'd meet up.

The drive home went quickly. I parked my car in the driveway and hurried down the hallway to my room to change my clothes. As usual, I didn't know what the final date was or what I had to wear, so a mix between comfortable and cute would have to do.

I settled on dark-washed blue shorts and a thin baby pink baby-doll-styled blouse. My white Converses would have to do just in case I had to be somewhat active, although I secretly hoped those types of dates were over at this point.

Now the easy part was over, I had to tackle my hair. I had settled on a high ponytail for school since it was just for finals, but that didn't seem like it would work for a date, especially now that we were official.

Bottles clattered to the floor as I scrounged in drawers for at least one of the containers Sage had sent me home with after the concert date. I had no hope of recreating her magic, but wetting my hair and putting curly setting gel had to help, right?

The horn honked a few times out front, thankfully right after I finished combing the gel through my hair with my fingers and then putting cold air on to somewhat dry it.

I snatched my clutch purse, keys, and phone, then locked up.

Wyatt stood leaning against his truck, watching me as I turned around. "Hey."

"Hey," I replied, sending swirls around my stomach. How goofy did we look? Just saying hey caused my stomach to flop and my cheeks to warm.

"Are you ready for this final adventure date?"

"Yes. I am tired of having a book determine what I do."

He chuckled.

"And yes I know I could have said no, but I was too weak for that."

He propped the door open, then helped me up into his truck, before walking around to the other side. "I would never call you weak." He laced our fingers together and then used his other hand to place it on top. "But this last date involves fears, which is why I saved it."

I groaned. "Fears? Really?"

"Yep. It is fight your fears. So, what is your biggest fear?"

"Mine? We can't do yours?"

"Nope. This is your party."

"Ugh. I don't know. Spiders?"

"Think bigger."

I sighed. What was my biggest fear? Well, I didn't want Andrea to know I had lied. All that attention from her would have been the worst thing in the world. "I guess being the center of attention."

He nodded and tapped a finger to his chin, then his eyes widened. "I've got the perfect idea."

"That doesn't make me feel comfortable at all."

He gazed back at me with those perfect brown eyes, all melty and warm. "If you feel like it is too much at any point, we will leave. I've got you, Marley. I promise."

If it wasn't for his look in that moment, I would have told anyone else no, but how couldn't I believe him? He had been so generous with his time these last few weeks, I could do this one date.

"Okay."

He grinned, then put the truck in gear and backed out of the driveway. "How was your final today?"

"Good, easy, honestly. I am the most worried about Latin, I guess. What about you?"

"I think it was good. Mr. Andrews's tests are always hard to gauge until after. At least it is over."

"Yes it is. When will you hear?"

"Should be tomorrow, I think. He told me I could expect to know if I would make it before Saturday."

"That's good of him at least."

He shrugged.

"What about the music demo? Is it finalized?"

"Yes. Just have to wait for them to play it Sunday."

"They'll love it."

He chuckled. "You haven't even heard it."

"I don't have to. I've heard you guys before. It will be no less than your best, and your bests are pretty great."

He squeezed my hand before returning it to the wheel. "Thanks."

"So where are we going?"

"Nope."

I crossed my arms. "Nothing? Really?"

"Really."

"It's like two o'clock in the middle of the week. I don't see how you have an idea with what I said when it's such a random time."

"Well, I happen to know lots of things that happen at random times and once we're there, you'll know."

"Ugh, fine. If you won't tell me where we're going, will you tell me what your greatest fear is?"

He glanced at me. "Being forgotten."

My eyes widened. "Forgotten? By everyone or specific people?"

"In general, I guess. I want to matter and I hope that I will make enough of a difference to matter enough to someone that they won't forget me."

I didn't know what to say to that. I didn't even expect that as his answer. It wasn't a typical teenager answer. It felt like he was older and saying that, realizing his life was more over than what was left. We had so long to make an impact. But then again maybe it connected to what Ms. Wasko had mentioned.

He nudged my elbow. "But we're talking about your fear, so the perfect place is around the corner."

I peered out the window. The surroundings were familiar enough for me to realize, but the sinking feeling in my stomach grew. How was Lucy's going to help? But what was worse was the fear that I secretly knew somewhere what he might have planned.

I clamped my eyes shut. "What can we find at Lucy's at this hour to do this date?"

"Well, center of attention could be tested in a few ways, but they're doing karaoke all day."

I groaned. "You want me to sing. In front of strangers? Are you crazy? I can't even sing!"

"You'll be fine. Most people can't sing at karaoke. And I'll do it with you."

My stomach flipped. While it was sweet he wouldn't let me be utterly alone, I still didn't want to do it.

The truck stopped and I could feel my stomach drop like on a rollercoaster. As much as I didn't want to get out of his truck, I opened the door and hopped down. My eyes closed once again, I tried to regain control of my stomach. My arms felt itchy and my cheeks felt warm. I was so anxious my body was physically reacting.

Arms circled around me and held me close. "You can absolutely do this, but if you don't want to, we can stop."

I peeked one eye open just enough to see Wyatt staring into my face, gentle and caring. "This is the last date. If I can't do this, then it's like I did none of them."

"That's not true."

I sighed. "I know it isn't technically, but I can't quit now."

He nodded and pulled me into his chest. After a few

moments, he pulled us apart, then interlaced our fingers. His calluses, rubbing against the soft skin of my palm.

"Distract me?"

"How?"

"Tell me something that most people don't know about you."

He arched a brow, his expression contemplative. "I had my tonsils removed when I was eight."

"Really? That's all you got?"

He smiled and nodded toward Lucy's. I knew it was his way of encouraging me to go in, but I was terrified. Ultimately, I took that first step and followed him, though.

Surprisingly, for the middle of the afternoon on a Wednesday, Lucy's was busy. The tables closest to the bar had been moved more toward the stage. The tables were packed near the stage but thinned out farther away.

Wyatt led us to a table in the back and signaled a waitress to bring us over two sodas. Before she left, he also asked for the list to sign up.

My stomach sank as he wrote our names in the fifth spot. I didn't know if it would feel any better if I could go on the stage right at that moment or not, but four people in front of us felt like an eternity.

"Don't stress so much. You have like a permanent crinkle by your eyes."

I huffed. "My body is oscillating between utter panic and agitation that I can't just get it over with."

He chuckled. "What song do you know or want to sing? We will have to pick before we go on."

"Ugh, I didn't even think about that. This is so bad. I'm going to make the glasses shatter or something."

"That's incredibly hard to do."

"You know what I mean."

He leaned closer and rested his forehead on mine, staring

into my eyes with those perfect soft brown ones of his. "This is about the experience. No one knows us here and you can just sing with me. Honestly, I've got you." He kissed the tip of my nose, sending shivers down my arms for completely different reasons.

"Wyatt and Marley, you're up," the announcer said.

"We didn't pick a song," I said.

Wyatt stood and pulled me with him as we moved to the stage, then winked. Did that mean he had an idea? Because he may be good at following the random words to a song on a screen, but I wasn't.

The announcer handed the microphone over to Wyatt, who placed it back on the stand. He adjusted it to fit our heights respectively, then leaned over to the announcer to tell them the song.

Their tones were too soft for me to hear, even if I could get my body to focus on them. The lights shined in our eyes, but it did nothing to lessen the number of eyes I counted that were staring at us.

Sure, he was the lead singer of a band, but I was a nerdy nobody who *never* sang or got in front of a crowd.

My stomach lurched. I was going to be sick.

Wyatt leaned toward my ear. "Let's do an encore to Iris."

My eyes widened. "You chose Iris? But you did all the work there. How do you know I know all the words?"

He winked in response, then surveyed the crowd as the music keyed up. The first few notes of *Iris* by the Goo Goo Dolls played over the speakers and Wyatt began following the lyrics on the screen, although he barely glanced in that direction.

I gulped a few times before I even opened my mouth. My body was rigid and my palms sweaty. I snapped my eyes shut and a few words escaped my mouth.

I didn't dare to open my eyes because I wanted to have no

idea how the audience was reacting. It was bad enough that my imagination wasn't strong enough for me to pretend I was in the shower or in my room, home alone.

Not to mention the energy wafting off Wyatt was palpable and I knew he was watching me. I could sense it all over my body.

After a few seconds, it didn't feel as scary to sing, so I ended up a little louder, until by the end of the song I sang like I did at home.

When the last chord of the song went through the speakers, the silence was interrupted by applause.

Wyatt squeezed my hand. "Bow."

Only then did I open my eyes and most people smiled as they clapped boisterously for us, whether it was more about him or me, or us both, I wasn't sure, but at least I did it and it was over.

He whispered to someone sitting close to the stage and asked them to take our picture, before he moved back to stand beside me, then pulled me in close. His lip grazed my cheek as the person took the picture, then we went back to our table.

My cheeks were flushed from the adrenaline and attention Wyatt kept giving me. I wasn't used to someone seeing me for who I was and liking that person.

After several sips of my soda, the constant staring from him had me fidgety. "What? I told you I couldn't sing."

"You honestly weren't bad. The way you were selling it, I thought it would be like nails on a chalkboard, but you can hold a tune."

"Then what's with the look?"

"You went up there and actually sang even though you were so nervous. That took a lot."

"Oh, well, that wraps all the dates from the book at least."

Wyatt pulled my chair closer to him, so our arms grazed

each other. "Is that the only good thing to come from the book?" He trailed his finger along the underside of my arm.

"No. I never expected to get an actual boyfriend from doing fake dates."

"Remind me to thank your cousin when I see her Saturday." He leaned forward and settled his lips over mine gently, before kissing my jaw line.

I giggled.

"Want to go somewhere else?"

I arched a brow. "Like where?"

"I'm not sure, but we've done all these dates because of that book. I'd like to see one without it."

"Okay." I finished my soda, then followed Wyatt back out to his truck. Today was turning out to be better than I could have expected.

Chapter Twenty-Two

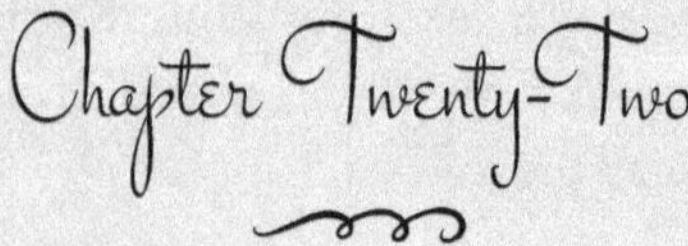

He took us to a small kid's playground tucked into the town of West End. I didn't even know it had existed, let alone understand how he did.

We walked in each other's arms toward the playground, still deserted from everyone being in school.

The clouds moved hastily across the horizon. "Do you think we have to worry about rain?"

Wyatt smiled. "Nope." He let go of me and took a few steps ahead. "Race you," he shouted then tore off toward the swings.

"That's no fair! You had a head start."

He laughed but didn't stop.

My legs would never catch up to him at that point, so I continued to walk toward the equipment, the same as before.

He turned and scrunched his brows when he saw my pace. "You do know what a race means right?"

"Of course. But you cheated so I didn't participate."

He shook his head. "Don't go reverting to your goodie-two shoes rules."

I crossed my arms. "What's wrong with rules?"

"Nothing." He moved closer and wrapped his arms around me.

Just as I settled into his embrace, he poked my side.

"Hey!"

"It's just boring." Then he stuck his tongue out.

I glared. "You just wait. I'll remember that."

He chuckled. "I'm counting on it."

The purple swings looked beat up, but at least the chains were sturdy. I didn't have to worry that they would drop me at least. I grabbed the closest one to me, while Wyatt took one a few swings over.

Was his house close to here? Did he come here as a kid?

It may not be as new as it used to be, but I could imagine it shiny and new once. It had teeter totters, although those were more than dangerous. I didn't even think they should be on playgrounds anymore. And then in the middle of the tire chips was a large rectangular jungle gym, fitted with a steering wheel and tic tac toe. At the base of the steps on both sides were the speakers to communicate.

"So why here? All the freedom in the world after our dates and you chose the playground. How come?"

Wyatt's face contorted. "Do you not like it?"

"N-no. That's not what I meant. I like to swing just like anyone but was curious. You never do things just haphazardly."

He raised a brow. "Are you sure about that? Mr. Andrews would disagree with you. Or at least would have disagreed before."

"I'm positive. Despite my initial assessments of you, you are purposeful."

"It's close to my house and my mom used to bring me here all the time as a kid." He shifted his gray beanie. "It didn't always look so worn down. I would come every afternoon after school and then on weekends we would walk here to play. We didn't have a yard, so the park was my way of getting out."

"That sounds so nice."

Once again, his expression twisted, then relaxed. "So, any update from Andrea?"

I groaned. "No. She won't waste her time texting me. I told her you were coming and she just sent back a smiley face emoji. We will just have to wait after graduation and see how it goes."

"How it goes is just fine. We are actually together now, so who cares if it was ever fake?"

"True. But I just don't like her being so critical. I don't want her to taint it somehow."

"Then don't give her the option to. We don't really have to go. We could spend time together, just us."

I shook my head. "No. I have to get it over with. Otherwise, I'll never hear the end of it and I can do this one thing this time, and then we can forget about her."

He smiled. "I like that idea."

"So ... I wanted to ask you something. Well, something else."

"Shoot."

"Well, since we're ... official. Would you ..."*Pull it together, Marley.* "Would you want to come to my graduation party? It's not until the middle of June, but thought maybe ... Well, if you want."

"I'd love to."

"You would?"

"Of course."

My chest instantly felt lighter. I didn't know if he would think it was lame or didn't want to meet my parents, but I was glad he agreed.

Something large and wet hit my hand as it rested on the

swing. I looked up in the sky to see the clouds had darkened while we swung. "Did you feel that?"

"Feel what?"

And then more drops fell.

"That!" I shouted as I tried to cover my head with my arms. But it was pointless, because the more I covered, the harder the rain came.

Wyatt and I fled toward his truck, but I was soaked by the time I reached his door. Everything stuck to me as it vacuumed sealed to my body.

I hopped in, but tried to stand, albeit somewhat cramped to avoid sitting on his truck seats.

"Marley, you can't hurt the seats, just sit."

"Are you sure?"

"I'm positive."

Reluctantly, I sat. I tried to pry my shorts from my thighs, but it was no use. Any space I managed, it sucked it back to my leg with force. My hair hung down over my face as the curls were tamed only by the onslaught of water. When they dried it would frizz out and expand. I groaned as I combed my fingers through my hair.

Wyatt without warning busted out laughing.

"What is so funny?"

"We look ridiculous. How about we get a change of clothes and then maybe get food?"

"A change of clothes? Where?"

He jerked his chin toward a row of houses in the distance but said nothing more.

Did that mean we were driving to his house? Would his parents be home? Did I even want to be alone in his house with him? What did I even know about them other than a few details of his past with his mom?

The rain continued to pour from the clouds, not letting

up once on the short drive to the neighborhood behind the park. And the closer we got, the more my stomach swirled.

He parked in front of a squat yellow house. He hadn't been kidding about the amount of yard space. The sidewalk looked to be a short six steps to the front door. It was a single story home, and two windows with black shutters. The shutters had seen better days and while the yard appeared to have been trimmed, the grass was still higher than the rest of the neighbors.

Wyatt shifted uncomfortably in the driver's seat. I didn't know if it was from his wet clothes or being at his house, either way I could understand how he felt.

He turned the key and shut off the truck. "I think I have an umbrella in the back somewhere."

I giggled, despite my nervousness. "What for? We are already soaked."

"True. Okay. On three we sprint to the front door."

I nodded and waited until he hit three before I launched the door open, closed it quickly, and ran toward the door. The small overhang provided a little reprieve from the downpour as he unlocked the door.

He pushed it open and we moved into a small hallway, which had several doors branching off. At the back of the hallway, it looked like maybe a kitchen, but we didn't stay in the light-gray painted hallway long enough to be sure. Wyatt took the first door on the left and opened into a dark-blue bedroom. A dark gray bedspread rested over the bed in the corner and a simple desk sat under a window on the opposite side. A guitar stand and guitar case leaned against a side door, which I assumed was a closet.

Wyatt pulled his soaked beanie from his head, revealing his hair beneath.

My stomach flipped. I couldn't remember when I had really seen him without a beanie on his head. His hair was longer than I had thought. He looked so good, I couldn't help but stare.

He must have felt my stare because he made eye contact with me in that moment.

The air sizzled. Could he feel the spark too? Or was I the only one? For all I knew, it could have been a fantastical hallucination brought on by my inexperience.

That was until he took the three steps toward me and our lips met with such fury that it stole my breath.

His hands were wrapped around me, then in my hair, as my hands roamed over his back. His muscles from carrying his instrument and band gear, ever present underneath the soft cotton of his shirt.

His lips were soft, like pillows or clouds. Which made no sense. How did he keep them so soft? Did he use Chapstick all the time? Or was it naturally that way?

Really, Marley? You're kissing the hot musician who is your boyfriend *and you only care about his lip routine?*

Our bodies stuck together.

Literally, from all the rain soaked materials. When we finally stopped kissing, my breaths were heavy and his eyes were glassy. At least I wasn't the only one who reacted to our kisses.

"I have been wanting to do that all day," he said.

"You have?"

He nodded as his thumb rubbed over my bottom lip. "You're too cute not to want to kiss you all day."

I coughed or attempted to clear my throat and ignore the butterflies that felt like they just went on a Merry-Go-Round.

But it didn't work. His expression had me glued and it didn't hurt that I had never been told that by a guy before. It was unusual territory for me.

"Then maybe ... you should have done just that."

His brow arched before he chuckled. "I think that was the most adventurous thing you've said yet."

"Well, you just wait. I'm a fast learner."

"That's for sure."

Our gazes stayed locked as he gently rubbed his fingers over my bare arm.

Goosebumps erupted all over my body and I shivered.

"Crap. Are you cold?" Wyatt took a step or two toward his closet and the heat from his body was immediately missed.

I crossed my arms, attempting to hold in the heat as he looked for something.

He brought over a pair of baggy athletic joggers and a graphic T-shirt. "You can change into these. It should help a little bit."

I nodded and bit the bottom of my lip. I may have really enjoyed kissing him, but I certainly didn't want to change in front of him. Not yet. I knew I wasn't ready for that.

His eyes twinkled with mischief, before he turned me around toward his bedroom door and then into the hallway. "The bathroom is through that door. I'll change in here while you change over there. Okay?"

I nodded after lifting onto my tiptoes to reach his cheek. Then I walked the few steps to the bathroom. The walls were a light green, almost mint and minimal decorations except for one or two fake plants.

My clothes clung to my body. At least I wasn't in jeans or this outfit change would have been nearly impossible. Eventually I was able to shimmy out of my shorts and shirt and tried to dry my legs with toilet paper before I pulled the joggers and graphic T on. My hair was unsalvageable. The frizz had already begun to set in and poof out. So, I took the scrunchie off my wrist and made a messy bun, with many pieces exploding out to join my flyaways.

My reflection wasn't as put together as I would normally

hope for, but Wyatt had already seen me and kissed me, so it couldn't have been that bad. I listened for any sign that Wyatt was done changing too, but the house was quiet. Somewhat even unsettlingly quiet.

I found a plastic bag under the sink and wrapped my sopping wet clothes inside. I knocked lightly on Wyatt's door.

"Come in," he called.

He stood by his bed, adjusting his shoelaces. His beanie was a dark red one and he wore dark-gray khaki shorts and a loose turquoise T-shirt. His wet clothes were nowhere around. "Does it fit okay?"

"It works, thank you."

He nodded and watched as I stood near him. "We could watch a movie while we wait for the rain, if you wanted?"

I was in his clothes and now we would watch a movie in his house? It felt unreal.

"Oka—"

The front door slammed and loud bangs emanated from the hallway.

Wyatt's eyes widened and his expression contorted, reminding me so much of those days when his mood was off.

Was this noise the cause of those interactions?

"Wyatt!" someone shouted.

"In my room, Dad."

My eyes widened and met his gaze, only to see him cringe before the door pushed all the way open. He mouthed *I'm sorry*.

"Wyatt ... what you doing home, boy?" he slurred.

"It's the last day of finals. We got out early."

"Oh—" His dad froze when he finally noticed me in the room. His eyes were unconcentrated, his step jerky and sluggish.

Was he drunk in the afternoon on a random Wednesday?

His dad whistled. "Who is this pretty lady?"

Wyatt pushed to stand before me and in between his dad and me. He placed a tense hand on my arm. "We're just leaving."

"What's your hurry? You're never home. Why don't you stay?"

"We'll be fine."

His dad didn't move from the front of the doorway. My stomach clenched. All the good feelings were gone and instead were replaced with anxiety about what was happening between them.

They clearly didn't get along, or at least on Wyatt's side. The negative feelings oozed from him.

"We're leaving, Dad. I will see you later."

His dad gazed at Wyatt's expression, albeit he wobbled on his feet. His dad was still taller than Wyatt by a few inches. If he really wanted to, drunk or not, could probably keep Wyatt from leaving.

Was this what he was hiding? And where was his mom? Did she let it happen? Was this what happened to him? His father was a drunk?

Their standoff lasted only another minute, before his dad stepped aside and hobbled down the hallway. He looked away as he waved us away, dismissing us from his presence.

Wyatt said nothing, communicating only through cold and standoffish body language. He grabbed a bag from his closet and stuffed it with several pieces of clothing before he strapped it over his shoulder and then grabbed his guitar case too.

"It should be done raining."

He walked from his room and out the front door.

I had no plans to stay there any longer than I had to. After one final look, I followed him out and closed the door.

Wyatt had already started his truck and was sitting in the

driver's seat. His expression was hard to read, but he wasn't carefree anymore like when he kissed me.

This was definitely related to his rougher moods.

The passenger door closed and the radio was silent, the only sounds coming from the engine. He reversed the truck and left the neighborhood.

"Are you okay?" I asked.

He glanced in my direction but didn't answer.

Of course he wasn't okay, Marley. Jeez.

"I'm here if you want to talk about it."

Silence.

We drove around, not talking. I tried a few times to say something or do something, but nothing I asked garnered a response.

And in that silence my feelings festered. I had spent time with him almost daily for three and a half weeks and I knew nothing about his family. I knew nothing about his mom or his dad, about that little house by the park.

How could we be so vulnerable with each other and him not actually tell me anything?

But that was it. As I replayed our conversations, *he* wasn't being vulnerable. He avoided every chance there was to tell me about his dad. He didn't elaborate when I asked him why they didn't hike. He didn't even tell me a big secret at karaoke.

I had been vulnerable.

How stupid could I have been? We agreed to date and I didn't know anything *real* about him. How could a relationship start like that and last?

He parked in the lot at West End Bakery and stared out his driver window. "I'm sorry about my dad. I didn't think he would have been there. If I would have known ..."

He would have what? Not brought me? Would he have just continued to keep it from me? I needed to know.

"What happened junior year?"

Wyatt's shoulders slumped, but he wouldn't look at me. "What do you know?"

"That something changed in junior year."

He sighed, still staring out his driver's side window. A minute passed in silence before he started. "We were happy. The three of us went hiking and spent weekends together, like I imagine you did with your parents. My mom was diagnosed with cancer at the end of sophomore year. She was strong. She planned to fight it and we believed her."

Oh no.

"By the end of the summer, she was on a ventilator and was in the hospital. I went to the first day of school and by nine a.m. I was called to the counselor's office. I just knew. She had died while I was at school." He readjusted his beanie. "My dad tried to put on a big show that he was fine, but I could hear him crying at night. He didn't bounce back. He lost his job. He drank all the time. And as you can see, that hasn't changed."

That was why he left the hospital. We delivered to the cancer ward. It must have reminded him of his mom.

"But why not just tell me that?"

He scoffed. "Was I supposed to say, 'Hey, Marley. My dad's a drunk. My mom's dead. Your life is perfect, yet you worry too much about what others think of you, especially your cousin?' I don't think so. You were my tutor."

My eyes widened. "A tutor you didn't even need. Mrs. Wasko let it slip today that you had top grades in good classes. So why even go along with it? *You* pulled yourself out of your hole. You didn't need me to help you with a thesis. Which was obvious with the papers you sent me."

"It's not as simple as saying I just flipped a switch and magically fixed everything. Do you really think I would fail everything just so I could be rescued later? I didn't know you'd come along, Marley. I was drowning. My dad couldn't maintain a job with his drinking. I had lost one parent and suddenly had to be the responsible one for my only other parent alive. I had to help with bills. I used the money from gigs and other odds and ends to pay things so we didn't end up on the street."

"Okay, so I structured something, big whoop. You still knew that you once upon a time were academically oriented. You had to know that didn't disappear."

"Yeah, I was smart. But you know what happens when you miss classes because you fell asleep from being up all night stressing? You stop hearing or caring what they say."

"So why not *say* that? I asked you to tell me something today most people didn't know and you said your tonsils were taken out. None of this seemed relevant to you? You didn't even want to trust your girlfriend with what you were going through?"

"It's not about ... No, you know what. Why should I have to explain? I'm telling you right now. It happened and I explained, but that isn't good enough for you." He shook his head. "This. This reaction is why I don't tell people."

He thought I was being ridiculous? Was I not allowed to process what he told me? Was I not allowed to feel upset that he kept such a big secret from me? I may not have had other boyfriends, but weren't they supposed to be honest with each other if a relationship was to work?

His lie of omission tainted everything. And if he could keep something so important to himself and not mention it, then what else could he have lied about?

I crossed my arms. "I think you should take me home."

He finally looked at me and studied my expression before he put the truck back into gear. He drove the ten minutes to my house in silence and then parked in the driveway.

My anger bubbled to the surface. So maybe it didn't make sense at first to tell me, but when I had put myself out there, he could have attempted the same even a little bit. But to hide it and then turn it around on me wasn't fair. I had been honest about my situation.

He never had been.

I was a silly, foolish girl. How could I think I knew someone enough to be their girlfriend after three weeks? I should have been smart enough to know that when something seemed too good to be true, it usually was.

Like he said that first day, he didn't want to be someone's bucket list before college. What if I had been his? A little goody-two-shoes, could I get her out of her shell?

Well, the joke was on me, but I wouldn't let him hurt me again.

"I'll wash your clothes and make sure to get them back to you. Thank you for doing our arrangement, but I think we were kidding ourselves. We clearly don't mean enough to each other to be honest about our lives." I opened his truck door and hopped down, then grabbed my bag of soaked clothes and watched him one more time. "I'm glad you will graduate. You've always deserved that. And I hope your band does well on Sunday, but I can't do this. I can't be someone's girlfriend when they can't even be vulnerable with me."

His gaze snapped to mine. "Be vulnerable? What do you call this conversation, Marley? How is this not *the* most vulnerable someone can be?"

"It's after he walked through. Tell me something. If he hadn't come in today. If we had stayed and watched a movie and kissed more, would you have told me? Would I have known about your parents?"

He stared but said nothing.

"I thought so. You only told me because you had no choice. That isn't real vulnerability. I admitted I hadn't kissed anyone. I told you my greatest fear. No, my vulnerabilities aren't as serious as yours, but I was honest and I disclosed them to you. How can I trust that what you've said to me is even real?"

The skin at the corner of his eyes crinkled. "You'll never trust what's real unless you believe you're worth it. And that's not something I can fix."

Believe I was worth it? What was he even talking about? That had nothing to do with this.

"Goodbye, Wyatt."

I ran to the front door as the first tear slid down my cheek. I should never have trusted him. I leaned against the front door and listened as his truck pulled out of the driveway and then disappeared.

How did a day go from so happy to an utter failure?

Chapter Twenty-Three

The loud knocking on my front door wouldn't cease.

My mistake had been texting Sage that Wyatt and I broke up. She practically flew to my front door after finding out and even though I still wouldn't open the door, she wouldn't go away.

The tub of ice cream and large spoon that sat next to me kept whispering to ignore her, put on a random show, and eat my feelings.

It would have won too, if she didn't FaceTime me.

"Marley June Wix!" Sage yelled as soon as I picked up. "Open this door."

More knocking.

"Why? I told you what happened."

Sage glared into my screen. "Now."

I groaned, threw off the fuzzy blanket my mom kept on the back of the couch no matter what season it was outside, and trudged toward the door.

"It's about damn time, Marley."

I shrugged and slunk back to the couch and hit the power button on the remote.

"Ben and Jerry's? My gosh, what happened?"

"I told you. It didn't work out."

She crossed her arms.

"All the details. Don't leave anything out."

So, I told her about our date, the kiss, and then his dad. I had to give her credit, she didn't interrupt me, which was a positive for her.

"I don't understand. Why did you two break up?"

My eyebrows scrunched together. "Why wouldn't we? He kept a massive secret from me."

"But came clean about it in the moment. He doesn't owe you his whole life story on day one."

"Of course he doesn't. But at no point in the last few weeks could he give me any inkling? Nothing? I asked him how he had turned his grades around so fast. I asked him to tell me something. He didn't take the bait at all."

"And?"

"And how am I supposed to start a relationship on that foundation, Sage?"

"You *just* started officially dating, Marley."

"To quote you ... and?"

"And so, you're still in the getting to know you stage. He took you to his house, right? Isn't that a step?"

"A minor one. I asked if he would have told me and he didn't answer."

"Are you sure this is really about the secret and not about you?"

"I'm pretty smart, Sage. I think I can comprehend a situation happening in front of my own eyes."

"Not when it's about you."

I crossed my arms. "What's that supposed to mean?"

"Are you sure you aren't self-sabotaging?"

"Why would I do that?"

She chuckled. "Because you're scared!"

"I'm not."

"You aren't worried about what would happen if things had gone further and then this came out? How much more it would have hurt?"

"No."

"You're lying and maybe you aren't doing it intentionally. Maybe you don't even realize you're doing it. But damn it, Marley, you're pulling the rip cord before he can."

"So what if I am? Sure, I enjoyed kissing him and he is handsome. A girl could have worse first kisses, but our futures aren't even on the same path. I go to UPenn in the fall. What, we have three months of great dates and getting closer and then he could go on tour and I go to college? The statistics on long distance dating are terrible. I bet if I factor in him being a musician, it would be even worse."

She crossed her arms. "Well, you don't just eat Ben and Jerry's when you're happy. If you really believe this is for the better, then why are you so upset about it?"

"Haven't you done something you know is bad for you, but you still do it anyway? I still developed feelings for him, that doesn't disappear just because he lied. I'm not heartless."

"Mm-hmm." She went to the kitchen and came back with another spoon. "What are we watching?"

"Haven't picked yet."

"Good, so I can." She snatched the remote and turned on some documentary I hadn't heard of.

She didn't bring him up again, but it didn't stop my thoughts from swirling. Why had they both brought up how I felt about the relationship? He lied. End of story. I could have standards about my boyfriend lying, couldn't I?

～

It got worse.

By Thursday I realized he had the finished adventure book. Not me. Him.

I had figured I would still bring it to see Andrea on Saturday and then it wouldn't be a big deal at all. I would do the original plan, and then move on.

But without the book?

How would I manage that? I couldn't just show up and say I had done it without any proof. Andrea would call me pathetic or a liar at best.

I wouldn't have believed her without evidence, why should she believe me? I was sunk.

Except, Sage thought it was the *perfect* reason to send him a text or call him and chat.

But the more I thought about it, the more my stomach twisted, my resolve wouldn't be able to withstand seeing his face again. If I saw those soft brown eyes and those long eyelashes, I could convince myself that maybe his lies weren't so bad. That maybe it didn't matter our futures were on drastically different paths.

Not to mention I couldn't imagine how he had gotten this far with his home situation. Losing both parents because one had died and then being responsible for myself? It would have been difficult for anyone.

My parents were important to me. They supported me. They were my stable foundation. Would I have done the same as him without them? Could I have watched my dad decline without my mom and still kept up my grades and ambitions?

But then my thoughts would spiral into why he couldn't have just trusted me with that information. I could have helped him. I could have carried some of that burden.

I couldn't text him. I wouldn't do it.

I trudged to the kitchen table for dinner. It was a rare occurrence that both of my parents were home at a normal time.

"Mar—" My mom's eyes widened. "Wow! It's like you knew telepathically it was ready."

I giggled. "Or I just know what time you said dinner would be."

Dad placed a casserole dish on the trivet in the middle of the table, then strode back to the kitchen. "I hope you brought your appetite."

"What's on the menu?"

"Your favorites." Mom walked to my side and tucked my hair behind my ears. "We're so proud of you honey. You stayed so focused on high school. Instead of partying and making silly choices you focused on what was important and your dad and I are so proud of the young adult you've become."

My stomach teetered as I soaked in the compliments. I was never one to handle them well. I just did what I felt was right, so it didn't feel like I had earned the compliments, but they warmed my insides at the same time they singed my stomach.

"Well, thank you. I had good role models."

She pinched my cheek, then nudged me toward my usual spot.

Dad carried two more containers over, then removed the lids.

Yummy smells drifted up toward the ceiling and invaded my nose. Crab legs, mashed potatoes with dark gravy, macaroni and cheese of course, and then Boston cream donuts for dessert.

My stomach rumbled. At least the comfort foods would hopefully help ease the ache from this whole situation.

"Is Sage having a graduation party?" Mom asked while she passed the potatoes.

"I think so, but it's sooner than mine."

"Well, let us know. We want to send over a gift."

Dad nodded as he scooped macaroni and cheese on his plate. "I'm surprised you're not off getting graduation things accomplished." He looked at Mom. "Can you believe she graduates in two days? It was like yesterday we brought her home from the hospital."

"Don't start that, Hank."

He sniffed dramatically. "You're thinking it too."

"So what if I am? I'm not saying it and more importantly I'm not thinking about it because I want to enjoy what time we have with her before college."

He chuckled.

"You both need to stop. I don't want to rush the summer and all. I want to relish it. I have only been free for like a day."

"Okay, you're right," Dad said.

Mom gave me her famous attorney stare. "Doing that with a certain boy in mind?" She arched an eyebrow daring me to contradict her.

And with that question went the hope of not thinking about Wyatt.

Without looking her in the eyes I said, "No."

But even without making eye contact I could feel the pressure of her gaze. It was an impressive gift and did wonders for keeping me out of trouble if I dared to even deviate from the rules, but if I avoided direct eye contact, I could pretend she wasn't boring holes into my head.

"Well, I'm glad you aren't spending time with any boys. You can wait to do that in college too," Dad said.

And darn it if that didn't grab my attention and cause direct eye contact with my mom.

"So what happened?"

My food suddenly became less appealing than at the outset. "Why did something have to happen?"

"Because, you've been preoccupied for weeks and now we get a chance to see you during prime daylight time. The evidence states something happened."

"Don't lawyer me."

"Can't help it and that's not an answer either."

"It was just tutoring, Mom."

She gave me a knowing look. "If that's all it was, then take my law license and call me a clown."

I crossed my arms. "We view things differently."

She laughed. "Honey, you don't have to align all your future prospects right this instant. There's no harm in having fun and being a *kid*."

"Why have fun if it goes nowhere in the end?"

"Because that's the point at your age. You don't have to find a husband yet. I love your planning and organization, Mar, but I also think it gets in the way of spontaneity and joy that your age can bring. You never get to be so carefree again, don't waste that time."

"I think you might be the only parents in the world that would find organization and logical reasoning as a negative. You might as well shout YOLO from the windows with that speech."

"I for one agree with Marley here. Are we really saying she should be reckless?"

Mom rolled her eyes. "Hank, our daughter could never be reckless, but a little fun without everything having to have some link for long-term is too far. She needs a little balance don't you think? I mean, you and I weren't so rigid in high school."

"Maybe not, but it's her choice. If she doesn't think it makes sense, we should trust that too."

Mom eyed me warily. "I don't think she actually believes it, or I would trust her." She shrugged. "But what do I know?" She winked and continued eating, dropping the topic altogether, but it was too late.

My brain was now on overdrive. That was now three people that didn't believe what I was saying. Wyatt might have been wrong, but Sage and my mom knew me well. Could I really dismiss their advice so completely? Should I have given us time for the dust to settle?

So instead of sleeping restfully that night, my thoughts swirled. How could they have seen something I couldn't see? Shouldn't the person in the relationship know best?

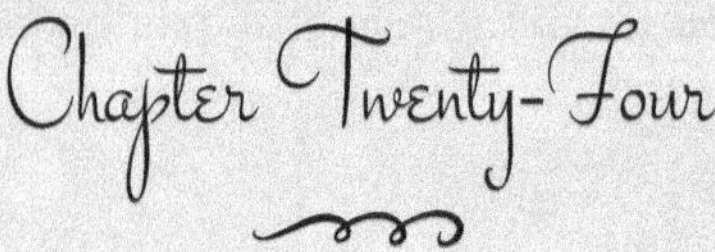

Chapter Twenty-Four

Sage nudged me for the fourth time since we arrived at the parking lot for school. "What?"

"Do you see him?"

"No! Because I'm not looking for him. Will you drop it already?"

"You aren't the least bit curious about whether or not he passed? Didn't you say something about your precious little reputation in tutoring would depend on his results too?"

"I don't even care about that anymore. And I really am trying to concentrate on this rehearsal we have for tomorrow. Yanno the moment we walk across the stage and everything changes?"

Sage snorted. "*Everything* changes? That's a bit much don't you think? It's a ceremony, it isn't the start to college, which *will* actually change everything." She tugged my arm, stopping our walk into the front doors. "Why are you avoiding him so intently? You're not even a little tempted to see him and find out how he's doing? See if he's upset about the breakup too?"

"Sage," I said as I pushed away her hand and scrunched my nose to release the pressure from her persistence. "I don't even know if he's here. He hasn't called or texted me since that day."

"Neither have you."

"And it seems silly to do it now. What would I say? What good would it do? We still want different things for our future. I couldn't ask him to come with me to see Andrea after everything that happened, then ghost him again afterward. It wouldn't be right. Honestly, I can't believe we fake dated to begin with. You never should have encouraged it."

"Oh no. Don't blame this on me. You finally did something that was out of Marley's little plan and it was so good for you. Look at all you pushed yourself to do in the past three weeks that you would have never done!"

"Yeah, and that's great, yay for new experiences, but honestly, if I could go back and avoid feeling like this, I would."

She glared at me. "You would not. You can't honestly tell me that you'd rather not have had your first kiss and all those moments with him, just so you couldn't feel hurt from how it ended."

"At least before I could live in my ignorance and bliss and pretend that I was happy. Maybe not even pretend. I *was* happy because I was satisfied with who I was and what I had. Now I know that kisses can feel amazing and how a guy's arm around you can make your heart flutter."

"Sorry to break it to you, but that doesn't happen every time. That tells me your connection was important."

I groaned. "Why? Why are you saying that? We broke up. I don't see it changing, so please just stop."

She rolled her eyes and strode away.

Sage didn't give up very easily or walk away when she was

being challenged, so she was either regrouping or completely fed up with me.

Which was fine. If she was fed up, then she could stop nagging me.

She got farther and farther from me as she headed to her homeroom to get in the proper order. We all had to sit in alphabetical order, so she was nowhere near me having a last name of Marshall. Wyatt would be even closer, but he still would hopefully be a fair distance away.

I had hoped that Shaw would be far enough away from Wix, but when we lined up in the hallway, he was close enough to see.

My stomach flopped.

It was unfair how quickly my body could betray me. Just the sight of him in the hallway cracked at my determination. My thoughts slipped to the park and how happy we were before it all crumbled.

Why did I crave his presence so much?

He didn't look my way. He didn't even search the hallway. At least if he was in rehearsal it meant he had passed his final with Mr. Andrews. He would graduate. The thought that even with all he had going on in his life, he could walk across the stage made me smile. But it was short lived.

My thoughts oscillated between the good moments and our argument.

Thankfully our practice was shorter than I had expected. We lined up in alphabetical order, processed into the gymnasium where chairs were already set up, then processed back outside. That was it. No big speeches, just a reminder that we had to be there by ten a.m. with our cap and gown.

I walked to my Honda Fit, where Sage's presence shortly joined me.

"Did you see him?"

I nodded.

"Did you talk to him?"

"Nope. And before you ask, he didn't talk to me or even look around for me either. I just need to face it that when I said goodbye, that was it."

She rolled her eyes and stomped toward her lime green VW bug. "You're being ridiculous." Then she gave me the peace sign and got in.

She didn't even wait for me to respond or look back my way again. Well, I would just follow her anyway.

I hopped in my car and made sure to get behind her in line.

She peered into her rearview mirror and sped up, but I stayed with her. She wove around cars as she entered town, but I was only a second or two behind her as I parked at her dad's bookstore.

She slammed her door as she got out. "What are you doing?" she shouted.

"Following you. What is your deal?"

"You!" She poked me in the chest. "You have a chance to be with someone who likes you and yet you are wasting the opportunity because you're too stubborn to talk about it."

"I'm not being stubborn. I don't even know if he would want to talk to *me* at this point. What if he didn't even acknowledge me?"

"Then you'll have to deal with that, but it is stupid not to try. And honestly is such a waste."

I crossed my arms. "What do you expect me to do Sage? I can't make him talk to me. It is probably just too late. I need to understand that and so do you."

Sage's nose twitched as she listened to what I said, before her expression soured. "It's only too late if you don't even try. You could text and see if he answers or wave to him at graduation. Those are all choices you could make, but if you make none, then yeah, there's a good chance it's too late." She sighed and rested her hands on her hips. "Marley, I love you, but you can be too much sometimes. It's up to you to decide what to do. It's your life, but I don't want to see you waste it because you're scared. You've been more adventurous lately and you needed that. Don't forget that just because the person who brought it out in you, might not be around anymore. But I have to start my shift. Talk later?"

I nodded and watched as she jogged toward the backdoor of Marshall's Books. Once again, I had nowhere to be.

Instead of going back to my car right away, I moseyed down main street and found a bench to sit. The day was warm and perfect for June. The humidity wasn't unbearable yet. In a few short weeks it would be suffocating to sit on the bench in the middle of the day, but today it was still clinging to spring time.

The streets were mostly vacant. A few older couples strolled along the sidewalks here and there, but no one else my age was anywhere I could see. I sighed then pulled out my phone.

His contact card taunted me. If I texted him and he still didn't want anything to do with me, then I would have to own that.

My fingers hovered over the letters.

Wyatt, I'm so...

So what? So sorry? Did he deserve the conversation over a text message?

Wyatt, I shouldn't have expected you to tell me. Your family is your business. I was just scared that if you could keep that, what else would you keep from me ...

I exited out of the message and shoved the phone back in my pocket. This was getting me nowhere. Pushing off the edge of the bench, I stood and trudged back to my car. Tomorrow was graduation. One more day and the meeting with Andrea and I could forget about it all. Sage and I had plans for the summer when she wasn't working anyway, why did that have to change? I would focus on that and forget about the whole arrangement.

Chapter Twenty-Five

It was hard to believe that graduation day was finally here. My parents had driven separately since they both worked after the ceremony, and I had to arrive earlier to school.

It was because of days like today, where life seemed almost impossible. Graduation was one of those things I waited my whole life to achieve, and then once it came, it didn't feel like I was actually living, at least for a few split seconds before teachers corralled us into our homerooms and insisted for the tenth time we put on our gowns and get in position.

My red gown didn't match my eyes or hair color or even my complexion, but it was mine and it symbolized so many things for me. I was eighteen, a graduate, going to college, and my life was sitting in my hands ready for me to take over.

Except, I had practically craned my neck *every* chance I had to see Wyatt.

Obsessively so.

If Sage had even seen a second of it, I would have earned myself a lecture. And maybe at this point I deserved one. I could say something, right? I could congratulate him. That could be done without it being awkward. We could be tutor and tutoree, although that seemed ridiculous now too.

But I didn't say anything, even though I knew he was located a mere twenty feet down the hall in his own homeroom waiting for us to process into the gym where our parents sat waiting.

Did he even have anyone there? Was his dad sober? In all my own suffering of us not talking, what if I had taken away the chance of someone being proud of him that he graduated and there for him today?

Marley, this is maddening.

What was happening? My brain was practically unraveling the more it focused on this scenario.

Of course he had someone here. It was graduation. There was no way his dad would just not come.

No way.

"Everyone in your gown and out in the hallway," the teacher shouted.

At this point, I couldn't even tell who said it because it was so loud and busy as we filed around the room.

Adjusting my gown and my cap one final time, I followed out in order down the hallway.

Wyatt's head stood out compared to those around him, enough that I could see him lumber toward the gym. Again, he didn't look around and he was too far away to tell how he was feeling.

My stomach flipped. I needed to do something to stop this feeling.

The line moved briskly toward the gym. The girls hobbled in too high heels and the boys wore their dress shoes with their khaki pants peeking through the bottom.

I took a deep breath and walked through the gym doorways. It was packed. Everywhere I looked the bleachers were full. Not a single bleacher had empty space. I scanned the crowd while still making sure to keep up in line. Eventually, I spotted my parents in the middle section to my right, up high near one of the top rows. I waved, then it was my turn to sit.

The white metal fold-out chair was cold against my leg even with the gown between. So many faces of my classmates were mixtures of joy and sadness. It was strange that after spending so many years together in school we would be going our separate ways in a few short months. And while Sage was the closest person I had in this school, there were many in the NHS and SADD that I would miss too.

Our principal, Mr. Monty, stood and walked toward the microphone. "Good morning, students and families. Today we are celebrating this group of seniors as they prepare to embark on one of the biggest journeys a teenager can take … adulthood."

As he continued his speech, I searched the crowd for Wyatt. It took a few minutes, but he sat four rows up and on the other side of the aisle, which wasn't the best location for trying to catch his attention.

Sage was even farther up front and even though I thought I could see the back of her head, there was no way I'd catch her attention when it was time to throw our caps.

"Please stand and come forward when I call your name for your diploma," Mr. Monty said.

Here it was. Time for the diploma, although it was really just an empty case. The real diploma was kept at our homeroom until after the ceremony.

In no time at all, Sage's name was called and I screamed as loud as I could for her. Her parents were in the audience near mine. Finally, it came to S names. Wyatt would be called soon. His row stood and walked toward the stage.

"Wyatt Shaw," Mr. Monty said.

My heart leapt in my chest and a smile spread across my face. He graduated. Even with everything my heart was feeling,

I was so proud that he had accomplished that goal. No one could ever take that from him.

And then it was my turn. My stomach flipped as we processed forward. All I could do was hope to not trip and fall as I walked up the stairs and onto the stage. That would be the absolute worst thing in the world and would forever be imprinted on the memories of all my classmates.

Lucy Waters took her place up the stairs and then I was next.

"Marley Wix," Mr. Monty stated.

Somewhere in the background I could hear my parents and maybe even Sage shouting. It was like my body floated onto the stage and then back down before I even realized it happened.

Another constant in big events in my life.

The metal chair welcomed me back and then it was only a few more minutes until we would be shifted back out the doors.

A lifetime of waiting for a ceremony that was shorter than a final.

Mr. Monty returned the microphone after our Valedictorian spoke. "West End seniors, it is my honor to officially crown you *graduated*."

On the word graduated, we took off our caps and threw them into the air. I watched as it drifted upward and then floated back down.

It was done.

My homeroom was a flood of students as we clambered for our diploma. I didn't rush, I didn't have anywhere to be yet, and I certainly wasn't excited for tonight with Andrea.

When the line thinned, I headed toward Ms. Howard for my diploma, thanked her, then went to find my parents and Sage.

I walked through the doorway and at the end of the hallway, Wyatt was facing my direction.

Our eyes locked on each other for the briefest moment. I smiled, but he had looked away.

Had he seen me smile? I only hoped he knew how proud I was of him. And then like I had imagined him, he disappeared from the hallway.

My parents texted me to meet me at my car, while Sage said she would come that way after she took pictures for her parents.

The parking lot was littered with families and my classmates, taking pictures, cheering, and enjoying our day.

"Mar," my mom shouted. She crushed me against her chest. "I'm so proud of you! My little girl."

Dad eyed me steadily. "How are you feeling? Can you believe it yet?"

I shook my head. "Seems like a movie and I'll wake up and find myself with drool all over my chin and my hair matted to my cheek."

He chuckled. "Well, it's real honey. Congratulations." He moved his hand from behind his back holding a beautiful bouquet of flowers.

I recognized daisies, but I wasn't a plant person, so the rest I had no idea of their names. But the pinks, blues, and purples were captivating.

"Thank you." Their sappy smiles twisted my insides. I would miss this when I left for college. "I wish you two didn't have to work. Then we could have an early board game day."

Mom caressed my cheek. "I wish we could too, but you know how it is. I promise though that tomorrow morning you can pick it all. Maybe even next weekend too." Her head tilted to the side, her ear inching closer to her shoulder. "Okay?"

"And maybe even some special brunch orders?" Dad asked.

"Of course." They squeezed me in a group hug, then Mom pulled out her phone and attempted to take our picture.

"Can I help, Mrs. Wix?" Sage asked.

I giggled as I could practically hear her cringe watching us take the photo.

"Oh, Sage. Congratulations, sweetie! Yes, that would be perfect."

Sage grabbed the phone and took several steps backward. "Say cheese!"

I smiled and attempted not to blink for as long as possible.

"I took several," Sage said then handed my mom back the phone.

"Thank you, hon." She scrolled through the pictures, then checked the time on her smart watch. "Well, sweetie, it's time for your father and I to head out. See you at home tonight?"

I nodded. "Remember I'm having dinner with Andrea."

"Ah, yes. Tell her we said hello."

I waved as they headed in the opposite direction, arm in arm.

I sighed.

"Still no progress?"

"Nope."

She grimaced.

"Well, actually I guess that's not entirely true. We locked eyes for a second, but I have no idea if he saw me or just around me, yanno?"

"Yes, which is why you should have said something. It wouldn't be too weird to say congratulations."

"Maybe, but too late now. I think he already left."

"What's your plan for tonight? Want me to come and tell Andrea to shove off?"

I giggled. "You're busy and no. I can handle it myself, I guess."

"Ooh, I'm scared. You're going to show her!"

"Ha ha, not funny. I have time to figure it out."

"Well, if you go like that, you certainly won't sound confident." She nudged my hip with hers. "Listen, Mar, you don't need her validation. The gift was stupid a month ago, but now even more so. If anything, maybe you could give her a thank you."

I crinkled my nose. "A thank you? For *what*? She upended the whole last month with that book."

"Exactly. Who had their first kiss and boyfriend because of that book?"

"Me, but it disappeared just as quickly."

She shrugged. "Still happened." She tapped my arm lightly. "Think about it." She sauntered off toward her car as I contemplated what she said. I would soon find out who was right.

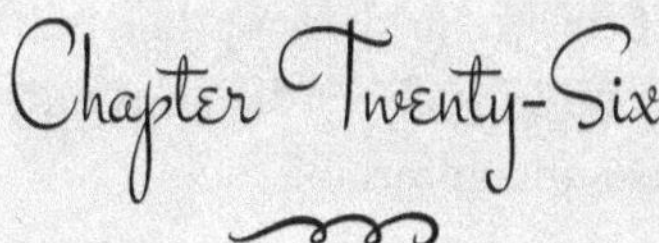

Chapter Twenty-Six

al's Diner's parking lot wasn't as busy as I had expected. I had only been here once or twice over the years. My parents liked to stay in West End, but when it was needed, Andrea's family would have parties or get togethers here.

Hal's had a strange aesthetic. The room was split into multiple decades and the wait staff had to dress up for their decade as their uniform. I preferred our bakery or Rosie's, but at least it had decent food. If I would be subjected to a night with Andrea, then at least I could shove food in my mouth every time she tried to ask me a question I didn't want to answer.

Actually, that might be the best plan I had. There was five minutes until five, having no other options, I pushed out of my car and closed the door, locked it, and headed toward the hostess stand.

A girl with a blue wig greeted me. "Hello, how many?"

"Actually, I'm supposed to meet someone. I'm not sure if I'm here first or not."

"Sure, no problem. Name?"

"Mine is Marley Wix. Hers is Andrea Wix."

"Marley, yes. Right this way."

I nodded and followed her toward a table. Her uniform was like a bad costume for an eighties metal concert. I shivered at the thought of having to dress up like that. There was no way I could dress up in such a ridiculous outfit for my job. I would have been so uncomfortable.

I was led into the part of the diner for the seventies. *How groovy.*

A few of the tables were taken, but I couldn't see Andrea anywhere. And she wasn't hard to miss. Her voice alone was enough to alert her presence.

We stopped at a booth, with multi-colored flowers all over the upholstery. Someone sat facing the opposite direction, but it clearly wasn't Andrea. It was …

"Wyatt?" I looked from him to the hostess and back again.

"I'll make sure Andrea comes over once she arrives." Then she left me standing there, gaping at Wyatt.

Was it even real?

He wore his typical beanie and a salmon-colored shirt. On the table sat the adventure book. He had brought it and showed up even though we hadn't talked in a few days.

I hated how much I wanted to touch him. To hold his hand or kiss his lips. He had shown up even though he had no obligation to do so.

"I'm surprised to see you."

"I figured you would need the book."

"But—"

An all too familiar squeal interrupted me.

"Marley! Congratulations on graduation."

I stood to greet Andrea. She crushed me into a fake hug then a pretend kiss to each cheek. "Thanks."

She gasped. "Who is this handsome man?" She leaned toward my ear. "Seriously, who is he? He's delicious."

I grimaced. Who talked about someone like that? Delicious? I mean he wasn't food.

"I'm her boyfriend," Wyatt said as he stood.

My stomach dropped clear to my feet. His ... His *what*?

Did he still plan to fake it? After everything, he was going to stick with the plan? What did that mean for after?

"Boyfriend?" Andrea squealed. "You know, Marley, I didn't think you were serious about that. But look at this." She gestured toward the table. "Shall we sit?"

I rolled my eyes but sat on the booth seat Wyatt had been sitting on. He sat next to me.

Andrea sat across from us, wearing a light pink crop top and what had to be uncomfortable jean shorts. Why she had dressed for a party when she was coming to see me, I had no idea.

"So, you've seen that he's real, can we move on from this now?"

Andrea laughed, although it was more of a cackle, like some evil witch from the Wizard of Oz. "Of course not, silly."

"It's nice to finally meet you, Andrea." Wyatt moved his arm around my shoulders, resting it over my skin like we did that all the time. "I've heard so much about you."

Andrea smiled at him ... and was she batting her eyelashes? Really?

"I'm afraid I don't really know anything about you ...?"

"Wyatt. My name is Wyatt."

"I see, Wyatt. So how did you two meet?"

"At school," he said easily. "We ran into each other in the parking lot. We ..." he chuckled. "We had a little misunderstanding, which turned into a date."

How could he still joke when this felt so awful? I wanted Andrea to get up and go away so I could talk to him. Anything instead of this.

A waitress came to the table wearing bellbottom jeans, a

huge afro, and dangling earrings. Another who looked the part. "What can I start you all off with?"

"I'll have a Pepsi," Wyatt said.

Andrea ordered a sweet tea.

"Pepsi, please," I said.

She nodded and walked toward the drink station.

My stomach growled and dropped all at once. How could I still be so hungry with all that was happening right now?

Andrea was watching Wyatt like he was a piece of meat and sizing him up for how best to cut him up and eat him for dinner. It was disturbing.

He sat there like nothing was wrong. His fingers trailed up and down my arm as his arm rested there.

It felt so normal and yet so wrong at the same time. I couldn't keep this up for long.

Andrea squinted her eyes at me. "So how come you didn't come to her birthday party? Seems a little rude not to show up."

"I was busy. I had band practice."

"You're in a band?"

"Lead singer and I play the guitar. We actually have a meeting with a producer tomorrow."

She gasped. "This can't be real." She stared me down. "You're dating someone in a band?"

I nodded because words would betray me.

Wyatt pushed the book toward her. "We filled out the book and did your silly dates, but you know, I don't enjoy being called a liar."

Andrea's eyes widened. "I'm not ..."

"This is real between us, which isn't the point. Andrea, it's not really up to you on how and who Marley dates. I would hope her *cousin* would know that."

"Why ... of-of course."

He smiled, one of the infectious ones he reserved for the

stage. "Good, because it seemed like you might have hoped to embarrass my girlfriend and I don't really like that."

She audibly gulped.

Was she nervous? I had never seen her anything but confident in my entire life. Was it possible she was like this with others and just used this as a mask with me? Goody-two shoes Marley wouldn't stand up to her, so she could push me around all she wanted.

"I wouldn't."

I coughed as the waitress set down our drinks. "Can we move on?" I pleaded with them both. This was awkward on so many levels.

"Of course." Andrea flipped through the adventure book, glancing at the pictures, though she never lingered on any page long enough in my opinion. Then she set it aside and pushed it toward us.

"So, what's the name of your band?" Andrea asked.

"Broken Axles."

Her eyes widened. "That's you?"

Of course Andrea knew his band, why wouldn't that happen?

Our conversation devolved into her talking nonstop about his band and what he liked to do. It was as if she was writing a documentary and wanted all the specifics before anyone.

Wyatt glanced toward me here and there, but it never shifted back to me, which on some level I was fine with. When the food arrived, I ate my food and listened. It wasn't even close to how I pictured my night.

I watched as Andrea got into her car and Wyatt walked back to where I stood. My cheeks were flushed. So far, the only positive out of the night was that Andrea backed down. The downside? I think she was in love with Wyatt and secretly hoping I would just disappear.

Despite all that had happened between us in the last few days and tonight, I so badly wanted to reach out and hug him for what he did for me.

I glanced at my feet, unable to focus on his expression for too long. "Thank you for tonight. I don't deserve all the help you gave me."

His hand reached toward my chin and lifted my head to peer into his gaze. "You still don't get it, do you? You deserve that and more."

My eyes welled. Even after focusing on myself, he treated me with such care. "But I don't. I should have given us wait time. I should have calmed down and waited it out before just saying goodbye. I pulled the rip cord."

He shook his head. "Maybe, but I also didn't give you a chance to react to my life before I assumed how you would be. I took my past experiences with girls finding out about my parents and put that on you. You're a different person. I should have known that you wouldn't judge me for what happened."

"It's only been four weeks, Wyatt. Not even. I shouldn't have expected to know your whole life story. I'm sorry. I-I ... I was scared. You were right."

His brow arched. "Of?"

I blew all the air from my lungs in a huff. "Of everything. Would you decide I was too unlike you? Would I be boring once I wasn't doing those dates anymore? Would you still like me? How could you like me when no one else had?"

He pulled me toward his chest and wrapped his arms around me.

My face settled against him, and I listened to the beat of his heart.

"I know who you are, Marley. I knew that from the first

day you stopped me in that parking lot. And I know that standing here with you now. I told you, if other people can't recognize what you would bring to a relationship, that's their loss."

My lips twisted to the side. "But we only got to know each other because of a stupid gift. This whole month might not have happened without it."

He shrugged a shoulder. "Maybe it was the catalyst, but I still noticed you. I *did* know your name, yanno? I just didn't think I was in the position to bring someone else into my messed up life. But when you showed up, persistent, and willing to drag my sorry self out of a hole I had created with school, then why not?"

"Why are you so amazing? I mean I seriously walked away, and you still showed up for me tonight."

"Because Marley June Wix there is no one else out there like you. You give all of yourself over to people and that is so incredible. You wanted to help me, and I will never forget that. I needed you not just to remember I could and should do better in school, but to remember who I was. I felt like myself around you again. And sure, you said goodbye, but you needed time to process what happened. I owed you that."

"I didn't handle it well and not because I was judging, but because I worried about myself in all of that. It felt like it was too good to be true. There was this amazingly sweet and thoughtful, hot musician and he was telling me that he liked *me*. Instead, I should have focused on how hard it must have been to be in your position and tell me when your dad showed up."

His fingers brushed my cheek. "It's okay. I'll forgive you if you can forgive me."

I nodded.

"Good, because I've been wanting to do this all night." He leaned closer to my face as his head tilted to the side.

I smiled knowing what came next as I closed my eyes and found those perfect lips against mine. He didn't push or deepen the kiss as first. Just kept our lips together as if they could say everything else that needed to be said.

And then his hands found their way into my hair and on my waist as he pulled me closer. When we finally pulled away, our breath was ragged.

"I missed you," I said.

He leaned his forehead against mine. "Me too. The band has been furious with me for not texting you."

I giggled. "Sage yelled at me too."

He laughed as his arms snaked around me in a hug. "So, do you still want to be my girlfriend, Marley?"

"More than anything."

"Good, because your presence is mandatory tomorrow."

"Oh, so now I get it. You were almost exiled from the band because I wouldn't have arrived."

"Simple semantics."

I shoved his arm and pretended to be outraged, but I broke as soon as he gazed into my eyes again, because I could tell it had nothing to do with the band.

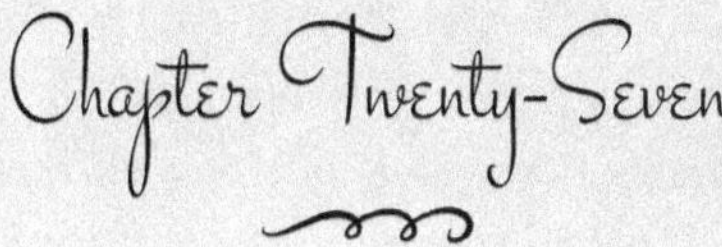

Chapter Twenty-Seven

Claire squealed so loud in the parking lot, I thought my ear drums would burst. Not to mention I didn't expect her to be the type to squeal.

"You came!"

Jack nodded in my direction, but his expression was tense. Did he not want me at the meeting or was he too focused on the meeting to tease me like he usually did?

Wyatt's arm stayed firmly over my shoulder, pulling me close to his body.

And I certainly wasn't complaining.

"I was informed it was mandatory."

Wyatt chuckled. "She's joking."

"Nope. I was informed that, but I wanted to come too."

Claire linked arms with me, pulling us in front of Jack and Wyatt. "I'm sure this is a silly question, but are you two better now?"

I nodded. "We were being stubborn about different things. But we're good." I looked back and winked at Wyatt who grinned easily.

It felt so good to be together again.

Claire blew a breath of relief. "That's good because I want all of us in the right head space for this meeting. We only get to impress them once."

I nodded. "Is it a live performance or from a demo?"

"Demo, but we will watch them listen to it in real time."

"Gotcha."

Wyatt's expression revealed nothing about how he felt. Besides the smile that tugged on his lips, it was as if he wasn't going into the most important meeting of his life.

Jack rubbed his hands together quickly. "Can we go in?"

"Yep, now that we are all here." Claire grimaced. "I wasn't sure if you would be here or not, Marley, so I think you have to wait in the waiting room."

"No worries." I pulled out my latest book from my purse. "I came prepared."

Wyatt chuckled and nudged my arm with his hand as we followed Claire and Jack. "You sure? I could try sneaking you in. Maybe you could be our fourth band member."

I snorted. "Yeah, right. We've been over this. I don't have musical talents."

"I don't know if I would say that. You didn't do horribly at karaoke."

"I had a good lead singer."

He smiled and leaned down to kiss the top of my head.

The music producer's building was concrete and modern. Dark lines and glass walls were everywhere. It didn't blend in at all with the area. I expected a building like that in New York, not in Maryland. The few walls made of drywall were painted white.

Through the front doors was a large waiting room with several receptionist desks. People bussed back and forth, going in two large stone doors. More people went in than come back out.

We took seats all together huddled by the window. The

summer sun streamed through the glass. For the number of people milling about, it was hard to believe it was a Sunday.

"Broken Axles," the nearest receptionist said.

"Good luck. They'll love it."

Wyatt squeezed my hand, then followed Jack and Claire toward the two large stone doors.

And now I waited. I believed in their band. If the record producer didn't want them, then that was their loss, but I knew how talented they were.

I pulled my book from my purse, opened to the first page and sunk into the pages of the romance novel. I finally didn't have to study or worry about school, so my long awaited book pile could finally be read. And the day after graduation was as good as any to start.

They reemerged about forty-five minutes after they disappeared with the receptionist. I hadn't seen their initial expressions, having been absorbed in the pages of my book.

When I noticed them getting closer, each of their faces gave nothing away as to how it went.

Wyatt waved me toward them, then we walked to the parking lot. No one talked. No one said anything.

My stomach lurched. Had it gone poorly?

"So ...?"

But they didn't answer.

Ten feet from the vehicles, I stopped. "Someone better tell me how it went or I'm not moving."

Jack's expression cracked first, followed by Claire.

Wyatt still stayed perfectly passive.

Claire took a few steps toward me, then burst into a huge grin. "We got an offer!"

"What?" I jumped in place. "You did? I knew it!"

Wyatt finally grinned, lighter than any I had seen on his face before. He was satisfied with the news.

"We don't sign anything today. We will have to come back in a week or so to finalize the contract, but they really liked the demo."

"When can I hear it?"

"Now," Wyatt said as he took out his phone.

"Okay, but you have to celebrate. How will you celebrate?"

"Later at Lucy's if you're up for it. It seems right to celebrate at the place that believed in us the most."

"Yes! I'll be there."

Wyatt ushered me toward his truck. "See you then," he called over his shoulder.

My nose scrunched. "Aren't we listening to the song?"

"Yes, but alone in my truck."

"Oh. *Oh.* Wait, why alone?"

"You'll see."

He opened my passenger door, then walked around to get in. He placed his phone in the middle and I waited for the first notes to play.

The melody was soft and built slowly. When Wyatt's voice began, it sent chills down my spine. It was haunting and elegant. By no means would it be a pop hit, but it felt infectious.

He watched my eyes and expression closely.

As the chorus began, my eyes widened. It was about finding someone special. Someone to change how they saw everything. Had he ...? It couldn't have.

Being alone was my identity
Until she became my serenity
Eyes that muddied my edges

I would never be the same

The more I listened to it, the more I heard tidbits of our dates, albeit hidden. No one else who had been with us or seen the adventure book would have guessed, but I knew.

As the final notes of the song finished and he took back his phone, I was speechless.

I had a song written about me and the producer had liked it.

"What do you think?"

"I don't know how to process this. I've never been a part of someone's creative process like that. It's beyond what I was expecting. It's ... It's perfect."

Wyatt's expression softened as he tucked a strand of hair behind my ear. "I mean every word. You have changed me, Marley."

His hair was soft and curly as my fingers combed through what peeked out from under his beanie. "You've changed me too, Wyatt."

His right hand entwined with my left, then he lifted it slowly to his lips. "Where to?"

"Anywhere as long as it's together."

He nodded like he knew exactly where to pick.

"And can we listen to it again?"

He grinned while he plugged his phone into his truck's radio and let the song play on repeat. A soundtrack to the beginning of our relationship.

Epilogue

It had been a month since I had graduated from high school, which seemed impossible. Every day was better than the last.

My *boyfriend* and I had been together for a month, and it didn't seem real. He brought me flowers randomly or dropped off a book from an author he knew I wanted.

I went to his gigs every Monday at Lucy's and traveled with them when they went a little farther out of town too.

"Mar! Come here and help with the banner."

I groaned. "I'm not tall enough to do the banner. Can't we do that later?"

"There's less than an hour until people show up. I think we've waited as long as we can."

My mother stood practically wrapped in a large *Happy Graduation* banner with a salmon background and rainbow letters.

"Where's Dad?"

"Picking up the cake. I told him to get it yesterday, but you know how he is."

I giggled. "Yes, I do."

A knock sounded from the front door.

"I'll get it."

Wyatt stood on the other side, dressed in dark gray khaki shorts, a graphic T-shirt and his everyday wearing beanie. He held a present wrapped in blue shiny wrapping paper.

"Hey, boyfriend."

"Hey, girlfriend."

I giggled. I still never would get over saying that.

"Marley, stop being corny with your boyfriend and have him help with the banner. I'm going to be a walking sign soon if we don't get it fixed."

Wyatt chuckled and kissed my cheek, before placing my present on a chair by the door. "Sure thing, Mrs. Wix."

Without even leaning onto his tippy toes, he tacked the left side of the banner to the column, then tacked the right.

Mom clapped her hands. "Perfect. Thank you."

"Of course. Can I help with anything else?"

She shook her head.

"Good, because I wanted to show you something."

He arched his brow as I drug him toward my room.

"I can't imagine your mom wanting us in here by ourselves."

I rolled my eyes. "It's not for any reason like that. I found this cute little bistro that's about halfway between New York and my college. We could meet there on weekends or our off days. It even has open mic nights if you all aren't too busy touring."

He wrapped his arm around my waist and pulled me closer. "Stop fretting about the fall. We don't start touring until December and only a few things here and there. We have to put out a single and all first." He kissed the side of my face. "And besides, I could never be so busy touring that I wouldn't see you."

"I know. But—"

"It's your personality to plan and worry."

I rested my head on his chest and nodded.

"Let's see this bistro then."

Clicking on my keyboard, the laptop whirred awake and displayed a Google Street View of the place. It was nestled in a small town in Pennsylvania and looked comforting.

"It looks like a cute place, although, I told you I don't mind driving to UPenn either."

"Yes, but in case it is too far, this is a good backup plan."

"Okay, but that's enough of that for today. We have a special woman to celebrate and I for one want to be first in line for that party."

I giggled. "You're silly. You know it's mostly going to be my family."

"I don't care who comes as long as I get to celebrate you."

No matter how many times he complimented me, my cheeks still flamed. "Well, just make sure to keep it rated G."

He crossed his finger over his heart. "On my honor."

I checked the time on my phone. "Sage should be here soon, and hopefully Claire and Jack too."

"Claire will be on time, but Jack has never shown up early to anything in his whole life."

I giggled. "Fine. Fine." I gazed into those beautiful brown eyes with lashes that could land a plane. "I'll miss you while in Greece. Why did my parents have to buy that as my gift?"

"Really? You get to go to Greece and you're worried about missing me."

I nodded. "It'll be the longest we've been apart since dating."

He tugged me close to his chest and settled his chin on my head. "Yes, it will. But then you can tell me all about the sights when you get back."

"I guess. Do I have to wait to open my gift until later?"

He winked as he pulled us back to the main room.

"Nope." He passed over my present and my fingers fumbled with the wrapping paper. A box was inside, so I had to pry open the tape on the sides to reveal a salmon-colored T-shirt with the lyrics to our song, which even though was going to be heard by other people, still was more important to me than it would be to anyone else.

I hugged it to my chest and smiled. "Thank you. This is the best gift."

He leaned close to my ear. "I figured you could wear it while you're being, Marley the lead singer's girlfriend and groupie."

I laughed. "You wish."

He tucked me against his chest and leaned down so our lips were millimeters away from each other. As his lips brushed mine he said, "I do wish. You're everything I want, Marley June Wix."

The touch and words sent shivers down my skin. How did I get so lucky for my first boyfriend? Wyatt was my perfect person, and I could spend forever making sure he knew it.

Acknowledgments

Writing can feel so solitary and working on the seventh book, I really felt this, but I have so many wonderful people who have helped me. Some who know and some who didn't realize they gave me inspiration when I was stuck.

I have had the honor of working with many wonderful people for this novel. First, I want to thank my publisher Creative James Media. Their continued support makes me forever grateful.

I also want to thank Staci Petroski for her edits of this novel. Alt 19 for the amazing cover work.

To my beta readers: PK and DKM. All your notes and feedback are invaluable to me. Thank you for putting your effort into helping me. You both help make these novels what they are and for that I am grateful.

Finally, to my family for supporting me. It isn't easy sacrificing time with them to write when time is always so limited, but they do it with grace. I love you all!

Please consider leaving a review after reading.
Goodreads Review
Amazon Review

For the latest news and updates, please sign up for her
newsletter from her website.

Twitter: @Marie_McGrath_
Instagram: marie_mcgrath_
TikTok: marie_mcgrath_author
Website:
https://mariemcgrathauthor.wixsite.com/books

About the Author

Marie McGrath lives in a small rural town in Maryland. She hopes to inspire others with her stories. When she isn't listening to her own characters, you can find her deep in any novel she can get her hands on, especially YA and contemporary fiction. She loves the color turquoise, lions, and listening to music.